SHARK
ISLAND

SHARK ISLAND

—

CHRIS JAMESON

St. Martin's Paperbacks

This is a work of fiction. All of the characters, organizations, and events portrayed in this novel are either products of the author's imagination or are used fictitiously.

SHARK ISLAND

For information address St. Martin's Press, 175 Fifth Avenue, New York, NY 10010.

ISBN: 978-1-250-10912-5

Our books may be purchased in bulk for promotional, educational, or business use. Please contact your local bookseller or the Macmillan Corporate and Premium Sales Department at 1-800-221-7945, ext. 5442, or by e-mail at MacmillanSpecialMarkets@macmillan.com.

Printed in the United States of America

St. Martin's Paperbacks edition / July 2017

St. Martin's Paperbacks are published by St. Martin's Press, 175 Fifth Avenue, New York, NY 10010.

10 9 8 7 6 5 4 3 2 1

For my brother, Jamie.
"Daylight's wastin'."

ACKNOWLEDGMENTS

Profound thanks to Dr. Michael Moore and Greg Skomal at Woods Hole Oceanographic Institution for their insight and knowledge, and to my sister, Erin, for tales of Race Point. Thanks also to my agent, Howard Morhaim, and to Michael Homler, Lauren Jablonski, and everyone else at St. Martin's Press. Finally, love and gratitude as always to my wife, Connie, who keeps the sharks away.

CHAPTER 1

She doesn't scream at the sight of blood. She screams at the realization that the blood belongs to her, that it used to flow in her veins but is now a frothing pink in the Atlantic surf. The impact against her leg underwater had been so sudden—a bump and a hard tug—that it stunned her for several seconds. She blinked in confusion, saw the blood, made the connection. Now she is screaming, her voice shredded and hopeless, as if she's being murdered. And why not? It's her blood, after all.

She thrashes in the water, underwater camera dangling from her neck by its strap, utterly forgotten. The small boat she came in floats two hundred yards out, her girlfriend sunning herself, music pumping. A trio of wet-suited surfers paddles not far off, waiting for the right wave. Frantic, bleeding, she spins toward shore and sees the massive herd of seals on the sand and in the shallows, blocking her way.

Her screams become words. Become pleas. Beyond the seals, a handful of tourists carry flip-flops in one hand and bottles of beer in the other . . . they've heard her. Seen her. Can they see her blood from there? She thinks not, but still she strikes out toward them, seals be damned.

Trouble is, she can't feel her left leg anymore. Swimming is difficult.

What's funny is that it's only when she spots the fin slicing toward her through the waves that she realizes this is the first time she's noticed the shark. It has to be there, of course. The moment she understood herself as the source of the blood, logic supplied a shark as the most likely cause. But she's been busy screaming, so it's only the actual sight of the fin that solidifies the presence of the actual shark . . . and the knowledge that she isn't going to make it to the flip-flop, beer-bottle tourists or the herd of seals.

The fin slides beneath the waves.

She goes silent, swallowing her screams as if somehow the shark might pass her by.

Knowing it won't.

Her day didn't start this way.

It won't end this way, either.

Naomi's never piloted a boat before, but Kayla wants her to learn, so here she is—Naomi Cardiff, just turned twenty, not just riding onboard a sparkly new twenty-foot Boston Whaler along the northeast tip of Cape Cod, but driving the damn thing. *Piloting*, she thinks, *not driving*. Kayla would *tsk* and correct her. She'd do it lovingly, with a sweet indulgence, but it'd still make Naomi feel awkward and apologetic. Kayla wants her to be more confident, which somehow always accomplishes the opposite.

Still, here she is, both hands on the wheel, ass perched

on the edge of the high-rise captain's chair. The sun bakes down, warming her to her bones after a rainy, chilly month of June. The boat skims the waves and as they pass the more populated beaches, Naomi settles down, enjoying the feel of the wheel in her hands, the power of the Whaler beneath her. It hums, and she likes that hum. It feels like control, something her life has sorely lacked.

Naomi's a student at Boston University. Kayla Chaudry's two years older, just graduated from B.U. and headed to med school in California in the fall. What will happen to them then is something Naomi doesn't want to think about. She's been in love before—or what she thought was love—but she doesn't think she's ever needed anyone the way she needs Kayla.

Stop. Don't think. Just be.

How many times has Kayla used those words on her? Dozens? She'll put a finger to Naomi's lips and then kiss her softly and touch her hair—she loves having her hair touched—and then she'll say those words. *Stop. Don't think. Just be.*

With good reason. As Americanized as Kayla's parents might be, they are from Pakistan. They have no idea Naomi is more than their daughter's best friend. The idea likely hasn't even occurred to them or they'd never have agreed to let her get a job on the Cape and live with them down here for the summer. Kayla has mastered *just being*, pushing all of the complications out of her mind to focus on the moment, but that means they've talked very little about what will become of their love a month from now, when Kayla moves west.

Naomi exhales. Tries to just be.

Music blasts from the boat's sound system—this summer's latest pop princess—and Naomi turns up the volume, the thumping bass shaking the deck beneath her feet. Up on the prow of the little boat, Kayla glances up with a curious smile. Only then does Naomi realize she's only been half paying attention to their location. Her thoughts have drifted, but her eyes have been riveted on the sight of her girlfriend sunning herself on the front of the boat. Kayla is long and lean, fit and muscular, brown skin glistening in the sun. Now she sits up and raises her sunglasses so Naomi can see the laughter in her eyes.

Kayla calls out something, but the music's too loud. Naomi turns it down, regretting the absence of that thumping beneath her feet.

"What's that?" she asks.

"You trying to get us lost at sea?" Kayla says. She pulls the thick elastic out of her mass of lush black hair and fixes the ponytail again, so beautiful that Naomi's throat goes dry just looking at her.

So beautiful. So damn smart. And so *leaving*.

"I told you I never piloted a boat before!" Naomi protests.

Kayla's grin is lopsided, a perfect imperfection. She rolls over and digs into their cooler, drags two bottles of Molly's Hard Lemonade from the ice, and stands up as if they weren't bouncing across the waves. *Girl has her sea legs*, Naomi thinks. *And they go for miles.*

"Throttle down, darling," Kayla says, the endearment an affectation she picked from old movies. She loves old movies, so now Naomi loves them, too. She's not sure if this is purely because Kayla adores them or if she's developed a genuine interest herself, but she supposes she will find out this fall, when it's over between them. As she thinks it must be.

As Naomi indeed throttles down, Kayla opens the

bottles and hands one to her. Naomi thinks she is going to take the wheel, but instead Kayla nudges her forward and slides behind her. A shy smile touches Naomi's lips as Kayla whispers encouragement into her ears, so Naomi barely notices that her girlfriend *has* taken over. Naomi has her left hand on the wheel—drink in her right—and so Kayla does the opposite, reaching one long arm around so that they are piloting the ship together.

Kayla turns them toward shore. Naomi can feel the warmth of her body, can smell the coconut tang of her sunscreen. Kayla kisses her neck and Naomi melts back into her, eyes closed, no longer caring where the boat takes them. They cruise the Atlantic and drink their hard lemonade and listen to new-femme pop, and all is right with the world. Naomi knows that she's supposed to be her own woman and believes that most of the time she's doing a decent job of it. But with Kayla, she forgets that she's supposed to stand on her own two feet.

Soon she will have to, and though her heart withers at the thought, deep inside—where the sensible Naomi is hiding—she thinks this is for the best, that with Kayla around to love her, she might never become the person she ought to be. It's a power she shouldn't have given away, but she has, and she's afraid she wouldn't have the strength to take it back.

Go away, she thinks as Kayla kisses her neck. And then, *Don't leave me*.

"Get that camera ready," Kayla says. "You're going to get the greatest pictures ever. Take a look."

Naomi shakes herself from her reverie and glances over to see a long stretch of narrow beach that has become a gleaming, undulating mass of gray and black bodies. There must be hundreds of seals, just as Kayla promised, and now all heartache is forgotten. Even the quickening of Naomi's pulse and those kisses on her neck are pushed from her mind. The seals are beautiful and there are so many of them that a childlike glee overtakes her and she utters a little squeal that makes Kayla laugh.

"Come on. Get ready," Kayla says, nudging her away from the wheel and taking the half-full bottle of hard lemonade away from her. "I'll finish yours."

Naomi is happy to comply. She strips off her thin lime-green cotton top and threadbare denim shorts. She's not as tall as Kayla and not nearly as fit, but Naomi feels healthy enough. Every girl she's ever met has body image troubles and she's no exception, but most days she's more focused on what she eats than how her ass looks. Her main interests are photography, marine biology, and crime fiction, but beneath that layer is another that is constantly at war with itself—a civil war between her fascination with nutrition and her torrid romance with ice cream. She's found a balance she can live with.

Kayla cuts off the engine and lets the boat drift, then comes over to help make sure the camera strap isn't going to come loose. It wasn't cheap, and unlike her girlfriend's, Naomi's family isn't rich.

"Be careful," Kayla says. "You get too close to the babies and they can get pissed. They might get pissed anyway, so—"

"Don't get too close. Yes, Mom."

Kayla grins. "I just worry."

Naomi rolls her eyes the way she always has when people who love her express concern for her safety. She gives Kayla a quick kiss, then steps to the side of the boat and drops into the ocean. Water goes up her nose, but she tries not to look uncool when she surfaces. It's over her head here, but not by much, and she only has to swim a dozen feet or so before she can stand. Something brushes past her foot and she squeaks and scrambles a few feet closer to shore, imagining a crab down there, snapping at her toes.

"Have fun, babe!" Kayla calls, raising her drink in a toast. "I'll check on you in half an hour."

But Naomi is no longer listening. The seals are bellowing on the shore, slipping in and out of the water. The ocean currents are soothing as they swirl around her and she lifts up the camera and snaps some distance shots. Secretly, she thinks that if she could make a living just doing this—taking photos of wildlife, in or out of the water—she'd be the happiest person on earth. In her element now, she is fully herself, and as she moves closer— the boat drifting away behind her—she thinks that maybe she's more independent than she thought. Maybe she's going to be just fine after all. Maybe more than fine.

The underwater bump comes thirteen minutes later, and then the blood and the screaming. And then the fin, and the terror, and the certainty that she is going to die.

The numb leg is actually still there. This should be good news, except the only reason she knows is that she feels another tug. Something rips—she can feel it give way, muscle shredding—and pain spikes up into her brain with such ferocity that for a second she blacks out. Another tug and the agony pulls her back to consciousness and she's screaming as the shark begins to shake her, jerking back and forth.

It drags her under. She knows she should fight, but despite the terror and pain and the force of her will, her body is sluggish to respond. For a few seconds Naomi is in such shock that she forgets to breathe, which helps, in a way, because breathing means drowning.

Then she breathes. Gags on the water.

Choking triggers something primal, something the blood and pain couldn't reach. This isn't terror; this is savagery. She claws for the surface, flails her arms in the water, and then her face is above the waves and she's coughing and sucking greedily at the air even as the shark twists at her flesh and bone.

Savagery. She drives a hand down, fingers straight out, aiming for its black button eye.

The shark releases her. Blood bubbles up in its wake as it darts away, and Naomi knows it will be back. Even now, the fin begins to circle. Thoughts blurring, she spots the flip-flop tourists trying to get down to the water, shouting at one another and waving their arms, but the seals are barking and bellowing and advancing on them and the tourists scamper backward.

Naomi hopes she bleeds to death before she can drown. The feeling of choking, not being able to breathe . . .

It bumps against her back and she manages to scream, jerking away. . . .

Hands grab hold of her arms, start to pull, and she turns to see a mop-headed surfer straddling his board. It bumps her again as he drags at her and that's the moment when the worst thing of all happens. Worse than the blood and the tugging and the screams.

It's hope.

Nothing so far has terrified her more than this moment of hope.

She grabs at him, pulls at the wet board, and he's yelling at her to be still, to let him help. Naomi's screams rip from her throat, heart racing so hard that she starts to black out again, and the surfer can see he's got no choice. He drops off the board into the water, puts a hand under her butt, and tries to hoist her onto the board.

They both see the shark coming back.

He jerks the board from her grasp and turns it into both weapon and shield. The shark glides through the cloud of her blood and the surfer bashes it with the board, twists and blocks its attack, and then bashes it again.

"Go, go, go!" he's screaming, and Naomi blinks because this makes no sense. Where is she going to go?

Then she hears Kayla crying out to her and she turns and somehow the boat is right there, ghosting across the water toward her. Kayla has cut the throttle and is leaning over the side, reaching for her, and there's that monstrously cruel hope again.

"Oh shit!" the surfer shouts. "Oh shit oh shit oh shit—"

Then a grunt. Very loud.

Ice spikes through Naomi's veins and the darkness continues to encroach upon her thoughts, but she manages to turn and see that there is a second fin now. And a third, coming in fast. Naomi's blood has drawn them, and this commotion in the water, but it's the surfer they take. He tries to smash one with the board, but another gets its teeth into him and the board shoots from his hands, floating along the surface of the red waves.

The surfer is dragged under. He flails. The sharks tear him apart.

One of them splits off now, knifing toward Naomi even as Kayla hauls her out of the water and onto the boat. Screaming.

Then it's Kayla who is screaming. She stands up and staggers back, hands flailing as if she doesn't remember what they're for. Kayla's staring at Naomi—at her legs— and all Naomi can think is how much she'll miss her.

Eyelids fluttering, darkness sweeping over her, she lolls her head and manages to catch a single glimpse of the wreckage of her left leg, the bloody strips of torn muscle, the exposed bone gleaming in the sunlight, the absence of anything below the calf.

Drive, she thinks she says to Kayla, knowing it's not the right word. Not caring. And maybe she smiles just a little as blood loss finally takes its toll.

It occurs to her that maybe she can't live without Kayla after all.

Then the sun goes black, and Naomi is gone.

CHAPTER 2

—•—

Eddie Wolchko liked to have his hideaways. As far back as the fourth grade, he would slip out the back door when his parents were fighting and find his way into the woods, where he'd climb into a tree fort some older kids had built. *Like a hermit crab*, his mother had said once, when she found out where he'd been running off to. Wolchko had liked the description back then, and he still did. A hermit crab could find any castaway domicile and feel at home. It was a good skill to have.

The desire to be on his own sometimes made people uncomfortable, but Wolchko had never cared very much about the comfort of others. He liked people well enough, knew how to take a joke and when to make one, but he had difficulty reading them. Sometimes his ability to process human relationships started to fray and he needed to run off on his own for a bit, until his anxiety level returned to something normal and healthy.

He smiled at the phrase. *Something normal and healthy.*

They were the words his wife, Antonia, had used when describing the life she hoped he would seek out, after she was dead. Breast cancer had whittled her down to nothing by then. Her second time at bat. The first time, the doctors thought they'd had it whipped, but cancer was a sneaky little bastard and some of those breast cancer cells had spread to other parts of her body and bided their time. Two years had gone by in between, but when her cancer had come back it came with a vengeance.

People have a hard time understanding you, Antonia had whispered to him, clutching weakly at his hand while he sat at her bedside. *And you have a hard time understanding them. I need you to promise me you'll make an effort to let the world in, to interact with it and build yourself a life. Something normal and healthy.*

Wolchko had promised, not certain if the promise was a lie. Antonia had died three days later. That had been nearly four years ago, and most days he tried to keep his promise. More often than not, he failed. But he gave himself points for trying.

"Anything else I can get you, honey?" the waitress asked. "More iced tea?"

Wolchko gave her a rare smile. "That would be great. Thanks."

She took the empty cup and headed inside while Wolchko took another bite of his lunch. The lobster roll at Barlow's Clam Shack was just about the best thing grown-up Eddie Wolchko had ever tasted, and he lingered over his lunch. It was one of the reasons Barlow's was his favorite hideaway, one of the reasons he had never invited any of his co-workers to meet him here. It was his secret place, and if he could have drawn it around him like the shell of a hermit crab he would have done that in a heartbeat.

He always saved the slivered pickles for the end, almost like dessert.

The sunshine beat down on him and he relished the feeling. Whenever he came here, he chose one of the tables out on the sandy patio—one without an umbrella. Wolcho had never understood people who chose to eat outside but then hid from the sun. He knew his skin had paid the price—at thirty-eight, he looked older than his years thanks to the tough, weathered appearance that years in the sun had given him—but he lived on Cape Cod and did much of his work out on the water, studying sharks and other marine life, which was worth the trade-off. And he didn't mind the idea of nurturing the *Old Man and the Sea* look. It wasn't like he was out to impress anyone.

The screen door hinges squealed as the waitress popped back out with his iced tea. When she set it down he made sure to meet her eyes as he thanked her, trying to practice a higher level of courtesy in his life. She smiled, maybe just to be polite, or grateful for the moment of humanity. Either was fine with Wolchko.

As he continued eating, he studied the other tables on the patio, all but one of which were occupied by people talking and laughing together. Wolchko liked to pretend they couldn't see him, and it nearly always worked out that the more he pretended to be invisible, the more people treated him that way. He preferred it that way.

The patio ran beside the restaurant, with Falmouth Harbor in the back and the parking lot out front. Gulls cawed as they wheeled above the water, the breeze carrying the smell of the ocean. White sails dotted the water in a peaceful panorama.

Wolchko felt at ease, right up until he heard the crunch of gravel and turned to see the gold Ford Focus pulling into the lot and Rosalie Suarez stepped out from behind the wheel. The hair rose on the back of his neck and he wished his ability to turn invisible were more than imaginary. Barlow's was his favorite hideaway. How the hell she even knew to look for him there Wolchko had no idea, but Rosalie scanned the patio and made a beeline toward him.

He ate his pickles, all three slivers at once. He would not be denied those pickles.

"Eddie," Rosalie began. "I've been calling, but your phone goes straight to—"

"Voice mail, yeah, because my phone is off," he said sharply, brows knitted, wanting to make his consternation clear. "Lunch is *my* time. You know I can't focus on the research if I don't escape for a bit."

"I do, yeah." She slid into the wrought-iron chair beside his. "But you wouldn't want me to wait for you on this."

Her eyes were bright and skittery with something that was not quite panic, a look that burned right through his irritation.

"What could . . . ," Wolchko began, and then he thought of the one thing that would bring her out looking for him. The thing they had been talking about at the beginning of every tourist season since he started his research at Woods Hole Oceanographic Institution.

He glanced around to make sure no one was paying attention, sipped his iced tea, and scudded his chair a little closer to her.

"Where?"

"Truro," Rosalie said. "A little way up from Ballston Beach."

"Tell me the rest." Because there had to be more for her to be sitting there.

Rosalie glanced over her shoulder, leaned in conspiratorially. "At least two Great Whites. Maybe three. Feasting on the seal population as usual when this college girl who fancies herself a wildlife photographer gets too close, in the water, and the sharks get her confused with the seals. College girl lost a leg. She's in surgery now. A surfer named Luke Turner tried to rescue her. Turner's dead."

"Son of a bitch," Wolchko whispered.

Rosalie stole a fry off his plate. "That's not the worst part."

Wolchko leaned back in his chair and threw up his hands, forgetting about the people around them. "How can that not be the worst part?"

Several heads turned. Rosalie had not forgotten about the potential for being overheard. She ate a couple more fries and waited while people returned to their own conversations.

"The girl who lost her leg is Naomi Cardiff. Her mother is Ellen Cardiff."

Wolchko exhaled a string of quiet profanity. The last fatal shark attack in New England had taken place in 1936. Now the media, the Chamber of Commerce, the tourism board, the Division of Fisheries and Wildlife . . . they'd all be arguing over what to do about the shark problem, which was really the seal problem, on Cape Cod. Greenpeace and SeaLove and others would get into the fight. And at some point, all eyes would look toward the researchers at Woods Hole to come up with a solution.

After all, a man had died. But it wasn't the dead man who would be getting most of the attention. It was Naomi Cardiff . . . the daughter of the state's lieutenant governor.

"Shit," Wolchko said, staring out at the sailboats beyond the harbor.

I just wanted a little alone time.

CHAPTER 3

Kat Cheong did not resort to storming down the corridor toward her office, but then she didn't have to. She had been a Research Associate at WHOI for two years, and in that time the junior staff had learned her quirks by trial and error, none more so than Tye Ashmore.

Her heels clicked on the cold floor of the corridor and her spine was straight, her chin raised, as she reached her office door. As she passed through, heading for her desk, she left the door open because she knew Tye would follow in her wake. He was brilliant and ambitious, full of potential, but in that much at least he was predictable.

"Close it behind you," she said as she slid her laptop onto the desk.

The small office consisted mostly of shelves and books and journals, a few small potted plants, and a hell of a mess on her desk. Three unwashed mugs sat beside her electric kettle on a little table by the door. Kat knew she could have made a stink, gotten herself more office space, but given that she spent nearly all of her time in the lab, there seemed no point.

Tye closed the door. "I know you're pissed."

Kat leaned on her desk. "Ya think?"

"Look—"

"Me first. Then you can decide if you still feel like speaking."

Tye hesitated, then shoved his hands into his pockets like a recalcitrant teenager called to the principal's office. The image was all too accurate, as far as Kat was concerned. His brown hair hung a bit too long, almost shaggy, and the tilt of his jaw suggested a defiance that had probably started as far back as high school. The trouble with Tye was that he knew he was good-looking and he counted on it too much instead of relying on his brains to carry him through. But Kat was not going to say that to him. She had said it before and it hadn't made an iota of difference.

She straightened her shirt cuffs, needing to do something with her hands.

"You undermined me in there, Tye. I've been on this research since grad school, it's half the reason Woods Hole hired me in the first place, and now I'm starting to get somewhere and I need my funding to continue, and then you sabotage me—"

"I did no such thing."

Kat set him on fire with her eyes. Or she would have if she'd had the laser vision she had always wished for. "When I got you this job—"

He bristled, hands coming out of his pockets. Nothing recalcitrant about him now.

"Say what, now?"

"I set up your interview," she continued. "I gave you my

highest recommendation, and that means I put my reputation on the line. I got you in the room."

Tye nodded slowly. "You got me in the room. And I'm grateful for that, Kat. You know I am. Grateful and happy to be here, working with you. I accept that I might not be here if you hadn't gotten me into the room, but they didn't hire me on your say-so. They hired me because I have the credentials. I've done the work. So please don't tell me you *got* me the job."

"You think there weren't other candidates with your credentials?"

He threw up his hands. "You know what? No. I don't think there were. Not with my references and with the work I'd already done. And I've proved myself every day since I got here. I have to, don't I? Otherwise nobody here is ever going to take either of us seriously now that—"

She laughed a little, lifting a hand to hide her grin.

Tye stared. "Are you . . . seriously, are you laughing? First you're calling me onto the carpet and now something's funny?"

Kat exhaled. She'd always had this problem, laughing at the absolute worst moments. She'd worked up a righteous fury in the quarterly funding meeting they'd just left, but now all that steam had burned off. She adopted a serious expression and crossed the tiny office. There were frosted windows on either side of the door, but the door itself was solid wood. Nobody could see inside.

"It's ironic, you know," she said.

Tye backed up, frowning, still ready for a fight. "What is?"

"The more time I spend researching ways to alter instinctive behavior, the less capable I am of controlling my own."

With a nudge, she backed him up against the door, wrapping his purple necktie in her fist. "You're adorable when you're defending your masculine integrity."

"Kat, I'm not kidding around," Tye said.

"Ssssshhhh. Neither am I."

It was far from the first time they had kissed in her office. Some nights, when the research had gone very late and almost everyone else was gone, they had done far more than kiss. She was still pissed at him. What had happened in that meeting might turn out to be a recipe for disaster down the line. But she was also in love with him, and she admired that he was a man who fought for what he believed in. They had that in common.

"Kat—"

"Don't worry. I'm not done fighting. Call this intermission."

Tye kissed her back. It was a very good kiss.

A quick rap at the door startled them both. Before Kat could say anything, the door opened and whacked Tye in the back of the head. He cried out in protest as Kat darted away from him, smoothing her top and wondering how flushed her cheeks might be.

"Damn it," Tye said, rubbing his skull.

The visitor was their boss, Dr. Carin Aluru, the senior scientist at Woods Hole. Tall, imposing, fiftyish, Dr. Aluru was an insightful researcher who exhibited great kindness on a personal level but a colossal intolerance for nonsense in a professional setting. She knew Kat and Tye had this thing, and she definitely did not approve of them indulging themselves in the office. So Kat was expecting a dressing-down or at least a glare of disapproval.

What she got was something else.

"Open your laptop," Dr. Aluru said, her dark skin

uncommonly ashen. "I just got a call from Eddie Wolchko. There's some video you need to see. And cancel any plans you have for the immediate future."

"What's going on?" Tye asked. "What happened?"

Kat, however, understood immediately. She hadn't yet seen the video of the morning's attack, but she did not need to. The call from Eddie Wolchko and the look on Dr. Aluru's face said it all.

Kat rushed over and opened her laptop, glanced up at Tye.

"What happened," she said, "is that we just got our funding."

CHAPTER 4

—

Naomi inhaled sharply. She opened her eyes to slits, but the bright lights forced them shut again. Tightly. Music wove through her confusion—Springsteen singing "It's Hard to Be a Saint in the City." The familiar scratchy voice and raspy guitar were a comfort to her. She exhaled in a huff and drifted off again. The funny thing was that Springsteen was still with her, down in the gentle sway of her not-quite-dreams. Her thoughts ebbed and flowed, pulling at her like an undertow, and in that blackness she imagined herself underwater. Struggling against the tide, neck deep in the ocean . . . and she was not alone. Something was down there with her, knifing through her dreams. A blanket of numbness coated her brain, muffling everything but the oldest instinct—fear. And that fear drove her back up into consciousness.

Groaning, she struggled for breath. Her hands flailed at the bright lights and she realized that her eyes were already open. Springsteen was gone. Maybe he had never been there to begin with. He was her mother's obsession. All of her lullabies to baby Naomi had been Bruce Springsteen songs, so Naomi knew every one of them backward and forward. But Bruce wasn't there to comfort her now. Her mother was not there to sing her fears away.

Drugs muddled her thoughts, somehow made her body feel both too heavy and light as air, as if she were floating. Her mouth tasted like salt and wet cardboard and the smell in her nostrils was like piss and furniture polish combined, but it was not the stink that made her gut flip and roil with nausea. It was the memory.

The surfer had to be dead. She knew that. So much blood in the water. Kayla hauling her up onto the boat. Naomi remembered it all, saw a flash in her mind of the ragged flesh and gleaming bone that was all that remained of her left leg.

She knew she ought to be screaming. Instead, her heart broke and she lifted a trembling hand to her mouth, as if to inspect her lips in search of the expected scream.

"Naomi? Oh my God . . . you're awake."

She blinked, surprised to see Kayla rise from a chair near the hospital bed. The television droned on, the day's ugly news unfolding in silence, closed captions delivering the tragedies in a scroll along the bottom of the screen. Kayla had been waiting for Naomi to wake, but now that she had, it seemed clear she had no idea what to do.

"Hey," Kayla said softly, coming to her, taking her trembling hand. "I'm here, babe. I'm—"

Naomi ripped her hand free, bloody images still playing in her head. She propped herself up. Kayla kept talking to her, trying to get her to lie down, to calm down. Naomi stared at the flatness of the sheet where her leg ought to have been. It was like some kind of magician's trick. The outline of her body was distinct, everything where it ought to be, except that the outline ended below her left knee, where the sheet lay flat on the narrow hospital mattress. An illusionist had snapped his fingers and made the lower leg vanish.

In her mind she could still see the shark's dull black eye.

"I can't . . . ," she said, shaking her head. Staring at the flat sheet, afraid to move.

Kayla took Naomi's face in her hands, tilted her head, locked eyes with her. "You're okay. Breathe, babe. The doc was just here and she says you're gonna be okay."

Naomi stared at her, wondering what Kayla thought *okay* even meant. She wanted to shout, but this was the woman she loved, the woman who called her darling. Maybe most important, this was the woman who had dragged her out of the water and saved her life. So Naomi didn't shout. Instead, she just turned her head away.

She heard Kayla begin to cry and wanted to comfort her, but then, Kayla wasn't the one missing a leg. In a little over a month, Kayla would be leaving for California, where she would find another girl to take out on the water, another girl to kiss in the sunshine, with the taste of hard lemonade on her lips.

Naomi hated self-pity in anyone. Herself most of all.

"I need to call my mother," she whispered, face still turned away.

"I talked to her already and she's on the way," Kayla replied, twining her fingers with Naomi's. "My parents are out in the waiting room. They'll talk to her when she gets here. They're being really great, actually. They want to help."

Naomi stiffened.

"Your parents?" Naomi said, turning reluctantly to study

Kayla's face, her rich brown eyes. "Your parents, who wouldn't be out there and sure as hell wouldn't let you be in here with me if they knew I was your girlfriend?"

Kayla winced. "Hey. They love you. They're afraid for you."

"Only because they don't know who I am. And they don't know who you are, either."

"Babe?"

Naomi glanced away again. "Could you please get the doctor?"

There was a moment of hesitation and then she heard Kayla sniffle, felt her weight lift off the edge of the bed.

"Yeah, of course. I'll find her."

From the corner of her eye, Naomi watched Kayla cross the room, open the door, and go out, closing it with a soft click.

"I love you," Naomi said quietly, and to her own ears it sounded very much like good-bye.

Taking a deep breath, she reached down and drew aside the sheet. Tugged up her blue-patterned hospital johnny. The bandages covering the stump below her knee were a startling white against the faded-to-gray bedsheets.

The drugs made her numb below the waist and muddled her thoughts, but not enough. Nothing could ease this pain. Her breathing came quicker, a scream building in her throat. Tears burned the corners of her eyes and she laid her head back on the pillow only to find that the scream had gotten lost somehow. She uttered only a hitching, painful breath and tried not to think about the next hour or the next day or the next year, because then she would have to think about all of the things she had lost today, just to take some pretty pictures.

If she'd had the camera in her hands, she would have

smashed it, blaming the camera and the seals and her own ridiculous self because there was no point in blaming the shark. It had done what sharks do. What it would keep doing.

She froze, thinking of the surfer's blood foaming on top of the water, mixing with hers. Thinking of the fins slicing the waves. It struck her that the sharks were still out there. Of course they were still out there, down in the cold and the dark. She stared at the place where her leg should have been.

They're out there hunting.

CHAPTER 5

Dusk was just settling over Boothbay Harbor when Jamie Counihan pulled his rattling Chevy pickup into a spot at the back of the lot behind the Salty Dog. The name was a cliché, but he loved it. Boothbay Harbor had its share of wealthy folks and tourists, but there were still some corners of town where a working man could have a few beers and play a round of darts with the assholes he called his friends. Jamie loved them all, except when he hated them.

The Dog's clapboards were peeling badly and Jamie knew that sometime this fall Nathan, the owner, would offer free lunch and beer to his army of regulars if they would help paint the place. They would all do it, too, mostly because the decades of shitty paint jobs had created an outer skin on the bar that was pretty much the only thing keeping it from falling down.

Jamie had taken a shower and changed his clothes, but he still smelled like the morning's fishing haul, which wasn't a big deal at the Dog. Half the clientele were fishermen and the friends, girlfriends, and spouses of fishermen. Most of them could barely smell that stink anymore.

Jamie's stomach growled as he pushed open the door. Hinges squealed as it swung open and closed behind him. Voices were raised in greeting and Jamie clapped shoulders, nodded, and grinned as he made his way through the bar. The warped floorboards stank from generations of spilled beer. Nathan stood behind the counter pouring pints with Alice Hoskins, whose husband, Ray, had a heart attack some years back while reeling in a ten-foot sword-fish. Ray had hauled that beauty out of the deep, but by the time he'd won that fight he could barely raise his arms, and while it was thrashing around on the deck it had stabbed him in the leg. Nobody knew if the heart attack had killed him or if he'd bled to death, and Alice didn't like to talk about it, even now.

God, she's beautiful, Jamie thought as he tipped her a wink, passing by the bar. He had the same thought every time. Winked every time. And every time, Alice gave him that heartbreaking smile, as if they shared some kind of secret, some kind of pain. He would have loved to take her out some night, but he had never had the courage to ask. She had turned down everyone he'd ever known to ask her, so what was the point?

Alice pulled a pint of Guinness from a tap and as she started to pace him along the bar, he realized it was for him.

More voices called out and Jamie tore his gaze away from Alice. Walter sat waiting for him, had saved him a spot at the bar, and the two men engaged in a three-part greeting that involved a little sideways-five, a fist bump, and a single jostle of the hand in the classic Hawaiian shaka, the one surfers used to mean "hang loose." Walter and Jamie had been greeting each other that way since they had built a fort together back in the fourth grade.

Walter Briggs was six-four, shaved bald, and a deeper mahogany than the gleaming counter of the bar, which was the only part of the Dog that Nathan kept in decent condition. Jamie and Walter would both turn forty in November, three days apart. Like every year, they'd celebrate together, unless Walter's boyfriend, Joe, had something to say about it. Walter kept saying Joe wouldn't mind, but Jamie felt pretty confident that he would. Time would tell.

"I believe this is what you're looking for," Alice said as she set Jamie's Guinness on a coaster on the bar.

"It's a start, m'dear," Jamie said, raising the pint and tipping it toward her in a salute before taking a sip. When he exhaled with satisfaction, it was not for show. All the tension went out of his shoulders. He was a casual alcoholic. Kept out of trouble, claimed he could quit whenever he wanted to, but he would never find out because he did not want to. And what the hell difference did it make? Half the guys he knew drank a little something every day. Half the women, too. It wasn't like they were driving into telephone poles or beating their wives like Tom Paulson, who had done both. Now *that* fucking guy was an alcoholic.

"Wings?" Walter asked.

"What else?" Jamie said.

Alice smiled. She knew what they were going to eat just as well as she knew what they were going to drink. Jamie had to force himself not to stare at her. Her eyes were hazel, but they had golden rings around the irises, completely hypnotic. He saw those eyes, her lopsided smile, and the gap between her teeth that made her real, and he wondered if she found predictability in a man boring or reassuring.

"Hey, Alice, can I get a salad to go with that? Maybe some peppercorn dressing?"

"Salad?" she asked, arching an eyebrow. "You feelin' all right, James?"

"Figured I'd eat something healthy for once."

"Coming right up," Alice replied. She shot Walter a disapproving look. "Maybe you'll start a trend, be a good influence on some of the other guys in here."

Walter toasted the sentiment with his beer, and Alice snickered as she walked away.

"You are hopeless," Walter said.

Jamie sipped his Guinness, wiped the froth from his beard. "What?"

"Please. You're so in love with her you've got little cupids flying around your head. Probably fartin' Shakespeare sonnets in your sleep. Can you just put me out of my misery and ask her out?"

"I'm working up to it. Can't rush these things."

Walter rolled his eyes. "Life's too short, man. The clock's ticking away and every one of those seconds is one you could already have her answer, for better or worse."

"It's the worse part that worries me."

Walter shook his head, took a gulp of Old Speckled Hen, or whatever other British ale they had on tap tonight. Then he nodded toward the television behind the bar.

"You seen this yet?"

Jamie glanced up, thinking it must be the Red Sox game and that Walter would start ragging on the team as usual. He had never met anyone who loved to hate a team more than Walter loved to hate the Sox.

Instead, the television was tuned to an NECN report about the morning's shark attack on Cape Cod.

"Shitty luck," Jamie said.

"Luck, nothing. All them fucking seals down there, anyone who's been half paying attention knows that's the sharks' feeding ground. This girl apparently was in there swimming with the seals, taking pictures or whatever. Surfer tried to save her and now he's chum."

Jamie stared thoughtfully at the television above the bar. Fishermen down that way hated the seals because they ate the fish, and over the past decade or so, the seal population had been exploding. The way the guys he knew down on Cape Cod saw it, every seal that got born was taking money out of their pockets. And the seals . . . well, the more seals there were, the more sharks showed up to eat them.

"What about the girl?" he asked. "She gonna make it?"

"Lost a leg, but she'll live. Turns out her mother's the lieutenant governor of Massachusetts, so of course we're gonna be seeing nothing but this shit on the local news for a month."

Jamie paused with his pint halfway to his lips. A smile spread across his face as he set the glass back down and turned to stare at Walter.

"You gone looney all of a sudden?" Walter asked. "What the hell's that look for?"

Jamie laughed. "This is good, man. This is real good."

"How do you figure that, you morbid bastard?"

"No, no. Think about it. This thing is a P.R. nightmare," Jamie said, nodding to himself. "The Massholes are gonna have to do something about the seals now. They won't have a choice."

Walter's eyes lit up. He raised his glass.

They toasted.

When Alice came back, Jamie ordered another round.

ELEVEN
MONTHS
LATER

CHAPTER 6

Naomi sat on a threadbare towel, faded images of dolphins and whales swimming beneath her. Her sweatshirt lay beside her, with her car keys and the copy of Shirley Jackson's *Life Among the Savages* she'd been reading. The book made her smile, and smiles were good for her.

A Frisbee hit the sand a few feet away and rolled past, followed by a pale little boy of about nine or ten. He grinned as he raced after the Frisbee and snatched it off the beach while it was still rolling. Triumphant, he tried to turn and throw it back to his father, but instead he tripped over his own feet and tumbled onto the ground. Naomi propped herself up farther, started to rise in alarm, but the boy began to laugh, which was always a good sign.

"You okay?" she asked.

A dozen feet away, clutching the Frisbee, he seemed to notice her for the first time. His grin vanished. He blinked with fascination, staring at her leg.

"Wow."

Naomi smiled. What else could she do? Kids, at least, never tried to pretend the prosthetic wasn't there.

"Were you in the army?" he asked, blue eyes wide as he walked toward her, Frisbee dangling at his side. It was a natural question. One people asked a lot. Sometimes she wished she could just say yes, make it simpler, but she would have felt ashamed to lie about military service.

"Nope. A shark got me." The truth was the best answer.

The boy's eyes widened even further and somehow he turned paler as he glanced up and down Lighthouse Beach. "*Here*?"

"No, no. Don't worry. It happened a long way from here."

It was only partly a lie, depending on how the kid might define *a long way*. Truro was down at the end of the Cape, a fair distance, but not so far at all. Not for a shark.

The boy's dad jogged over, casting a sheepish grin at Naomi. "Hey, Spence, come on. Let's not bother people."

Face wrinkling in irritation, Spence glanced at his dad. "I'm not bothering her. She's nice. Her leg got bit off by a shark."

Dad went almost as pale as his kid. "Oh. I'm sorry." Awkwardly, he took the Frisbee from the boy's hands and started to guide him away. "Come on, bud. Let's see what mom packed in the cooler."

Spence dug his feet into the sand and looked pointedly at her leg. "How come you can be on the beach with that? Can you swim with it, or do you have to take it off?"

Naomi lifted her prosthetic foot, bending it at the ankle to show him how well it moved. "It's waterproof, actually. There's pretty much nothing I can't do. It kind of makes me a superhero."

This made him grin.

"Thanks for putting up with him," the dad said, a bit less awkwardly now.

She told him it wasn't a problem. Told them to enjoy their lunch. Was it weird, she wondered, that she would have liked to tell Spence more about her prosthetic? The truth was that the thing was a miracle. She had grown up knowing that prosthetic limbs were remarkable, that wounded veterans and the victims of the Boston Marathon bombing were capable of things that people injured in earlier generations could never have done. But the X4 attached below her knee still filled her with a fascination even greater than Spence's. The battery lasted a week between charges and the charger was magnetic—she could attach it to the back of her prosthetic calf without having to plug anything in. Didn't even have to have to take off her pants. And the fact that it was waterproof just blew her away. It was a complex mechanism, but it felt simple.

Explaining all of that to Spence, seeing his wide eyes, might have helped her to fight the urge to go back to her car, crank the radio, and drive as fast as possible back to Andover.

Stop it, she thought. *Just breathe.*

Naomi listened to her own advice. She inhaled deeply, exhaled slowly. Other people on the beach had been glancing at her ever since she walked onto the sand, but she had ignored them all until Spence and his Frisbee. She wore a bright yellow bikini top and a pair of black Nike Pros, which her mom still insisted on calling booty shorts, a phrase that made Naomi cringe. If she'd wanted to go unnoticed out here, she could have worn sweats, but she had never liked to hide. *Not the way Kayla likes to hide.*

She didn't like to think about Kayla.

What the hell am I doing here?

The answer had been sitting in the back of her mind, shut away like a dark family secret. Lighthouse Beach was in Chatham, a stone's throw from a spot where seals sunned themselves on the shore. Just three days ago, the beach had been shut down for several hours thanks to sightings of multiple sharks. Nobody had been attacked.

Not yet.

Naomi stared out at the water, her book forgotten. She sat up farther, one hand propped behind her, and scanned the waves, knowing they were out there. It was only mid-June, so although the sun warmed the air and the sand, the water was still chilly, which meant there weren't many people in the water today. What amazed her was that they knew the sharks were there, and still they swam. But then, she hadn't been any different a summer ago, had she?

She closed her eyes and took a deep breath. Her mother's words lingered in her head, along with the image of her imploring eyes. The lieutenant governor was used to getting her way, but she never tried to order Naomi around. No, Ellen Cardiff was sneakier than that. She sowed the seeds of doubt and hoped they would prosper.

Are you sure you should be doing this? You haven't been in the water since—

I'm not going to be in the water, Naomi had told her.

But you'll be on *the water. What if you have a panic attack? You still have nightmares. I hear you sometimes, talking in your sleep.*

She was troubled by the image of her mother standing at her open bedroom door, listening to the things she murmured while dreaming. She was also disturbed by the fact that Kayla had said almost exactly the same thing.

Kayla. Just the name in her head made her tense up with something that was not quite anger, not quite regret. By the time the doctors had let Naomi out of the hospital last summer, Kayla only had a couple of weeks left before she was scheduled to fly to California for med school. She had talked about deferring a year, which had sent her parents into a frenzy. Naomi wondered if they suspected she and their daughter were not just friends, if their panic arose from the fear of having those suspicions confirmed. They had wanted Kayla to go far away, and Kayla had hesitated. For half a day, she had considered telling her parents the truth, professing her love for a girl.

Naomi had told her to go, told her that if she stayed neither one of them would ever be sure if it had been out of love or just guilt and that resentment would poison them. They would see each other at Christmas, they promised each other, at the tail end of the semester Naomi would be skipping, and then when summer came around again they would feel each other out, see if their feelings had changed.

Kayla hadn't even made it to Christmas. She had a new girlfriend by October. Naomi had expected it all along, knew that the separation would be the end of them, but somehow it felt so much worse than it would have before the attack. Before she had lost a limb and had to take the semester off to get fitted for her prosthetic and learn how to walk with it. Before she had to endure the constant looks of pity, the questions, and the feeling that she needed to reintroduce herself to the people in her life, as if she had somehow become someone or something new, when she was still just Naomi.

She didn't hate Kayla for not sticking it out, but she thought what they'd had together at least would have earned her the courtesy of a few months of lies. If Kayla had waited to tell the truth until after the holidays, when Naomi had started back to school . . .

But Kayla hadn't waited. She said she owed Naomi the truth.

Naomi told her the truth was selfish.

When she was being honest with herself, she had to admit that the attack had changed her. Of course it had. She might still be just Naomi, but she was a different Naomi now. A more focused, less patient, more honest Naomi. That honesty had complicated things for her mother, who had been raising hell in the media about the need to do something about Cape Cod's seals. Local fishermen loved Ellen Cardiff now, because she backed their calls for culling the seal herds, which basically meant a free-for-all for sadists who wanted to kill the cute little bastards. The governor had begged her to back off, because just the idea of a public seal slaughter was terrible for publicity. Tourists were especially turned off by the idea, but the media would have shown up in droves, filmed it all, and shown it on the five o'clock news.

Naomi was the one who told her mother there might be another solution. She had spent her free time during her semester off doing research, making phone calls in which she identified herself. Scientists who would have passed off the typical twenty-one-year-old college student to some assistant or just never returned her calls had proved very willing to talk to the one-legged shark-attack-survivor daughter of the lieutenant governor. By the time Naomi had started back at B.U. in January she had decided to add journalism classes to her marine biology major, and now she was combining those two with her passion for photography. For the first time, Naomi knew exactly how she saw her future unfolding . . . and it all started here.

Her mother had set up a meeting for Naomi with a

friend at *The Boston Globe*. Ellen Cardiff had wanted to attend that meeting, but Naomi had insisted she go alone. She had to make her own way now. Her mother might be able to provide connections, but Naomi would have to turn them into opportunities, and that was exactly what she had done when she pitched *The Globe* her idea. She had gone in with a portfolio of her photographs and writing samples and come out with a commission for an article and photo essay for their Sunday magazine. Now that commission had brought her back to Cape Cod for the first time since the attack, and it was the reason she would be going to sea in two days' time. *The Globe* had been unable to resist the combination of the survivor-facing-her-fear with the political angle and the long-simmering community debate over the seal problem, which so many now thought of as a shark problem.

The idea of getting on a boat, going out on the water, made her blood run cold, but Naomi was getting on that boat Thursday because she *had* to.

The Woods Hole research team really did not want her along, but she needed this.

If she didn't go, Naomi felt sure her nightmares would never stop. That she would wake up in terror in the middle of the night for the rest of her life . . .

Her cell vibrated and she glanced down at it, surprised to be getting an actual phone call instead of a text. Even her mother mostly texted these days. When Naomi saw the caller's ID flash on the phone's screen, she stared at it for a few seconds. She exhaled a noisy breath, not quite a grunt, and answered.

"Hey. Everything okay?"

Because if Kayla was calling her something had to be

wrong. They texted occasionally, mostly awkwardly, and hadn't spoken by phone in . . . she couldn't even remember now.

"Hi," Kayla said. "I . . . wasn't sure you'd answer."

"Well, here I am."

In other words, *What the hell do you want?*

"I'm home for the summer, Nay. I was hoping . . . I mean, I'd like to see you."

Naomi went quiet. How was she supposed to reply to that? She watched the people on the beach, watched the umbrellas flapping in the wind, bending a bit too far. Watched the waves rolling onto the sand.

"You still there?" Kayla asked.

"I don't think it's a good idea," Naomi said. "Not for me, anyway. I don't see the point."

"Nay, listen . . . I have to see you. I don't want to say this to you on the phone."

"I guess you're going to have to. Whatever 'this' is." Her heart began to race. Her thoughts started coalescing around fantasies she'd had six months ago, eight months ago, but she reined them in.

Kayla sighed. "Naomi." Just the name—her real name, no pet names, no terms of endearment. "I want to tell you I'm sorry. I handled it all so badly. So damn badly."

"Handled what, exactly?"

"Everything, Nay. Everything."

Naomi breathed in the ocean air. Her skin flushed with heat that had nothing to do with the sun. For a moment she imagined she could feel the whir of power in her prosthetic.

"I'm not sure what I'm supposed to say to that, Kayla. I'm glad to hear your voice, but I still don't see the point of this. Apologies are nice—"

"I broke up with Stef."

Or she broke up with you, Naomi thought, *and now you're getting nostalgic. Don't play with me, goddammit.* Yet she felt a tremor in her heart. It pissed her off.

"Kay, I've gotta go," Naomi said.

"Wait, please. I wanted to see you face-to-face. I need to see you."

"I don't need to see *you*."

A huff of air on the line. "Okay. That's fair. It hurts, but it's definitely fair. I just wanted you to know that I did it, finally."

"Did what?" Naomi asked. But she knew. *It* could only be one thing.

"I came out to my parents. I blew up my life. They haven't thrown me out or anything and they're still going to pay for medical school, but it's like I'm invisible to them now. I did it because when I got on the plane to come home for the summer I realized I was more ashamed of hiding who I am than they could ever make me for *being* who I am."

Naomi wanted to say something snide. *How poetic.* Something like that. But even after the way she'd felt abandoned, she couldn't hurt Kayla like that.

"I'm proud of you," she said instead. "Really. I know it must hurt, but I hope you're okay and that you're proud, too. You should be."

Silence on the phone. The wind shifted and Naomi heard music drifting down the beach, someone's radio playing 1970s pop songs.

"I made a huge mistake with you, Nay. I think about the life I want five years from now instead of the old, safe life I was holding on to, and I see you there with me. Is it . . . is it too late to undo my mistake?"

Naomi smiled, but it was a sad sort of smile. She was glad Kayla couldn't see her. The wish had come true. So why didn't she feel like celebrating?

"I think it is," she said. "I think you're just afraid now and feeling alone and need a life preserver to cling to until you get something solid under your feet again. I don't want to be your life preserver, Kayla."

"That's not it. I swear it's—"

"I meant it when I said I was proud of you. But I've gotta go."

She ended the call before Kayla could reply. Better not to give her a chance to be persuasive. Not that Naomi would let herself be persuaded. At least she didn't think so.

As these thoughts crossed her mind, she spotted the fin.

Out there in the water.

A breeze kicked up, sand sweeping across her towel and grit stinging her eyes behind her sunglasses. She pulled them off, rubbed away the grains of sand, and looked again. The fin remained, cruising slowly, perhaps a hundred yards offshore. Fewer than a dozen people were in the water. She quickly scanned the beach and located Spence and his parents. Dad had jumped up to make sure the sudden breeze wouldn't blow their umbrella over and Mom was fussing over a tinfoil-wrapped sandwich that Spence seemed to be refusing to eat.

They were safe.

Naomi rose, the prosthetic so damn fine a piece of machinery that she barely noticed it doing its job. A drunk guy at a sorority party had told her she was a *fucking cyborg*, like that was the coolest thing in the world. But now she glanced down at her leg and fought back revulsion at the sense of detachment that still swept over her now and again.

She walked down toward the ocean. As she stood near the water's edge and stared out at the fin, people watched her warily, almost as if she were the danger here.

Then the fin vanished beneath the waves.

But the shark wasn't gone, she knew.

The shark was only waiting.

CHAPTER 7

———

Wolchko never rolled up the sleeves of his shirt, no matter how high the mercury climbed. He sometimes loosened his tie, but that was as far as he would take it. That morning he wore dark-green pants, a white shirt, and a purple tie in a pattern best described as chaotic. His late wife had picked out the tie six or seven years ago. He had lost weight since Antonia died, but all he'd done was tighten his belt. Without her to pick out his clothes, he knew he would be lost.

He pulled his car into the lot behind the Cosmic Muffin, NPR voices droning on the radio. The voices were soothing, even when he disagreed with them. They made him feel as if he were in the company of friends who did not expect him to participate in the conversation, and as far as Wolchko was concerned, those were the best sorts of friends. Not that he had a great deal of experience in the arena of friendship.

The Muffin was his favorite coffee shop, not because

they served so many specialty drinks but because when he asked for enough cream and sugar to turn coffee into a confection, they didn't bat an eyelash. Last summer there had been one college kid who had suggested to him that it would be easier to get himself some coffee ice cream, but Sasha, the Muffin's owner, had never allowed that kid to wait on Wolchko again and the kid hadn't reappeared at the beginning of this summer. Apparently he had moved on to greener pastures.

Wolchko killed the engine and climbed out, going over his order in his head. Rosalie liked her coffee with a double shot of espresso, the new receptionist liked iced mochaccino, Dr. Cheong took hers black, and Tye Ashmore always ordered straight-up iced coffee, no matter how cold it might be outside.

Wolchko only made it about fifteen steps before he heard a car door open and glanced over to see a thirtyish guy with close-cropped hair and stylish spectacles getting out. The guy adjusted his specs and shut his own car door, but when he started walking it wasn't toward the entrance to the Cosmic Muffin . . . it was toward Wolchko, whose eyes narrowed while a litany of possibilities cascaded through his mind. Cop, stalker, constable serving a summons, reporter.

"Mr. Wolchko?" the guy said just as Wolchko settled on the last option.

"Make an appointment."

"I've tried."

"If you've been put off by people in my office, I'm sure it's for good reason."

Spectacles put on a mask of sincerity and reason.

"Just a few questions for the *Times*," the guy said, as if he might mean *The New York Times* or the London *Times*, instead of the *Cape Cod Times*, which did not have quite the same ring of authority.

Wolchko kept walking and Specs fell in beside him.

"You're part of the Woods Hole research team running this seal experiment—"

"That's not a question," he said, unable to stop himself.

"Your personal research has focused on acoustics," Specs continued. "Some kind of negative reinforcement, attacking sharks and marine mammals with—"

"We don't attack marine life; we study behavior."

Wolchko regretted opening his mouth the moment the words were out.

"You want to manipulate their natural behavior. Don't you worry that could be detrimental to them?" the reporter prodded.

Wolchko gritted his teeth in irritation. It wasn't that the team had anything to hide. The media relations office had asked them to keep the details of their experiment confidential until afterward. Most of it had leaked out already. The public knew they were going to try to lure the seals away from the shores of the Cape and that they hoped to be able to entice them to make their home farther north this season. What the public did not know was *how*.

"Several organizations argued against your experiment during the federal permitting process. Do you think the Feds fast-tracked the permit, gave you a rubber stamp because of the Cardiff girl?"

Wolchko stopped twenty feet from the office door and turned to glare at him. "That's ridiculous. Everybody's motivated to get this done. It has nothing to do with . . ."

He trailed off. *The little shit is smiling behind his fancy specs.*

"Everyone's motivated?" the reporter said. "So you do think they rushed the permitting?"

"Never said that," Wolchko muttered.

The Cosmic Muffin's door swung open, reminding him that he did not have to stand there and talk to this asshole.

"*Sir*," Wolchko said, like the word was a stab at the reporter's heart, "if you want an interview, contact the media relations office—"

"One last thing," Specs continued. "What do you think of WHOI letting a college student go along under the auspices of the media instead of including an actual journalist? Do you think they're trying to control the story? Do they have something to hide?"

Wolchko paused, and all the tension bled out of him. He grinned and turned toward Specs. "That's what this is about? The folks at *The Globe* are making Naomi Cardiff part of the story, and it burns your ass. Truth is, I can understand why, but this behavior is hardly the way to get WHOI to reconsider, or to make sure they give you access to the team when the experiment's finished. Now, what's your name again? I'm sure I can describe you well enough when I phone your editor, but a name will make it easier."

The reporter smirked. "Any thoughts on the shark attack at Race Point this morning?"

Wolchko blinked, caught off guard. "What? There wasn't any—"

"Half an hour ago. Surfer lost a chunk of his arm. Nothing as bad as last summer, but still . . . do you think if WHOI had moved faster with this experiment that man's injury might never have happened? Don't you have a responsibility to the public?"

Wolchko wanted to smash Specs' face through the glass door of the coffee shop.

"You're not from around here, are you?" he asked.

Specs shrugged. "Seattle. Decided I wanted a change of scenery."

"You can forget any interview with anyone from the institution," Wolchko said. "Ever. We're done here."

The reporter nodded. This was not news to him. Still, he got in one last question as Wolchko let go of the door and it glided slowly closed.

"Would you go in the water at Race Point right now, sir?" the reporter asked. "Would you swim there today?"

Wolchko turned away as the door clicked shut, but he hoped the reporter heard his reply.

"You first."

CHAPTER 8

The jangling phone dragged Kat Cheong up from sleep, wisps of dreams muddling her thoughts so much that she had to shake her head to disperse them. She stared blearily at the phone as it rang again. The room was dark, save for the moonlight that turned the curtains pale and ghostly and the electric burn of the digits on her alarm clock. Twelve minutes past midnight and her phone was ringing, and that sort of thing never boded well.

Kat picked the phone up from its cradle, her voice a sleepy rasp. "Hello?"

No one spoke, but she could hear the seashell hiss of an open line. Someone was there and had not yet hung up. Anger flickered through her, and then concern. Her mother had been dead for seven years and her father lived alone. An image swam into her head of her burly, amiable gray-bearded old dad lying on the floor of his bedroom with his hand clutched to his chest. It was a nightmare she'd had before, both sleeping and awake.

"Dad?" she ventured, hoping the call would turn out to be some late-night pervert or a political robocall instead of this thing she feared.

Kat heard breathing, a small grunt of satisfaction, and then a click, which turned the open line into the flat nothing that told her the call had ended. A prickling sensation crept along her spine as her worry and annoyance were replaced by a flutter of fear. She shuddered as she rested the phone back on its cradle and burrowed beneath her covers. It was still early summer and the night breeze carried a chill off the ocean.

She turned over, back toward the nightstand, but she felt the presence of the phone as if it were a hand that might reach out at any moment and tap her shoulder with a single long finger. The curtains rustled with the breeze and she closed her eyes, fighting the suspicion that the phone would ring again. Midnight phone calls were dreadful things. They spoke of drunken car wrecks and sudden death. No good news arrived by telephone after midnight. Hell, after 9:00 p.m., now that she was old enough to be called Doctor. Late-night texts were one thing, but a call on her landline? Shit, who even had a landline now, unless the cable company forced it on them as part of a package deal?

Nobody, she thought, breathing deeply, telling her racing heart to be at peace.

Another deep inhalation and she could feel the tight muscles in her neck and shoulders begin to relax. The jangling of the phone still echoed in her ears, but the lure of sleep was powerful. A little buzz of irritation kept her from surrendering to it completely. She would have liked to know who made that phone call. Kat didn't have caller ID on the phone in her bedroom, but it occurred to her that she could go into the kitchen and check it there.

Then she was gone, easing into the soft comfort of slumber.

A loud rapping snapped her awake. Kat twisted around in the bed, tangling herself in the sheet, and stared at the windows. Her bedroom was on the first floor and there was a little deck just outside with a view of the woods and the water beyond.

A shadow stood outside the windows, a silhouette that vanished in a blink as she froze, unable to breathe.

What if he broke the glass in the French doors, out in her living room? It would be only seconds before he reached her.

Someone whispered her name. Fear closed her throat. The silhouette darted back across the moonlit deck beyond those curtains. Fingers drummed and scratched along the glass and she wanted to scream.

"*We're coming in, Kat,*" the voice said, so softly that she could barely make it out.

Something snapped inside her, and it surprised her to find that the thing she felt breaking was her fear. It burned off like droplets of water on hot tar, and anger surged through her.

"Who's there?" she shouted, lunging from her bed.

Only as she reached for the heavy crystal ballerina statue on her bureau did she remember the phone, the idea that it could be used to summon the police. Kat hesitated, gripping the ballerina, and she reached out to whip the curtains aside.

Her heart thundered as she stared out into the moonlit woods. Slivers of dark ocean were visible between the trees, but there was no sign of that silhouette. For half a second she wondered if she was experiencing a lucid dream, but then she heard thumping at the side of the house and a fresh wave of anger hit her. She snatched up the phone in her free hand and ran out into the hall and then into the front-to-back living room. Outside the French doors at the back there was only moonlight, but now she heard a shout from the front and some kind of scuffle and thump, as if her tormentor had fallen.

She pressed the TALK button on the phone. Dialed 9 and 1—and then her doorbell rang. She snapped her head up to stare toward the front of the house and the doorbell rang again. Someone started to knock. She hit the 1 button a second time, held the phone to her ear as she moved soundlessly to the front living room window.

A face appeared, eyes wide. Profanity streamed from her lips as she jerked back from the window.

A little buzz-click came over the phone. "Nine-one-one service. What is the nature of your emergency?"

The face called her name.

Kat stared at it, her anger taking on a different hue.

"I'm sorry," she told the 911 operator. "So sorry. False alarm."

"Ma'am, if you—"

Kat stabbed the phone's off button with her thumb and tossed it onto the sofa. She marched to the front door, unlocked it, and threw it open. Tye stood on the brick front steps and she felt the words rising in her throat, ready to cuss him out as she had never cussed out anyone in her life. She knew he had been holding a grudge about her breaking off their relationship, but it had been months and now he had decided to scare the crap out of her in the middle of the night? It was the move of a King Asshole, and she had never imagined he fit into that category.

"You . . . ," she began.

Then she saw the blood on his forehead and under his nose.

"Son of a bitch *hit* me," Tye said, as if he was trying the words out to see if he himself believed them. Somehow it was that disbelief that convinced Kat.

The pieces fell into place. Somebody had been out there intending to do her harm or just scare the shit out of her. The question burning the hottest in her brain was *why*, but she knew Tye couldn't answer that, so she moved on to the next question.

"Did you see his face?"

He sniffed, wiped blood from his upper lip with the back of his hand, winced at the pain of touching his nose. "He's wearing a black hoodie, cinched tight. All I can tell you is he's white, shorter than me, and willing to draw blood."

"Next question, then," Kat said, and he must have heard it coming in her tone of voice, because he stiffened, his injuries forgotten as he glanced up at her. "What the hell are you doing outside my house in the middle of the night, besides getting hit in the face?"

Tye stared at her. He scratched at the back of his head and exhaled, glancing around like he might find the answer on the front lawn somewhere.

"Don't say you came over here to profess your love like Romeo at Juliet's balcony."

"What if I did?"

Kat cocked an eyebrow at him. Insects buzzed around his head and some were getting into the house, but she preferred that to letting him inside at the moment.

"You're not Romeo, and I sure as hell am not Juliet," she said. "Plus, there's no way I'm going to believe that you just happened to be here on the one night when some freak decided to roust me from my bed. Too much of a coincidence, Tye. So I ask you again, what are you—"

"It's not the first time," he told her.

She frowned. "Which part?"

He threw up his hands. "Not the freak part, obviously. Not as far as I know, anyway. I'm saying it's not the first time I've had trouble sleeping and found myself walking past your place. It happens a couple of times a week."

Kat did not need him to spell it out any further. Tye had a history of insomnia and he lived half a mile away. If the crumbling of their relationship had been keeping him up nights, she could not allow that to be her problem.

But she opened the door a little farther. Maybe just for tonight.

"You might as well come in while there are still some bugs on the outside of my house instead of in here with me. I won't be able to fall right back to sleep anyway. I've got that herbal tea that helps you to . . ." The words trailed off and she gave a little shake of her head. "Anyway, I can make us tea."

Tye only stared at her. In the moonlight, the blood on his face glistened black and the rest of his skin seemed sallow and waxy. He looked like something dead.

"You should call the police, file a report," he said. "If they want to ask me about it, they can talk to me in the morning before we leave."

Kat's chest hurt. She should not have been disappointed, felt angry at him and at herself that she was.

"See you at seven," she said.

Tye turned and walked toward home, gingerly wiping more blood from his face. As she closed the door, she told herself she did not need him to protect her or to love her.

The first part was certainly true; she could protect herself. But she wasn't so sure about the second part. They had made a terrible couple—this was demonstrable fact—but somehow that did not erase her regret.

Kat locked her door, searched around for her phone, and dialed the local number for the police department, not daring to phone 911 again, especially now that the crisis was over. When the call ended she found herself sitting on the floral sofa in her living room. She wanted that cup of tea but had no interest in going into the kitchen to make it. Not yet. For the moment she could only sit there and watch the windows and listen very carefully and maybe hold her breath a little.

Wondering who had come to her window tonight and if he would come back.

Tomorrow morning she would be headed out to sea for two full days and a night. Part of her wished the trip would take even longer, that she could stay out on the water and not deal with this new and unwelcome fear or the other complications in her life. But in her heart she knew that it never mattered how far you ran to get away from your troubles. You carried them with you, always.

Literally, in this case, because she and Tye would be on the boat together.

A chill ran through her as she remembered that voice outside her window, calling her name, and the tapping and scratching on the glass. The jangling of her phone and the presence of someone on the other end of the line. She thought of the refrain of a haunting song by one of her favorite bands.

If I stay here, trouble will find me.

Tye would not be the only one unable to sleep tonight.

CHAPTER 9

—

Light rain spattered the dock as Naomi hurried toward the R/V *Thaumas*, the Woods Hole research vessel upon which she'd be spending at least the next forty hours. It was past seven o'clock, which meant that she was late, but thanks to the gray blanket of sky, the morning seemed barely to have arrived. Over her shoulder, she carried a faded canvas backpack containing a change of clothes, a toothbrush, and her camera case. Her tired eyes itched and she rubbed at them, stifling a yawn with the back of one hand. In the other she held the biggest cup of coffee Dunkin' Donuts would serve. Nothing fancy. No hazelnut or French vanilla. Just big damn coffee, cream only. Sugar was for amateurs.

When she had driven up to the front entrance of the Woods Hole Oceanographic Institution, she had been expecting protesters. Maybe some TV cameras. Though details had been sketchy, what little information WHOI had disseminated had inspired keen interest all over the

Cape—and beyond—for months. Yet, aside from a single minivan and a middle-aged woman with a hand-painted banner, the road leading to the institution had been deserted. Naomi found herself slightly disappointed. It might have been pure fancy, but she imagined that in her mother's era people who gave a shit about the world had a bit more fortitude.

Or maybe it's just that nobody cares that much, she thought. It was a possibility, of course. The world was full of people primed for reflexive outrage, people who moved on to the next tirade as easily as a seventh-grade girl changed outfits. She remembered those girls and the way they had judged her for her own wardrobe choices, for not caring enough to make herself look pretty—or what they thought pretty was supposed to be. At twenty-one, she remembered middle school as if it had been a prison sentence. It had forged her, steeled her for the future, for dealing with the shit the world had thrown at her ever since.

Naomi hurried through the WHOI complex, showed her ID three times, and finally made her way along the docks where the institution's various research vessels were moored. The *Thaumas* was a thirty-five-footer that glistened like new, its blue hull and white wheelhouse vivid with color against the dull gray of the day. A red stripe along the hull added a dash of style, the thought of which made her smile inwardly.

The one piece of advice the editor at *The Globe* had given her had been quite simple—*do your homework*. Naomi would have prepared anyway, but his advice had sounded more like a caution, and so she had doubled down on the research she had done in advance of this experience. In her experience, most people over thirty treated college students like unruly pets, and she was determined not to let Dr. Cheong's team perceive her as an interloper.

But that's exactly what you are, she thought, hurrying toward the boat.

The truth. Which made it all the more important for her to prove she had a reason to be there.

WHOI was a research collective, the scientific equivalent of an old-time hippie commune. Scientists survived at the institution based on their ability to raise the money to fund their own work. As long as they brought in the funding, they got to stick around. Naomi was sure it must be more complicated than that, but she admired the autonomy WHOI researchers seemed to have.

The rain picked up strength as she reached the *Thaumas*. Raincoated figures moved around on deck, shifting equipment, and she was relieved to see they had not been delayed by her late arrival. The research vessel rocked in the water, slamming against the bumpers on the dock. The folded arm of the crane on the rear deck swayed back and forth as the boat bobbed. She faltered a second as her subconscious mind gauged the amount of space onboard the Thaumas now that her arrival made seven. It was going to be close quarters and that unsettled her. She had known the math in advance, of course, but now that she saw the ship up close the idea gave her pause. Even if they slept in shifts, it was going to get intimate down below.

One of the figures up on deck spotted her and turned, raising a hand.

"Naomi, come aboard!" he said, grinning under the hood of his raincoat. She had met Amadou N'Dour two days before for a preinterview and a quick photo session. The skipper of the *Thaumas* was dead serious about his boat and his responsibilities but seemed lighthearted about everything else.

"Good morning, Captain N'Dour," she replied as she stepped across the gap between dock and ship, leaving the land behind.

The skipper frowned. "Don't know about that," he replied in his Senegalese accent, a little French and a little West African. "They're saying this big storm is tracking east, that it's going to miss us completely, but I don't trust weathermen. I trust the sky. And the sky's got me worried."

Naomi blinked, a ripple of worry going through her. "If you're worried, then I'm terrified."

Captain N'Dour laughed. "Don't be crazy. I don't like sailing in storms, but I've done it a thousand times. Plus, we won't be far from shore. You're safe with me."

Normally she bristled when men said that sort of thing to her, but Naomi smiled. Somehow the captain really did make her feel safe.

The introductions began then, starting with the first mate, a lean, unshaven man named Peter Bergting. Some kind of Scandinavian name, though Bergting had no trace of an accent. Naomi shook hands with Dr. Cheong and Dr. Ashmore. She had met them once before, but now that she had actually arrived and her presence on board had become reality they were a bit warmer toward her. She did not hold their reservations against them. Having her along during this experiment was a decision made in the upper echelons of WHOI, under advice from their media relations office. Allowing Naomi to join them would give Woods Hole great press, whether or not the experiment worked. Refusing her would accomplish the opposite. Even so, she felt pretty sure Dr. Cheong would not have invited her if she'd felt she had a choice.

"I'll try not to get in your way, Dr. Cheong," Naomi said, focusing on the lead scientist. The rain pelted them both and Naomi saw it beading up, running down the slick surface of the scientist's coat.

"Don't worry," she replied. "We won't let you."

Dr. Ashmore smiled. "She's teasing."

"Is she?"

"I am," Dr. Cheong said. "And call me Kat, okay? By tomorrow night we'll all be best friends, or we'll have killed each other. We might as well be on a first-name basis."

Kat introduced their assistant, a grad student named Rosalie Suarez, as well as Eddie Wolchko, the acoustics specialist and engineer who had installed the strange apparatus that now adorned the roof of the *Thaumas*'s wheelhouse. Wolchko wiped his hands on a rag as he stepped out into the light spatter of rain.

"A pleasure to meet you," he said, shaking her hand. His gaze flicked down toward her leg.

"Nice to meet you, too," Naomi said, cocking her head, trying to draw his eyes back to her face. Once upon a time, she had been more troubled by guys staring at her tits. Now she almost missed it.

"With your pants on, you can't even tell," Wolchko said.

Overhearing, Rosalie sighed loudly. "Christ, Eddie."

Wolchko flushed deeply, scrunching his face in self-recrimination. "Damn it, I'm sorry. I just . . . sometimes thoughts roll around in my head and I open my mouth and the wrong one comes out."

Naomi nodded. "I know the feeling. But I'm sorry to say you won't be seeing me with my pants *off*."

The others laughed.

Wolchko hung his head in shame. "There's a reason I try to avoid leaving my office."

Captain N'Dour gave a loud clap of his hands. "There you have it, my friends. The truth is out. Eddie Wolchko has no filter. You'll get used to it. And you get to watch him squirm every time he realizes there's something he probably should not have said out loud."

Then Bergting was there, telling them all it was time to cast off, and Wolchko shot him a grateful look before hurrying back into the wheelhouse. Naomi found herself feeling bad for him. She followed Wolchko into the wheelhouse. When he glanced at her, she nodded.

"No worries," she said. "I don't trust anyone with too good a filter."

Shortly after they cast off and the boat began to ply its way along the coast, Naomi went below to stow her gear, then came back up with her camera and an umbrella. The camera had its own rain shield, but the umbrella helped to keep the lens from speckling and gave her more room to maneuver. As she adjusted to the pitch of the boat, getting her sea legs, she began to snap photos.

She wore a dark-red raincoat and a weathered Red Sox cap that had once belonged to her father, though he'd been dead so long she only remembered his face from pictures. If someone had asked her, she might have been willing to admit this was one of the reasons photography felt so important to her, but she was not in the habit of volunteering the information.

Naomi had fallen in love with photography as early as the fourth grade. Her teacher had assigned a project detailing their family histories. Most of Naomi's classmates had left it to their parents, but once her mom had started pulling out books of old photos she had become lost in the mystery of every picture. Who were these people? What were their stories? Where were the photos taken? And then there was her dad, smiling and alive.

She'd begun taking her own shots with the family camera, snapping pictures of people, of trees and flowers and architecture, of her cat, Phineas, and the neighbors' dog. Her passion for marine life had come later, and she'd nurtured that passion enthusiastically, right up until the moment it nearly killed her.

Time vanished when she was behind her camera. When they'd been together, Kayla had been her favorite model. The camera had introduced them, really. It had given Naomi the confidence to approach a girl that beautiful, to ask if she minded being photographed. Kayla had arched a suggestive eyebrow and said, *Clothes on or off?* That had been the beginning of them. For the first time it occurred to Naomi that the camera had also been the beginning of the end. The camera and her stupidity for thinking that she had been far enough away from the seals that a shark would not confuse her with one of them.

Is it too late to undo my mistake? Kayla's words from the day before echoed in Naomi's mind now, haunting her. *Yes*, she thought. *It's too damn late, all right?*

But no matter how emphatically she issued that reply inside her head, it didn't feel convincing.

Now she stood on the deck and the boat churned onward, but Naomi paid little attention to their progress. She focused on the task at hand. Focused on what the camera saw.

Dr. Cheong—*Call me Kat*, she'd said, and Naomi would

try—craned her neck to look up at the dish apparatus on top of the boat.

"How certain are we that we're broadcasting?" Kat called into the wheelhouse.

Wolchko poked his head out. "The signal is going out from both arrays."

"You're one hundred percent certain?"

Wolchko tried to hide his irritation, but Naomi saw it ripple across his features before he managed to control himself. "One hundred percent," he said. "Topside and belowdecks."

"Thank you, Eddie," Kat said. If she noticed his irritation, it was pretty clear she did not give a shit.

Naomi snapped a few pictures of her. Kat was attractive in the too-serious way of people lost in their work, but she could not be blamed for her focus. She and her team had a lot riding on this experiment.

Bergting had gone below, leaving Captain N'Dour to pilot the boat. Tye stood at the prow with binoculars, watching the coastline and making notes with some kind of voice recorder. Naomi suspected the wind would turn half of those recordings into unintelligible gibberish, but these guys were the scientists, so maybe they knew what they were doing.

She moved toward the wheelhouse, peered inside, and snapped a few quick shots of Wolchko at work with Rosalie, whose job seemed to be to sit inside with a laptop and read data, which seemed boring as hell, considering they hadn't done anything to acquire new data as yet. Rosalie was only two years older than Naomi—the same age as Kayla—but that little span of time had somehow given her the gravitas of adulthood. They should have been natural allies, but Rosalie had barely acknowledged her presence after the initial introduction. Busy with work, Naomi figured.

Or maybe she was just a bitch.

Naomi snapped a few more pictures. They were boring shots, just Wolchko and Rosalie studying computer screens, and Captain N'Dour in the background, going about his business as if the rest of them were ghosts whose chain-rattling shenanigans he was trying to ignore. But *The Globe* would want that sort of thing, photos of the team doing their work, to go along with the images Naomi hoped to get of the seal herds and the occasional shark fin.

She shuddered, taking a moment to breathe.

"Naomi," a voice said, and she flinched, startled. It was Eddie Wolchko, his brows knitting in consternation at her reaction. "Sorry," he added. "Didn't mean to spook you."

In reply, she took his picture. "Apologies in return, but I can't let that facial expression go to waste."

He grunted. "I'm not much for having my photo taken."

"It's the least you can do after that awkward bit with my leg."

"Fair enough. I told you, though, I'm not—"

"Good with people." She snapped his picture again. "It's okay, Dr. Wolchko. People are so bizarre about it all that I've gotten into the bad habit of busting balls any time it turns awkward. I can't help myself, but I'm working on it."

The boat rocked a bit harder, sea spray pattering the deck. She raised the camera again, and this time he managed to muster half a smile for it.

Just like that, they were at ease with each other. Naomi liked him, this stiff, awkward man. Soon they were standing at the railing together as she took long-distance shots of one of the beaches around Chatham—she could not be sure exactly how far they had come.

"It's damn impressive, I must say," Wolchko observed. Naomi glanced up from her camera. "What is?"

"I figured you'd have a much more difficult time staying upright with the boat rocking. I have a hard enough time balancing out here, and I've got both my legs."

From someone else, it might have come off as insensitive, but she had Wolchko figured out. Or she was starting to. His curiosity and wonder felt genuine. Naomi had put up with a lot of people who made her feel like a victim or a freak or as if her life were over, but Wolchko treated this like any other conversation, like what had happened to her was just another version of normal.

"Honestly, it's pretty amazing," Naomi admitted, glancing around because she knew she sounded anything but normal when she talked this way. "Not like I don't wish it hadn't happened. I won't give you the list of truly suckish parts of going through what I've gone through. But it's pretty miraculous—"

Then Tye appeared and she fell silent. He joined them at the railing, using his binoculars to study the coastline more closely.

"Tye," she said, willfully changing the subject, "why is the boat named the *Thaumas*? Somebody couldn't spell *Thomas*?"

The binoculars didn't even twitch. "Thaumas is a Greek sea god."

"I thought that was Poseidon," Wolchko said.

Tye's lips twitched. It wasn't much. Not a sneer or even a smile, but there was something condescending in that little twitch, that almost disdain, and right then Naomi decided she did not like Dr. Tye Ashmore very much.

"The Greeks had a lot of sea gods," Tye said. "Thaumas is the god of all the wonders of the sea."

Naomi snapped a picture of Tye and his binoculars. "That's kind of happy sounding. Poseidon is always portrayed as being such a dick. I wonder why we don't hear more about Thaumas, 'god of all the wonders of the sea.'"

"Poseidon killed him and took his throne," Tye explained, still focused on the shore, where the herds of seals had stubbornly refused to respond to the siren call of whatever signal the boat had been broadcasting at them.

Naomi and Wolchko exchanged a raised-eyebrow glance.

"Well," Wolchko said to her, "you did say Poseidon was a dick."

Naomi barked laughter, irritating Tye, which made her even happier. Wolchko laughed as well, and since she had the idea he did not get a lot of laughs out of his typical day, this pleased her.

Then Rosalie called out, and they all turned.

"Come take a look at this," she said from the opposite railing, the starboard side.

Naomi and Wolchko joined her there, and Kat emerged from the wheelhouse to do the same. Rosalie had her thick hair tied back and a set of her own binoculars pressed to her eyes. She sensed their presence without turning and pointed southeast, toward a smaller vessel that almost seemed to be trailing them.

"They've been pacing us for the last twenty minutes," she said. Then she glanced back and realized she was talking to Naomi and her expression shifted to derision.

"Could be press," Naomi said. "Could be protesters."

"Greenpeace," Wolchko added. "SeaLove. There are half a dozen organizations who'd like to interfere, or at least keep an eye on us."

Rosalie seemed content with Wolchko's presence, seemed to look up to him, but Naomi could feel that she was unwelcome. She had decided to say something, try to break the ice, but then Kat pushed between them and took Rosalie's binoculars, having a glimpse for herself.

The Endangered Species Act and the Marine Mammal Protection Act required anyone whose research might alter the creatures' natural behavior to apply to the National Oceanic and Atmospheric Administration for a permit. Like any other government office, NOAA had a tendency to drag their feet, but in the case of this experiment, many forces had been in place to usher them toward a quicker decision. The attack that had killed Luke Turner and mutilated Naomi had forced the public to link the adorable seals with hungry sharks in a way that made them truly nervous. The local fishermen, the state government, and local business leaders all wanted both seals and sharks gone, which meant that funding sources had started lining up to finance Dr. Cheong's research.

Pretty much the only people who didn't want the WHOI experiment to work were animal rights activist groups. They thought Dr. Cheong's team was interfering with the natural order and endangering the seals. Those organizations had a lot of money for attorneys and a lot of social media power, and NOAA had taken that into consideration when evaluating the permit application. They had fast-tracked the approval. Naomi thought maybe they had moved so swiftly because the longer they waited, the more time SeaLove and Greenpeace and the rest would have had to organize their opposition.

Naomi zoomed in as much as her camera would allow and snapped photos of the other boat and the few figures she could see onboard. With the gray sky and the rain, it was hard to make out much of anything.

"It could just be some lookie loos, curious about what

we're up to," Kat said. "Either way, it doesn't matter. Just go about your business. This is an experiment, not a P.R. campaign."

Naomi stiffened. Maybe she was just being oversensitive now, but this felt like a jab at her. As Kat handed the binoculars back to Rosalie, Naomi again felt the need to say something, argue the legitimacy of her presence onboard.

The seals interrupted.

"They're on the move, Kat," Tye called out.

Kat nudged Naomi and Wolchko and Rosalie aside and dashed across the deck. They followed.

"Are you sure?" Kat asked.

Tye grinned and offered her his own binoculars, but she didn't need them. From this distance, they could all see the swathes of seals waddling on their bellies along the sand and slipping into the water. Bergting came out of the wheelhouse, craning his neck.

"They're on the move," Tye said again.

Kat let out a cry of victory.

Naomi got that moment of exuberance on film, then turned and started shooting images of the seals' exodus. As she watched the herd vanish beneath the waves, she kept an eye on the water, because she knew the sharks were there, waiting. The signal from the *Thaumas* was luring the seals en masse, persuading them to act against their instincts.

For the sharks, it might as well have been the dinner bell.

CHAPTER 10

~

The little crew of the *Thaumas* let out a cheer as the boat passed Race Point in Provincetown—the tip of Cape Cod—and the seal herd flowed off the sand and into the water, joining the mass exodus that swam behind the boat, following the signal. Kat did not want to celebrate prematurely, but she did allow herself a little fist pump. Even the first mate, Bergting, called out a loud woo-hoo of support and applauded for them, and she couldn't help grinning when he gave her a thumbs-up.

"All right, calm yourselves," she said loudly, making sure she would be overheard in the wind and the rain. "This is just proof of concept. It's a long journey from here to being able to claim success, so settle down."

As she glanced around, she spotted Naomi taking photos of her—recording the moment of triumph or something. Kat's face flushed with irritation, but she brushed it off. The girl was here to do a job, just like the rest of them, which meant Kat would have to get used to having her picture taken. Still . . .

"Naomi, the real story's out there," she said, pointing toward shore.

The girl nodded agreeably. Maybe she understood that Kat didn't want to be the center of attention, that she had no interest in being the story . . . or maybe she really did see that the seal herd moving en masse off the shore was a remarkable achievement for the whole team. Either way, Naomi focused on the sudden migration, which gave Kat a few moments to stand at the railing and appreciate what she was seeing. The seal numbers had been growing exponentially, and the sharks weren't the only thing that came along with them. The herds also brought their appetites, which meant they ate a lot of fish . . . and they covered their nesting ground with their shit. The stink downwind of that had worsened over the past few years to the point where it drove people away and kept them away.

So many little problems becoming big problems . . . *And we might be solving them all*, Kat thought. Then she smiled inwardly. *Now who's getting ahead of herself?*

The wind gusted harder and she pulled the strings of her raincoat's hood tighter. The dark sky had turned the water black and gray, so that it was easy to look at the seal migration and lose track of how many there really were. Their bodies arced out of the water as they swam, but their colors blended. She spotted hundreds of dark heads poking up and then submerging again, but the real numbers would be hard to gauge. Fortunately, that was Tye's job.

As if summoned by the thought, he appeared at the railing beside her. He hadn't bothered with his hood, and his wet hair plastered his head, rain trickling down his face.

"This is damn cool," he said.

"Thanks to Wolchko. He built the thing."

Tye bumped her with his hip. "Based on your theory, and our research. Maybe we couldn't have done it without him, but he couldn't have done it without us, either."

Kat turned to Tye. To speak without shouting, they had to be close, there in the rain, with the boat rising and falling on the ocean beneath them. She hadn't been this close to him in months and the intimacy unsettled her. Confused her. And she resented that confusion.

"Yes, it's a team effort, Tye. Is that what you want me to say? Don't worry, it may be my team, but everyone will get credit for their contributions, from Captain N'Dour to Rosalie."

Tye flinched, as if the words stung. And maybe they did. Maybe she had meant them to.

Tye started to argue, but then Naomi approached, grabbing hold of the base of the crane to steady herself. She wore a broad grin, and despite the intrusion Kat couldn't help but marvel at the girl's resilience. The prosthetic might have been a remarkable piece of technology, but Naomi had still needed to adjust to it, both as a limb and as a concept. Less than a year after a shark had torn her leg off, this college kid walked around on the surging deck of a research ship with a camera around her neck, apparently having the time of her life.

"Do you guys mind if I capture the moment?" Naomi asked.

"Actually, now's really not—" Tye began.

Kat elbowed him. "We don't mind at all."

She put her arm around Tye, startling him with her closeness. Starling herself a little bit, too. But this was their project, something they shared; she refused to allow the complexities of their relationship to destroy the camaraderie this team deserved.

"Naomi, I figure you don't need me to tell you this, but please make sure to get the whole team," Kat said. "If this experiment fails, I want to make sure everyone shares the blame."

The girl laughed as she snapped another shot and then strode away, moving carefully forward. Kat turned to look back out at the seals, only to find Tye staring at her as if doubting her sanity.

"What?" she said. "I'm joking, obviously."

"I know." He laid his hand over hers on the railing, just for a second. He squeezed and then pulled his hand away. "I'm just glad you can."

Kat might have jerked her hand away if he'd left his there any longer. Instead, the feeling of his touch lingered, reminding her of the comfort they had once taken from each other. She watched him move farther along the stern, binoculars in one hand and walkie-talkie in the other. He'd be making observations about the herd's behavior, trying to get a rough count, and making sure that the boat did not outpace them. The last thing the team wanted was to get too far ahead, so that the signal broadcasting from the two dishes—one on top of the wheelhouse and the other underwater, along the boat's keel—would no longer be able to influence the seals' behavior. Tye would radio the information in to Rosalie in the wheelhouse, and she would input everything, along with whatever data Wolchko must already be feeding her about signal strength and modulation.

The boat plied northward, straight for the Maine coast.

A trickle of rainwater slid down Kat's neck and inside her shirt and she decided to celebrate the morning's small victory with another cup of coffee. She headed for the wheelhouse, intending to go below and dry off a little and pop a pod into the Keurig. Everyone had a function at the moment except for her. A few minutes for an extra coffee was one of the perks of being in charge.

Then Tye called her name and she turned to see him still at the back rail. His serious expression had vanished, replaced by a childlike excitement that made him look like a rain-drenched puppy. Behind Kat, Naomi saw that something was going on, and started toward them again. In the wheelhouse, Wolchko poked his head out, frowning as he tried to read the strange excitement building there.

Kat didn't ask Tye what had him grinning. One glimpse at the churning mass of seals trailing in their wake and she did not need to ask. Instead, she lifted the binoculars that hung around her neck and peered out at their wake for a closer look.

She counted at least three large fins.

"Great Whites," Tye said.

Kat kept silent. They both knew what this meant. The signal had lured the seals away from the shore as planned. The hope had been that this would draw the sharks with them, that the predators along the Cape Cod shore would follow them north, but Kat had not anticipated such an immediate response.

"It's only a start," she told Tye, knowing her rationality would not extinguish the gleam in his eyes. Knowing her own eyes must have the same gleam.

They had to get the seals to follow them all the way to Bald Cap, the small island off the coast of Maine that was their destination. It was a hell of a long way, and the seals might give up interest in the signal. Even more likely, the sharks might give up interest in the seals. The sharks were following only their own hunger and instinct to hunt. The signal would not be affecting them. As they plowed north, the water would become colder, and the sharks might well break off the hunt. Kat and Tye both knew that.

But as she'd said, it was a start.

And even if the boat could lead the seals all the way to Bald Cap, even if the sharks followed, they would then have to repeat the procedure several times a year, at least. Unless they could figure out a way to get the seals to relocate there permanently.

Something clicked in her mind, thoughts like puzzle pieces locking into place. She nodded to herself.

"Y'know," she said without taking down her binoculars. "If this works, we could wire something up at Bald Cap to broadcast the signal at a low level all year round."

Tye also kept his binoculars to his eyes. "I was just thinking the same thing."

"Great minds."

Kat bumped him with her hip. He bumped her back. For the first time in so many months, all the tension between them was gone.

Then Wolchko shouted. Kat and Tye turned to see him pointing. The small boat they'd seen earlier had reappeared, closer than before. It kept pace with them, 150 yards to starboard. Naomi and Wolchko were already at the railing, watching the newcomers.

"Who the hell are these guys?" Tye asked as he and Kat moved to join Naomi and Wolchko.

"Media, maybe?" Naomi offered. "My story won't be filed until we get back, but all the seals trailing behind us kind of tell part of the story all by themselves."

"I still think it's a protest," Kat said. "But I guess we'll—"

"Son of a bitch," Wolchko said, lowering his binoculars. He pointed out at the other vessel. "I know that guy."

CHAPTER 11

The man Eddie Wolchko thought of as "Specs" stood on the deck of the smaller boat, a twenty-five-foot Bayliner Ciera that SeaLove had bought used with money donated from its membership. The boat had been built in 1989, but it still ran beautifully. Specs, whose real name was Tony Feole, wasn't going to be able to ram it into a whaling ship or do much to block the path of one of the massive Arctic research vessels, but it was small and quiet enough to glide up alongside a mooring for a little sabotage. The security at WHOI was too tight for late-night ecoterrorism, but Feole and his small crew had other plans.

"I still think we should just shoot that fucking dish."

Feole stabbed a withering look at Ash, who only lifted her chin higher, like a boxer not afraid of an incoming punch. Almost daring him to pull rank on her. Ash was not the most militant member of SeaLove he had ever encountered, but she was the most militant he would ever have taken out on a mission with him. Since a crew had

set fire to an oil rig in 2002, SeaLove had publicly dis-
avowed anything other than organized protest. Privately,
the leadership condoned the continuation of more drastic
action, as long as they couldn't be linked to it. Feole didn't
mind trying to scare someone off or posing as a reporter
to get information. He wasn't afraid of risking jail time.
But there were lines he had grown reluctant to cross.

"They've seen us. They've got us on film," Feole said.
"I'm not letting you pull out a rifle and take shots at the
dish."

"Who cares if they have us on film?" Ash sneered, glaring with hatred at the R/V *Thaumas* and the figures they
could see standing on the deck. "You used to be willing
to go to prison for the things you believed in, Tony."

"I still am," Feole replied. The boat hit a swell and he
had to grab on to something to stay upright. The ocean
spray coated his right side, obscuring his glasses. He took
off his specs and blew on them, clearing them as best he
could for the moment. "I'm just not willing to go to prison
because I was an idiot."

He knew Ash would be staring daggers at him but refused to give her the satisfaction of acknowledging that
look. They had been friends since college, thrown together
by politics and then left stranded together when most of
the others who claimed to share their passion decided they
had never been that passionate in the first place. Since then,
humankind had gone about the slow, inexorable process
of destroying the global ecoystem, poisoning the ocean,
exterminating species on both land and sea. Feole and Ash
moved from group to group, eventually settling into posi-
tions with SeaLove, admiring the intellect and aggressive
tactics of the organization.

"You calling me an idiot?" she asked.

Rolling his eyes, he shot her a sidelong glance. "Have I ever hesitated to call you an idiot to your face if I thought you were being stupid? I never have. And you've done me the same courtesy, Ashleigh. It's why we've been able to stay friends as long as we have. So the answer is no, I'm not calling you an idiot, but shooting at people—especially people who just took your picture—would be pretty damned idiotic. Now, do you need me to hold your hand some more, or can we get on with—"

She punched his shoulder, one knuckle pointed to dig into the muscle. It hurt.

"Fuck!" Feole barked, jerking away from her.

Ash marched after him, poked him hard in the chest with one stern finger. "I don't need anyone to hold my god-damned hand, and if I did, I sure wouldn't come to you."

He exhaled, guilt washing over him as the pain in his shoulder subsided. "I'm sorry. I shouldn't have said that, okay? But we won't help ourselves and we damn sure won't help our cause if all we succeed in doing out here is getting our asses tossed in prison. I don't know about you, but I don't think I could live on prison food, and I shudder to think what the coffee must be like behind bars."

"Shit," Ash replied. "I shudder to think."

She offered a weak smile, but it was more than he'd anticipated, so he would take it.

"So we stick with the plan?" he ventured.

"For now. But let me ask you this: If we can't jam their signal, and what they're doing doesn't end up killing a bunch of seals so we can have visual evidence that it's causing real harm, where does that leave us?"

Feole softened. "It leaves us where we've always been. Studying the data, searching for their secrets."

"You know as well as I do that any negative impact of

exposure to this acoustic signal could take years to show up in the seal population."

"Ash," he said, "this work is important. I've dedicated my life to it. But I'm not willing to die for it, and you shouldn't be, either. We follow protocol, simple as that."

She rubbed at the spot on his shoulder that she'd hit. "Okay." Then she gave him the mischievous smile that always worried him. "For now."

Ash cared a great deal for Tony Feole, but over the past year or so she had developed a powerful urge to strangle him. Her own desire to fight for their cause burned ever brighter inside her, but Feole seemed to be growing more cautious. It would not surprise her if this turned out to be his last field trip. He might not have been losing his heart, but he certainly seemed to be losing his nerve.

Rain plastered her hair against her head. She slid a wet lock away from her eyes as she strode across the wet, heaving deck and headed beneath the overhang that served as shelter on this tub. The boat wasn't big enough to have anything that could be called a wheelhouse and she had no idea what sailors would call this. The helm? The pilot's station?

Their pilot was a monstrous blond guy named Ivor Blount. A guy that size and with a name like that needed a beard, and Ivor sported a beauty, complete with three iron rings tied in its tangled length, both for decoration and to tame the unruly bush.

"Powell's below?" Ash said.

Ivor nodded, keeping his hands on the wheel.

Ash ducked down through the hatch and descended the steep ladder into the small cabin space. The door to the head swung back and forth, so she yanked it shut until it clicked, ignoring the shit and chemical smell that never seemed to go away.

Eric Powell sat at a small galley table with his laptop, tapping away. Though he must have heard her come down, he did not look up from the computer. Ash didn't like the way his brows were knitted together.

"Problem?" she asked.

He blinked and glanced up as if coming out of a trance. "Not really. At least I hope not. It's probably just the storm causing interference. Ivor might have to get us closer to them for it to work."

Ash propped her hands against the low ceiling and stood looming over him. Only in a space as cramped as this one could a woman of average height feel as if she were looming, and she liked it very much.

"But you do think it will work?"

Powell scowled. "Would I be here if I didn't?"

She planted herself next to him and leaned in to stare at the laptop. The numbers on the screen meant nothing to her.

"What I can tell you," she said, "is that right now? Your program isn't jamming shit."

Powell stopped typing. His eyes seemed to darken. "Give it time."

She nodded slowly. "Absolutely, Eric. I have faith. You know that."

The words were hollow, but her insincerity didn't shock either of them. Ash rose and went back to the ladder, then up through the hatch, which she closed behind her to keep the rain out. At the wheel, Ivor glanced at her, one eyebrow raised.

Ash looked around, made sure Feole was too far to

overhear them with this wind, and she moved over next to their skipper.

"It's not working?" Ivor asked, iron rings swaying from his beard.

"Not yet," Ash confirmed. "In a little while, if he can't get it going, he's going to ask you to get closer to the WHOI ship."

The captain opened and closed his enormous hands on the wheel and grunted, exhaling like an unhappy grizzly bear. "And if that doesn't solve it?"

Ash moved nearer to him, shoulder to shoulder, peering out through the windshield.

"They're fucking with the natural instincts of an entire species," she said, staring at the WHOI ship as it plied the dark water. "That's wrong, Ivor. It's a crime against nature, and unlike some of our friends, I know you take that as seriously as I do. So if Powell's tech doesn't work, we'll do whatever we have to do, right down to putting this boat in their path."

"You'll sink us," Ivor said in his gravelly earthquake of a voice.

"Would it also sink them?"

Ivor heaved another breath, another grizzly bear sigh. "It might well."

"Well, let's hope Powell can do his job, then, right?"

Ivor gave a snort that might have been laughter, but he kept his hands steady on the wheel. That was what Ash liked best about him. The giant man was nothing if not steady. When the time came, if he had to risk them all he wouldn't shrink from it.

CHAPTER 12

——

Wolchko stood watching the smaller boat, which seemed to be keeping pace with them but otherwise not doing much of anything. For the moment, anyway. Like the others he was wearing rain gear, but it made him feel claustrophobic and he wanted to get below and dry off, fix himself a cup of coffee now that everything seemed to be working properly. Rosalie would keep an eye on the incoming data stream, make sure there were no significant changes in the signal output. But something about this chase boat, their nautical stalker, had gotten under his skin.

"I'm telling you," he said, wiping rain from his face. He turned to face the others, raising his voice over the wind. "Specs is up to no good."

Kat still had her binoculars up, studying the chase ship. "No markings," she said. "Not even a name on her."

"Or they covered the markings for this jaunt," Naomi observed.

"I don't know," Tye said. "So the guy in the glasses—"

"Specs," Wolchko said.

"We don't know his name," Tye reminded Wolchko. "But okay, we'll call him whatever you want. Point is, 'Specs' was an asshole to you, but he didn't do anything other than antagonize you. No vandalism, no threats, no—"

Naomi swore. "I'll tell you what he was trying to do. Stir shit up."

Wolchko nodded. He had told them about his encounter with Specs outside the Cosmic Muffin, including the way the guy had tried to get him riled up and turn him against Naomi.

"No question, but to what end?" Kat asked.

"Maybe just to make things ugly," Naomi replied, shaking rain off her ruined baseball cap and then slipping it back on. "Maybe he's got something against me personally, though I don't think I've run into him before. Or maybe he thought if he got Eddie pissed off enough he would start a fight that would delay the experiment."

The boat pitched steeply to port and they all held on. The storm wasn't much in the scheme of things, but the seas were rougher than Wolchko had anticipated and there was worse on the way. They were only supposed to get the by-product of the larger storm, the wind and rain at the edges of it, but this was enough to annoy the crap out of all of them. He wondered if Naomi had taken Dramamine or if she was just a natural sailor. Most people Wolchko knew would have been at least considering heaving their guts up by now.

"Maybe he thought he could scare me off somehow," he said.

A frown creased Kat's forehead. She lowered the binoculars and turned to exchange a troubled look with Tye.

"You think?" Tye asked her.

"Could be."

"Could be what?" Wolchko said. "I've got a bad feeling about this, so I don't have a lot of patience for secrets or meaningful glances."

Tye nodded toward Kat to indicate it was her story to tell.

"It seems like a stretch," she said.

"Try us," Naomi chimed in.

Tye seemed irritated that she would speak to them as equals, but Kat didn't flinch and Wolchko admired the girl's confidence, particularly after all she'd been through.

Kat shrugged. "Middle of the night, I had an asshole outside my bedroom windows, banging on the wall and making threats."

"Hang on, what kind of threats?" Tye asked. "You didn't tell me that part."

"Just that he was coming in, but I don't think he really would have."

"You don't know that," Tye said. "If I hadn't shown up—"

Kat shot him a dark look. "I'd have handled it. I don't need your protection."

Tye threw up his hands. Wolchko hadn't missed the implication that Tye had been at Kat's place in the middle of the night, but it was none of his damn business and he had no intention of poking his nose into that particular hornet's nest. Naomi studied them with open curiosity. Apparently she hadn't missed that bit of information, either.

"We don't have any reason to think there's any connection here," Wolchko said. "It could've been bored teenage pricks or some pervert trying to get a peek."

Kat gave him a lopsided grin. "Thanks, Eddie. That's reassuring."

It was the sort of moment that always made him wish he could read people better. He wasn't sure if Kat's gratitude was sincere or sarcastic, so he chose to ignore it.

"So what do we do about Specs and his buddies?" he asked.

Kat shrugged. "We keep an eye on them. Otherwise, we do our jobs."

Heads nodded and Kat took a last look through her binoculars, but by silent consent they all began to move away from the railing. Wolchko caught Naomi taking his picture again and shook his head, rolling his eyes a little. It was a good-natured eye roll, though. The girl had started to grow on him.

Rosalie appeared from around the side of the wheelhouse. "Eddie, check this out!"

He followed her, Naomi trailing behind them both as Rosalie led him aft again. They passed the wheelhouse and he wanted to chide her for abandoning the instrument panel, but he could see she was excited about something.

The rain had turned cold and it slid down inside Wolchko's collar. He felt like his skin might slough off, as if he were not a person at all but a figure built of papier-mâché. Even with the rain gear, the moisture snuck in.

At the bow of the boat, Rosalie pointed at the seal herds spread out to port and starboard and for what seemed at least a mile behind them. Wolchko felt sure there were more than there had been.

"It's going as we'd hoped," he said, turning to Rosalie. "What am I looking at?"

But the answer came from behind him. From Naomi.

"The fins," she said.

Wolchko took another look at the dark seas, noticing now what he had missed the first time. He had expected sharks, so he had not immediately seen that things had changed. As he watched, a Great White surfaced with a seal in its jaws and then submerged again. Before he could turn away, another shark darted across the boat's wake and tore into two different seals with a twist of its massive head.

"There are more of them," he said.

"Way more," Naomi said, barely loud enough for Wolchko to hear. "Way the hell more."

"And they're going nuts," Rosalie added. "Bastards are eating like it's their last day on earth. All the arguments over the morality of letting people hunt them, and now they're getting culled anyway. The good news is, the sharks have to get full at some point."

Wolchko saw another attack, fifty yards or so back and off the port side. Rosalie had to be right, of course, but as he watched the sharks at work now, tearing through the herds, it didn't appear as if they were going to stop killing anytime soon.

CHAPTER 13

Jamie Counihan sat on his usual stool at the Salty Dog with a cold pint sweating on the bar in front of him. He took a gulp of beer and soaked in the fish-and-chips ambience of the place as he waited for Walter to arrive. In recent years Jamie had noticed the habit of people waiting at bars to spend their idle minutes staring at their phones, probably checking social media or sports scores. Jamie owned such a phone, but as a rule it never came out of his pocket in public. He didn't like the way society had embraced the hunched hostility inherent in that trend. People thought they were never alone as long as they were connected to the Internet, but he had never seen anyone as alone as the guy sitting three stools down from him. The Red Sox game played on the television and music pumped through the speakers around the bar. There were people all around, but the guy never lifted his eyes from the screen of his oversized "smart" phone. Jamie figured people like this guy weren't just antisocial . . . they got lost in their phones because they were afraid to be lost in their own thoughts.

Someone bumped his shoulder. Jamie glanced around to see Mel Rice, scraggly beard, rheumy eyes, and all.

"I know what you're thinkin', brother," Rice rumbled, voice low but close enough for Jamie to hear. "Guy makes me nervous. Probably the friggin' Unabomber, part two, right?"

Rice must have been on his way back from the bathroom. He wiped water from his hands—at least Jamie hoped it was water—and dragged his fingers through his scraggly beard to make himself presentable before returning to the group he'd come with.

"Maybe not quite that bad," Jamie said. "But he's not gonna make any friends."

Rice shrugged. "Some people don't want friends." He narrowed his eyes as if realizing for the first time that Jamie was by himself. "Say, you wanna join us until Walter shows up? We're talkin' politics and old monster movies. Two of your favorite subjects."

Jamie arched an eyebrow. With a quiet laugh, he raised his beer. "I do like old monster movies. If Walter hasn't shown up by the time I finish this pint, I'll come and crash your party."

Rice clapped him on the shoulder, but not hard enough to spill his beer. "Fair enough."

That's what I'm talking about, Jamie thought. He glanced around the bar, saw half a dozen people checking their phones, and shook his head. The Salty Dog had been attracting more tourists lately, which meant it was going downhill fast. He didn't like to think about the idea of having to find somewhere new to hang out.

Laughter erupted from a corner table. Then the door

opened and Jenni McGrath came in with her new husband. Voices rose in greeting and Jenni and her groom—whatever his name was—made their way to a table for two. On the way, they stopped to say hello. Jamie had known her since high school, so even though the groom seemed like just another handsome asshole from away, Jamie hugged Jenni and congratulated them both.

Then he looked at his watch. Going on seven thirty. Given that he and Walter would be up around three thirty in the morning to take the *Little Martha* out again, he was growing impatient.

When he glanced up again, he found Alice leaning on the bar, studying his face. Her eyes gleamed with mischief.

"Looks like you've been stood up," she said. "It's a damn shame, a perfectly good man like yourself cast aside for another man."

Jamie laughed. "You're a fresh little thing."

"That's news to you?"

"Not hardly. Anyway, Walter hasn't stood me up. He's just runnin' late. Got a text from him before I came in."

"Funny you didn't argue about him finding another man," she teased.

Jamie shrugged. "I'm kind of numb to jokes about Walter being my boyfriend. Hell, we joke about it ourselves pretty much constantly."

Alice slid her hands into her back pockets, arching her back a little as she studied him. The move stretched the cotton of her shirt taut against her breasts, but Jamie did his best not to let his gaze linger. Not that he didn't appreciate her figure or the work she put in to stay fit. He just figured it was polite to keep that appreciation to himself. Alice knew she looked damn good, but she didn't put the effort into it so men would leer at her.

"Still, it does kind of stink, doesn't it?" she asked. "Ever since he started dating Micah, you don't see him as much. Happens pretty much any time a friend gets a new boyfriend or girlfriend. They get caught up in the emotional whirlwind of it all, kind of lose track of everything else."

Jamie sipped his beer while she spoke, then gave her a nod. "You're not wrong, but I'm not worried about it. Walter's the best friend I've got, but I'm capable of entertaining myself. For instance, I can come in here on one of your theme music nights and listen to eighties pop songs that make me want to drive rusty spikes into my ears."

"Oh, please," Alice said. "I've seen you mouthing the words to Hall and Oates songs—"

"That stuff doesn't count. I'm talking about Debbie Gibson and her ilk. Hall and Oates are musicians. Daryl Hall can *play*."

Down the bar, one of Rice's buddies signaled for another beer. Alice waved to him to indicate she'd be right along.

"Okay, big guy," she said, and then she leaned over the bar so that her face was close enough for Jamie to feel her breath on his face. Close enough for him to kiss her, if he'd dared. Her eyes were bright, even in the gloomy bar. "All I'm saying is that if you're getting bored with Walter busy all the time, maybe you should get yourself a girlfriend."

A hopeful spark ignited in Jamie's chest, but he played it off with a scowl, afraid to read into it.

"Why?" he said. "You got someone in mind?"

Alice rolled her eyes and sighed in disgust.

"Don't be stupid," she said.

Then she kissed him. On the cheek, yes, but a kiss nevertheless.

Alice glided along behind the bar, scooping an empty

glass from in front of Rice's friend and replacing it with a fresh pint of Guinness, a perfect head of froth on top. Jamie felt mesmerized, struck dumb by that kiss. His face flushed with emotion, only part of which consisted of happiness and excitement. The other part was a simmering frustration with his own idiocy. Alice had turned down every guy who had asked her out in the years since her husband had died, and Jamie had used that as an excuse not to ask her. Now he wondered how many conversations with her he had missed because he hadn't had the guts to just ask.

Idiot.

The moment the thought struck him, he reminded himself it hadn't been stupidity that had prevented him from asking. It had been cowardice. Fear of embarrassment, no different from the little fears that had plagued him in middle school and high school.

Several minutes later, when she came back down the bar to see if he wanted to order dinner or keep waiting for Walter, he'd had time to get hold of himself.

"You still waiting, or do you want to—" she began.

"I'm glad you got tired of waiting for me to muster up the courage," he said.

Alice crossed her arms, staring at him. "You still haven't. Unless you whispered that question to me and I missed it."

Jamie smiled. "Can I take you out some night, Alice? The very next night you have off?"

"Where would we go?" she asked, brow furrowed, mulling it over as if the idea had never occurred to her.

"Anywhere but here."

She took a deep breath, nodding slowly. "It's a date. Now figure out what you want to eat, because your dinner companion has finally decided to show himself."

Walter strode purposefully through the bar, face etched with grim lines, like he'd arrived at the Salty Dog on a mission and didn't want anyone getting in the way. A man as big as Walter, with hands large enough to crush skulls, got pretty used to people moving out of his path, but when he looked pissed off he also silenced those around him. People paused in conversation as he passed them now, just for the few seconds it took to confirm that his ire had nothing to do with them.

"What's this about?" Alice asked quietly.

Before Jamie could even think to reply, Walter reached them. His usual stool waited for him, but he ignored it, bristling with nervous energy. Only then did Jamie notice the rolled-up newspaper clutched in his fist.

"You've got murder in your eyes, man," Jamie said. "You have a fight with Micah?"

Walter smacked him in the chest with the newspaper. "You see this?"

Alice asked what was going on. Normally Walter adored her, but he barely seemed to have heard her, gesturing for Jamie to look at the paper. He unfolded it, discovered it was that morning's *Boston Globe*. He frowned. Walter was typically up too early to get a newspaper. He and Jamie both got most of their news from their phones or from television.

"What am I looking for?" Jamie asked.

Walter grunted as he snatched the paper back, flipped it open to the page he wanted, and shoved it back into Jamie's hands, poking at a headline. Jamie scanned the article quickly.

"You remember that shark attack down on Cape Cod last summer? Surfer got killed; girl lost her leg?" Walter asked.

"Sure," Alice said. "Her mother is the—"

"Yeah. That one," Walter interrupted.

Jamie felt his brow knit. He didn't like Walter being rude to Alice like that. He opened his mouth to comment on it, but by then he'd skimmed just enough of the *Globe* article to figure out the part that had Walter fuming.

"Son of a bitch," he said.

Walter nodded, gesturing at the newspaper as if it were the enemy. "Uh-huh."

A voice called to Alice from along the bar, but she ignored it.

"Someone want to tell me what the hell is going on?" she asked.

Jamie stared at the newspaper article a few more seconds. "Scientists down at Woods Hole are doing an experiment. Think they've figured out some way to lure the seals away from their beaches. They figure the sharks will follow."

Down the bar, someone called for Alice again.

"Just a damn minute!" she barked, then took the newspaper from Jamie's hands. "That sounds like a pretty good idea. What am I missing?"

"They're trying to lead the seals up this way. Want them to make their nesting ground on the islands out by Bald Cap."

Alice stared at the newspaper. "We've got our own seals. Not to mention our own sharks. Though I guess maybe that far out, I don't see the harm. Not many people to bother out there."

"You don't see the—" Walter started angrily.

Alice shot him a dark look and he exhaled, shoulders sinking.

"Sorry," he said, putting up a hand in surrender. "This

thing's just lit a fire in my gut. The harm isn't in adding a few sharks. But you double or triple the number of seals out there and that means you double or triple the number of fish they're eating to survive."

"Fish we need to *catch* to survive," Jamie said. "We don't need the competition."

"Damn right we don't," Walter said. He ran a hand across the scruff he called a beard, brow knitted in thought. "Which means what we really need is for this experiment to fail."

"What are you suggesting?" Jamie asked.

Walter looked up, gaze intense. A silent communication passed between them, a grim determination Jamie felt keenly and understood very well. There might not be much they could do to interfere with the Woods Hole experiment, but he and Walter weren't the type to let that keep them from trying.

"They're on the way now," Walter said. "Probably hit the area a little before dawn."

Jamie scratched at the scruffy thickness of his beard. "I'm going to need another beer."

Behind the bar, Alice shifted nervously, looking like she wanted to come right over the top and knock some sense into them.

"Even if you two idiots could interfere with this thing without getting yourselves arrested, have you seen the forecast?"

"Idiots?" Walter said. "That's the sweetest thing you've called us, maybe ever."

Jamie slumped on his stool, shaking his head. "Is that nice?" he said to Walter. "I've just asked her on a date and now she calls me an idiot."

Walter shot a startled glance at Alice. "He asked you on a date?"

"I had to nudge him a bit, but he came around."

Jamie gave them a sheepish grin, but then his eyes were drawn to the television above the bar. The Red Sox game was between innings and the channel had broken in for a local news update. A woman mouthed a bit of news that seemed to involve some kind of sporting event for veterans; then that gave way to a report from the balding meteorologist. With the volume off, the details were impossible to make out, but the satellite map showed several possible paths for a storm that had been churning its way up the East Coast. The night before, the same fellow had predicted the storm would turn far out to sea, but now it looked very much as if it had shifted direction.

"Guy looks almost giddy," Jamie said.

Amidst the buzz and music and chatter of the bar, the three of them exchanged worried glances. When the weatherman got excited, it never boded well for conditions at sea.

"But we're going, right?" Walter asked.

Alice shot a disapproving look their way, then threw up her hands. "*Idiots* might be too kind a word," she said. "I'll go put in an order for the usual. You're going to want to eat well and get to bed so you can be up early enough to do something really foolish."

As she marched away, Jamie felt a pang of regret. Then he thought about the Woods Hole scientists and the seals and how small and defeated he felt any time he came back into port with a catch too small to earn enough to pay his bills.

"She's not wrong," Jamie said, then raised his beer to Walter in a toast. "But hell yeah, we're going."

CHAPTER 14

Naomi sat on a bench in the wheelhouse of the *Thaumas*, wet and shivering. The sea surged and roiled beneath them and she tried to tell herself the nausea would pass. She had been out on the water a hundred times, but never overnight and never in weather so rough. Two days earlier, she had asked the media relations manager at WHOI what would happen if this storm turned toward shore and been assured that the trip would be scrubbed, the experiment rescheduled. As recently as this morning, the forecast had called for the storm to continue turning east, making for some rain and wind but nothing like this.

This, Naomi thought, *sucks hard*.

Cold rain dripped down the back of her neck. Though she was shielded in the wheelhouse, she had been out on the deck a short time ago, just to get a look at the horizon, trying to steady her uneasy stomach. The weather and the lateness of the hour had put a damper on the entire team and any sense of adventure had bled away, leaving only the night and the cold. It might be early summer, but out on the Atlantic, with the wind and rain, it felt like the sky had not quite given up on winter.

Bergting had the wheel. Captain N'Dour had gone below for a few hours of sleep and the first mate seemed content to let Naomi just sit there, comfortable with the silence. He'd offered her a mug of coffee, but she feared putting anything in her belly at the moment, so she'd only thanked him and kept gazing out at the darkness, trying to keep her eyes on the horizon despite the way the storm and the night conspired to hide it from her. She had put her camera away, there being little hope of her getting any usable photos under such conditions, but without it in her hands she felt cast adrift. The camera gave her purpose. A reason to be there. A way for her to avoid thinking about the phone call from Kayla, the things she'd said.

She wants to fix it, Naomi thought now. *Not fix me, but fix her mistake. Fix us.*

Naomi had shut her down quickly, even harshly. But ever since, the conversation had been echoing in her mind. Kayla had abandoned her—not by going to medical school, but by falling so fast for what's-her-name . . . *and just ghosting me*—and now she had realized the error of her ways? Had she matured, or was she just feeling broken and lonely? Naomi wondered if it would be worth finding out.

No. Stop. No more thinking.

To take her mind off Kayla, she focused on what little activity there was on the boat this late. Tye camped at the stern under a voluminous raincoat, keeping an eye on the seals as best he could in the murk. With the crane blocking her view, Naomi could only see half of him, but she imagined he must be bored and wet and tired. He and Kat were taking shifts overnight, monitoring the seals to make sure they were still following. If something went wrong with the signal, they didn't want to wait until sunrise to discover it.

Rosalie had gone back to sit with Tye for a few minutes and Naomi watched their interplay, wondering if there might be something between them. As a child she had been pretty good at reading the body language between people, but the skill had grown rusty during high school and college, when she had become much more focused on her own emotions than those of other people. During her convalescence, with so much time to just lie in a bed or sit in a chair and watch people, she had begun to hone the skill again. She knew that Tye and Kat were exes just based on the way they dealt with each other, but this thing with Rosalie was harder to read.

As Naomi tried to figure it out, Rosalie stood and made her way forward again. She was supposed to be keeping an eye on the data streaming in from the acoustics equipment, taking turns with Wolchko.

When Rosalie reached the wheelhouse, she paused to stare down at Naomi. "Why don't you go below? You're not doing anyone any good up here."

Her tone made clear that she wasn't trying to be helpful. She just wanted Naomi to go away. Once upon a time, Naomi would have shrunk back from that hostility, tried to make herself a smaller target. Even invisible. Given that she had pretty much barged into the lives of these people, she had expected a chilly reception and had prepared to be as cooperative and amiable as possible. But losing her leg and witnessing the death of Luke Turner, the surfer who'd saved her life, had changed her. Parts of her had been shattered by those events, but what remained had been forged into something harder than before, something that rose up within her instead of shrinking. Something unyielding.

Naomi rose, barely noticing her prosthetic leg. She had mastered it, and it served her well.

"I'm going to give you the benefit of the doubt," she told Rosalie, "which means I'm going to assume you see yourself as the hero of this little adventure and you're not just some high school mean girl who's grown up into a total bitch. Maybe you've got other things going on in your life and I'm a convenient punching bag, because when we get back into port I'm gonna get off this boat and you won't have to see me again."

Rosalie cocked her head, pursing her lips, preparing one retort or another.

"No, hold up," Naomi said, one finger raised. "I'm only up here on deck instead of sleeping below because I'm trying not to puke. I'm not your enemy. I'm just a girl who got her fucking leg ripped off by a shark and who's trying to do something with her life. I'm not in your way, woman, so *don't* get in mine."

For several seconds, she thought Rosalie might lay hands on her. From the way Bergting had stiffened at the wheel, it seemed he also thought that a likely outcome. Instead, Rosalie bit her lip, took a calming breath, and gestured toward the hatch leading below.

"There's a massive bottle of Dramamine on a shelf just outside the head," she said. "Take a couple of those. They'll settle your stomach and put you to sleep."

Naomi stared at her in confusion.

"Oh, don't worry; I'm not being nice," Rosalie went on. "I just don't want you sitting up here while I'm trying to do my job, and I don't want you puking where someone has to clean it up." She made a dismissive gesture. "Now go, please. If you can't be useful, at least be gone."

Queasy stomach giving another twist, Naomi decided the fight could wait until the weather, her condition, and her mood had all improved. With a glance toward a relieved-looking Bergting, she thanked Rosalie and went to the hatch, quickly descending into the cabin.

The instant she went below, her nausea surged and she had to breathe through her nose. Tiny lights glowed at intervals throughout the cabin and that dull gleam allowed her to spot the fat white plastic bottle of Dramamine on a shelf built into the wall outside the bathroom. Trying not to wonder too hard whether she'd be able to keep them down, she quickly dry-swallowed two of the dusty pills and then stood leaning against the shelf, slowly inhaling and exhaling, full of cautious hope that she would not puke her guts up on a boat full of strangers and with no chance of going ashore anytime soon.

"You all right?" a soft voice rasped.

Still taking even breaths, she turned to see Wolchko sitting up on one of the narrow bunks. He rubbed a hand over his stubbled chin and gazed at her in that soft light with a certain clinical detachment.

"A little seasick. Hoping the pills will do the trick."

Wolchko nodded. "Better off on deck, but if you want to be down here, I'd suggest not lying down until they take effect."

Naomi agreed. Her stomach sloshed a bit and she breathed in. Her skin felt a bit clammy and she wanted to stay near the door to the head, just in case. Captain N'Dour had curled up on a bench next to the little table against the starboard side and Kat Cheong snored lightly on the bunk above Wolchko's head.

It occurred to Naomi that the skipper had left the rear bunk empty, probably for her, and the thought repaired some of the damage that her run-in with Rosalie had done to her spirit. Miraculously, just that bit of good feeling seemed to ease her nausea a little, too.

"How did your family feel about this trip?" Wolchko asked.

Naomi studied him. Such a strange man, and so direct, but she liked that about him.

"There really isn't much family. Just my mom and me, plus some aunts and uncles in Vermont, and a cousin at Tufts who we've sort of adopted."

She spoke quietly, not wanting to wake the others. The boat swayed back and forth, enough so that she could feel the blood rush to her face when it pitched to port.

"My mom encouraged me," she went on. "Honestly, she nudged me quite a bit and I'm glad she did. Some of my friends said stupid things, like they'd never go back on a boat if they'd been the ones attacked by sharks. As if sharks routinely boarded boats like they were pirates or something. Stupid, right? But I knew what they meant. They were just surprised that I wasn't nervous about being out on the water again."

"But you were," Wolchko said. It wasn't a question.

"Damn right I was. I am. Who wouldn't be? Yeah, it's stupid, but psychologically, I know there are sharks following us right now, and knowing it makes my skin crawl, which in turn pisses me off. I don't mind that they've made me afraid. If I'd been more afraid last year, I'd still have both of the legs I was born with. But I'm not going to let them make me a coward."

Wolchko's eyes crinkled as he smiled. "I think it's safe to say you're not a coward."

She shrugged. "I want things from my life. I've got plans that I didn't have before, and the path I'm on put me on this boat with all of you."

Wolchko leaned against the frame of the bunk. "How are you feeling now?"

Naomi almost said, *Sick*, but then she realized that she didn't feel very sick at all. A little queasy, but the feeling that she might vomit any second had gone away.

"A little better. Did you hypnotize me?"

"Distracted you is all. While the Dramamine did its job, or started to. I'd still wait a bit before you lie down."

"Thanks, Eddie. Really," she said, breathing easier now. "What about you? Do you have a family that thinks you're crazy to go out on two-day boat trips to play with sharks and seals?"

His smile bled away and he glanced awkwardly at the floor. Naomi knew she'd said something wrong and wondered if she ought to apologize for getting so personal.

"Look, I'm—"

"No, no, it's okay," he said, holding up a hand to stave off her regret.

The boat took its biggest roll yet and Naomi staggered forward, had to catch herself on the other side of the bunk frame, and ended up just a few feet from him. On the top bunk, Kat muttered some profanity and turned over, punched her thin pillow, and shot Naomi the angry look common to sleepers unhappy at being awakened. Then she closed her eyes and was out again. Captain N'Dour slept the sleep of angels, his face smooth and unconcerned.

"I don't talk about it much," Wolchko said.

"You don't have to—"

"She died. Cancer," he said.

Naomi's heart broke for him. She could hear the pain in his voice, could see that he had no idea what to do with it. There was no comfort she could offer him, but still she wanted to ease that pain.

"Do you think . . . I mean, I'm not sure how long it's been, but do you think you'll ever find someone else to be with? Not a replacement. I don't mean—"

"I know what you mean," he said kindly. Sadly. "Most people don't feel comfortable enough around me to ask. I don't . . . I never make it easy on them. If you haven't guessed, I can be a little prickly."

"Maybe so, but you've been kind to me."

Wolchko looked at her for a long time. Then he gave the tiniest tilt of his head. "You're on the outside of this thing. I don't like seeing people held at arm's length, like they don't belong."

Naomi frowned. "I guess you've had enough of that in your life."

"You're pretty smart."

"I've been told that," she joked. "I've also been told I'm an idiot."

Wolchko grinned. "Me, too. Mostly by my late wife. To answer your question, I don't think about it much. Finding someone else would be difficult, mainly because I'm so difficult. You think I'm nice, but chances are good I'll be rude to you more than once before we head home and I won't even realize it."

"You might find someone who understands the way you're wired, someone patient enough to not take it personally."

"Maybe," he said, "but I'm fine with being alone. I'm used to it anyway, and maybe that's for the best."

Naomi searched her heart for something to say, anything that might brighten his outlook, but she could think of nothing.

"Go and get some rest now," Wolchko went on. "Tomorrow's going to be a long day."

Naomi smiled one last time, but she knew he would see right through it. Neither one of them could have smiled sincerely just then. Her hip ached and she limped a little as she made her way to the bunk at the back of the cabin, heart heavy with sadness. She had lost her leg, but it seemed to her that Eddie Wolchko had lost so much more. There was no prosthetic replacement for the only person who had ever loved you.

CHAPTER 15

The Bayliner rocked from side to side on the roiling water, tilting so hard on the waves that Ash kept thinking about a plastic Fisher-Price boat she always had in the bathtub with her as a little kid. It might have been a floating soap dish, though—she couldn't recall clearly. What she remembered was how much she had loved to make waves in the tub and watch the little plastic boat sway as the water grew ever rougher, until at last she churned the waves up so high that the boat would capsize.

The memory did nothing to improve her mood, which was already as foul as the weather.

She had a vague recollection of the plastic Fisher-Price boat being chewed up by Panda, her husky. Damn, she missed that dog.

The small boat shot up a wave and slid down another. They were running in darkness, following the WHOI vessel at a distance. Ash had a pair of military-grade night-vision goggles she told people she got from an ex-boyfriend who was a Navy SEAL, but that was bullshit. She'd bought them from a guy she'd met in an Internet forum—they'd cost her three hundred bucks and a Snapchat photo of her ass, the latter of which she'd have sent the guy for nothing.

"Well?" a voice said beside her.

The boat went up another wave. She grabbed a rain-slicked railing and turned to glare at Tony Feole. The goggles meant she could see details of his face that the night would otherwise have obscured. He looked tired and older, and she knew this mission was taking its toll on him. Feole didn't have the heart for this stuff anymore and they both knew it.

Rain pounded the deck of the ship and curtains of it swept across the undulating waters. Somewhere not far off, thunder boomed overheard. The clouds were so thick that there was no trace of lightning.

"Well," she echoed, studying Feole. "Well, it's not working, if that's what you're asking."

He looked sick. "Are you sure?"

Ash tore the night-vision goggles off her head and handed them over. "Have a look for yourself. It's not working, which means we need another plan."

Feole took the goggles like he feared they might bite him. Ash knew what he would see—the water behind the *Thaumas* churned with seals. The tech they were broad-casting to jam the WHOI acoustic signal had not done its job. Worse, from what she could tell in the dark, the number of seals had only increased, as had the shark fins weaving in and out among the seals. She had tried counting within the past hour and had spotted at least eleven sharks. Nothing scientific about it—the real number might have been more or less, depending on whether she'd counted some more than once or others had been submerged—but in any case, there were a lot of sharks out there. Great Whites, primarily. She had an image in her mind of what the water behind the *Thaumas* would look like at sunrise, with an entire ocean of marine life following the WHOI vessel like its captain was the Pied Piper.

"Damn it!" she heard Feole snap as she headed into the wheelhouse. She ignored him. He might be angry or frustrated, but she knew he wasn't going to take the steps that were needed now.

In the wheelhouse, Ivor sat on his high seat at the wheel, drinking a mug of something that she knew would smell like coffee but would have been spiked with a little something else.

"No luck?" Ivor said.

"Give me a second," she said.

The boat rolled hard to starboard and she grabbed a handhold, grip slipping in the rain. Her face smashed into the side of the hatchway even as she caught herself. She cussed colorfully as she descended into the small berth below.

Powell looked up from his laptop, blinking like a raccoon that had just been caught raiding trash cans in the beam of a flashlight.

"I'm doing my best," he said weakly.

Ash gnawed her lower lip instead of unleashing the tirade that simmered inside her. What would be the point? His tone made it clear that he knew it wasn't working, even without going up on deck, and to her that cemented the certainty that it wasn't going to work. Not tonight, anyway. Probably not ever.

"Not so cocky now, are you?" she said, spinning on her heel.

Wind swept off the deck and drove cold shards of rain

into her face as she climbed back up onto the deck. In the dark, she could see Feole still standing at the railing with her night-vision goggles, as if Powell's tech would suddenly kick in and start working. She and Feole had been friends for a long time. She knew that was about to change, but her beliefs were more important to her than her friends. He had lost his spine.

The boat rocked to port and she held on for a second, then moved toward Ivor. His eyes were narrowed, his jaw grimly set.

"We doing this?" he asked.

"Fuck it, yeah. We're doing it."

Soaked to the skin, she went to the other station in the wheelhouse and took a seat. Ivor nodded slowly and with a strange rhythm, as if he were listening to music only he could hear. Slowly, he began to throttle up. It was subtle, but Ash thought if someone was paying attention they would be able to hear the difference in the engine's growl. Ivor started to shift course, angling the boat toward the WHOI research vessel.

Butterflies swarmed inside Ash's chest. Some of them had wings of fear, but others flew with excitement, anticipation. She had been fully committed to this cause for years and now, at last, the time had come for her to prove just how complete that commitment really was.

"Go," Ash said, skin prickling with anticipation. The buzz that filled her was like nothing she'd ever felt. "Do it!"

Ivor kept bobbing his head. "Yeah. Yeah. Yeah," he said in time with his nodding.

He throttled up harder, the engine growled, and the boat started to skip along on top of the waves. It threw them from side to side. The wind picked up, thrashing them harder, but now they were really moving.

A voice came to her in the air, strangled by the wind. At first Ash didn't turn, though she knew whose voice it had to be. When she heard the stream of profanity, she turned and saw Feole picking himself up off the deck. Her night-vision goggles were nowhere to be seen—somewhere back at the railing, she figured—and he had lost his glasses as well. As she watched, his fingers snatched them up from the deck and he slipped them back on, trying to clean rain-water off the lenses.

"Ivor, what the hell are you doing?" Feole barked as he stomped toward them, arms stretched out, staggering back and forth as he fought to keep his balance.

Ash stared at him, feeling a twinge of pity. Tony Feole still thought he was in charge.

Ivor did not reply to him, and neither did she. Feole ducked into the wheelhouse and reached for the skipper's arm. Ivor shot one hand out, propped his palm open on Feole's chest, and shoved him backward so that he sprawled back onto the deck in the rain.

"Jesus! What is wrong with you?" he shouted before he turned to Ash. "What is he doing? Are you even listening?"

Ash pointed at him, made sure he was paying attention. "Tony, I'm going to say this once. Go below."

Ivor scoffed loudly. "Might be best if you get yourself a life jacket, too."

Feole froze. The boat rolled to starboard and he reached out to Ash, grabbed hold of her to steady himself, and turned to stare out through the windshield. Through the rain and the sweep of the wipers, he spotted the *Thaumas*. Close enough to be intimate, Ash saw the moment of confusion cross his face, that frowning instant where he didn't understand why they were racing to catch up with the Woods Hole research vessel—a boat nearly twice the size of their own—and why they were angling toward it. And she saw the moment when he got it.

"Ivor, no!" Feole said, lunging toward the wheel.

Ash dug her fingers into his arms, held him fast. "We've got to stop them."

Feole spun on her. "You're out of your mind! I've got a family. You want to throw your lives away, that's up to you, but—"

"We're not throwing anything away," Ash assured him, grabbing his face, staring into his eyes. "We're doing the job."

"If the job is suicide!"

"They'll veer off," Ivor called to him. "I'll give them plenty of time to notice. And I'll keep doing it, forcing them off course, till they turn the hell around or come to a dead stop."

Feole ripped himself away from Ash and grabbed at the wheel. The two men began to struggle and Ivor shoved him away again.

"You know it won't work!" Feole cried, the wind and rain sweeping in through the open wheelhouse and whipping at him. "Their boat's too big to maneuver like that. You put us in their path and you know they'll clip us at least, maybe broadside. You'll stop them all right, and kill us all in the meantime!"

Ash grabbed his arm again. "Tony, get a life vest."

He stared into her eyes, saw the determination there, and she knew he understood then just how far she and Ivor were willing to go for their principles.

Which was when Powell came up from below. He

popped his head up, looking around like he'd just woken up from a winter's hibernation. "What are you guys doing up—"

Feole shoved Ash against the inside of the wheelhouse and lunged at Ivor, shouting for Powell to help him. Ash swore and tried to scramble after him, but as distracted as Powell so often seemed, he was quick when he had to be. A big man, he stepped between her and the scuffle at the wheel.

"Tony—" Powell started.

"They're trying to steer us right into the path of the WHOI boat!" Feole shouted.

That was all Powell needed. Ash grabbed him from behind, tried to pull him away, but he was too strong. He did not even bother to shake her off as he forced his way past Feole and grabbed hold of Ivor. Feole hadn't stood a chance on his own, but Powell wrestled Ivor away from the wheel and the two big men careened out of the wheelhouse. The swell of the ocean tipped the boat and they stumbled to the deck in a tangle of limbs. Fists started flying, and Ash knew they had passed the point of no return. She started toward Feole and he stared at her, eyes wide.

"What the hell is wrong with you?" he shrieked.

"This has to happen, Tony."

"Bullshit!" he spat, hands white-knuckle tight on the wheel as he throttled down and changed course, pointing them farther out to sea. "The only way Powell and I are letting you idiots put us in the path of that boat is if you beat us unconscious or kill us."

Ash hesitated, fists opening and closing.

"You've been to my house, damn it!" Feole shouted. "Eaten at my table. You think I don't want to stop those WHOI assholes, but I do, Ashleigh."

"We're not going back to port!" she roared at him. "I've had enough of letting these people get away with whatever they want to do, enough of them acting like human life is the only life that matters. I can't turn my back anymore. I'm not going home with my tail between my legs!"

"Fine!" he shouted. "But we'll find another way. I'll do anything for this cause, Ash, but I'm not going to die for it!"

Ivor hurtled back into the wheelhouse, yanked Feole away from the wheel, and cast him to the floor. Ash whipped around to see Powell standing, wiping blood from his mouth out on the deck in the rain. The fight wasn't over, and Feole was right. If she and Ivor wanted to do this their way, they were going to have to subdue Tony and Powell. Or kill them.

What the hell are you thinking?

She exhaled. A rush of bile burned up the back of her throat as she thought about the possibility of killing this man who had been her friend for so long. Hell, the possibility of killing anyone. That wasn't going to happen.

"Ivor, stop," she said.

He throttled up again, turning back toward the *Thaumas*.

Ash grabbed his arm again. "I said stop. We're not doing it like this. It won't work."

The massive Viking glanced at her and for a second she thought he might hit her next. Then he deflated a bit, snarling and cursing under his breath as he eased back on the throttle.

"You people are batshit crazy," Powell snarled, moving toward Ash.

Feole stepped into his path, struggling to stay on his feet as the deck rocked beneath them. "Eric, listen—"

Powell spat a wad of bloody saliva onto the deck. The rain washed it away. "Listen to them? They could've killed us just now."

"You've gotta be willing to die for what you believe in," Ivor said, barely looking at them. He stared out through the windshield, craning his neck to watch as the WHOI research ship plowed on through the water without them, moving farther ahead.

"It's not a damn war," Powell said. "We're not under attack!"

"Isn't it?" Ash asked. "I don't want to die, either, but I'm willing to risk my life—"

Feole's mouth gaped. He stared at her as if he had never seen her before tonight. Rain slicked his face and made him look younger, somehow, as if they were both still the kids they'd been when they met.

"Ashleigh, come on. You know what would've happened if Ivor had put us in the path of that boat," he said.

"They'd have done their best to avoid a collision," she argued.

"No way they could avoid it!" Feole snapped. "Not in this weather, with us running dark, just putting ourselves in their way. You two are lunatics."

"Tony," she began.

He stepped close to her, put his hands on her shoulders so they were face-to-face, physically close in a way they hadn't been for ages. They had never had sex, but their friendship had been close enough once upon a time that Ash thought of it as intimate. And it was intimate now, enough that she felt suddenly guilty for having struck him. She remembered what they'd meant to each other, once.

"All I'm saying is that if we're going to do something

extreme, we need more of a plan than 'let's do something terminally stupid that will get us killed and get SeaLove sued out of existence.' "

Powell scoffed, spat another wad of blood. "You three can do whatever you like. I'm not having any part of it."

He pushed past Feole and Ash and went down below. Ivor nudged the throttle forward, turning the ship so that it cut across the waves, lessening the back-and-forth a bit.

"What kind of plan are we talking about?" Ash said. "We've got to stop them."

"They can't prove who we are," Ivor growled. "I've got a case of whiskey down below. Why don't we pull alongside and toss Molotov cocktails at them? That'd send them home."

"Might still get arrested," Ash replied.

Ivor barked laughter that sounded harsh but genuine. "You were angry enough to let me cut them off, but now you're afraid to go to jail?"

Feole dropped his hands from her shoulders and turned away. He stood, swaying on the deck in the rain, watching the *Thaumas* draw even farther out of range. They could all see the massive seal herds following, dark heads glistening as they popped up from the water before submerging and carrying on. They had moved into the wake of the research vessel themselves and Ash glanced around to see that they were in the midst of the seals now. She caught a glimpse of a shark fin and then another.

"I can't believe I'm saying this," Feole announced, "but maybe Ivor's right about the Molotov cocktails. We've got to turn them around. I won't die for this, but if I'm not willing to go to jail for it . . ."

Ash felt a tremor of excitement go through her as his voice trailed off. She grinned at him. "Tony, are you sure?"

"Hell, no, I'm not sure! But I've already tried scaring them off. I wanted to scare the crap out of Dr. Cheong and ended up getting in a tussle with Ashmore. Never mind pushing Wolchko's buttons. I'm too old for this shit, but I'm out here anyway, and if I'm out here then I ought to do what we came here to do."

Ivor throttled down again, turning to stare at Feole. Ash understood the look of disbelief on his face. Her old friend had become almost conservative over the past few years.

"You serious?" she asked as the wind swept over the deck. Down inside her, a kind of war cry began to build.

Feole took off his rain-peppered glasses and massaged the bridge of his nose, and Ash knew he had already begun to have second thoughts. In a second he would regain his senses, all the boring logic that had gotten him promoted up the ladder inside their organization, and he would try to talk them down.

Instead, he glanced up with narrowed eyes and a look of determination she hadn't seen on him in ages.

"Screw it, yeah. If I don't do this now, what was the point of anything?"

Ash let out that war cry that had been building inside her. Grinning, exultant, she wrapped Feole up in a hug. Ivor growled at them, told them to stop wasting time, to go down and get the damn whiskey, but Ash barely heard him. For so long it had felt like she and Feole had drifted apart, but now they were tight again. All the awkwardness bled away and they were partners in crime once more. This time, literally.

"Time to go out in a blaze of glory," she rasped into his ear as the boat drifted into a trough, tilting hard to starboard.

Feole tightened the hug as the boat righted itself, then

began to tilt to port on an enormous wave. "I wouldn't want to go to jail with anyone else. But let's see if we can avoid—"

Something struck the boat underwater, not a simple bump but a heavy, thudding collision. Ash cried out as she felt them tilting, felt the wave rising up on the starboard side, and then another impact jolted the hull. She heard a crack, but by then she felt her feet slipping on the rain-slicked deck, felt Tony Feole try to break their embrace. Then they weren't just tilting; they were tipping.

She screamed and grabbed Feole's arm. Out of the corner of her eye, she saw Ivor holding on to the wheel, locking his arm through it to keep from falling, but in a flicker of foresight she saw how foolish this was, knew he would only trap himself under the boat.

They were going over.

Even as she slid, Ash maneuvered her legs beneath her and kicked off the deck, diving out and away and into the ocean. Heart slamming in her chest, she crashed down into the ocean, plunged beneath the waves, and then began to claw frantically toward the surface. Salt water shot up her nose and for a panicked moment she thought the boat would slam on top of her. Something bumped her, slid against her. Twisting in the water, unsure for a moment which way might be up and which down, she felt herself floating, felt the undulation of the current beneath her, and chose.

Kicking her legs, she let the surge carry her and burst from the water, gasping for air as panic seized her, fear coursing through her veins. There were seals everywhere, an endless herd of them darting past her in the water, swimming with a primal urgency. In the rain, she rode up the crest of another wave and then dropped into a trough, going under for a moment. Coughing, she felt the ocean rising beneath her again and whipped around, searching for Feole and the others, searching for her boat. In the distance, in the night and the rain, she saw the lights of the *Thaumas* sailing northward. Sailing away from her. The seals pursued it, the herd parting to go around her as if they barely noticed her presence.

Then they were gone, only a handful of stragglers still around her. The bulk of the herd had passed by. Already her limbs were tired and she knew she had to find something to keep her afloat. The water was cold and the shore so far away. Ash scanned the darkness for debris . . . and saw the upside-down hull of her own boat rise into view on a crest off to her right. She screamed for Feole, and for Ivor, and for Powell, but she heard no answering cry.

She screamed for them again, but the maelstrom seemed to swallow her words.

Thunder crashed overhead. Lightning flickered up inside the storm, and in that moment of haunting illumination she saw the huge fin of a Great White knifing toward her through the water. And beyond it another, even larger.

The lightning faded and they were only shadows in the rain.

Ash kept screaming. As another wave rose beneath her, she lost sight of those fins, but she could sense them there, could feel them.

Coming for her.

CHAPTER 16

Tye stood on the deck, cold and numb, watching the seals churn through the *Thaumas*'s wake. Standing on the deck for so long, leaning into the wind, had left him bone weary. He had no idea of the time but knew it must have been well after midnight. His stomach ached and he felt a flutter of queasiness, not from seasickness—he didn't get seasick anymore—but from sheer exhaustion. He hadn't slept well last night, and now this day had gone on forever. Another couple of hours and he could wake Kat, give himself the gift of a little shut-eye. It wouldn't be much more than a long nap, but it would have to be enough.

He shivered, hating the slick chill of rain against his skin. He wore a heavy, hooded Grundens coat, made for this sort of weather, but somehow the rain always managed to get inside it, down the back of the collar. In a gale like this, there was no staying dry.

"Why don't you go inside?"

Tye turned to see Rosalie had come up behind him. Over the howl of the wind and the sea, he hadn't heard her approach.

"Go on," she called, gesturing toward the wheelhouse. "Get some cover for a while. I'm starting to dry off and we can't have that."

"You sure?"

"Shit, yeah! You can monitor the broadcast signal just as well as I can. Both jobs are boring as hell. Might as well switch it up for a while."

The ship rode up a swell and Tye grabbed her arm to keep his balance. They shared an anxious grin.

"This is crazy!" he said. "We should've postponed!"

"Every forecast had this crap going out to sea," Rosalie said.

Tye became aware of their closeness, the intimacy of the moment, so late at night and out to sea. He released her and they stared at each other for a moment. They already shared a secret, which was its own sort of intimacy— its own excitement—but he told himself he didn't want to get any closer.

He started toward the wheelhouse, and then paused. "Can I ask you a question?"

She grabbed hold of the railing to steady herself. "So serious. What's on your mind? Having second thoughts?"

Tye glanced toward the wheelhouse, but it was a foolish thought. The others were below, and in this storm even Bergting wouldn't hear their conversation, though the wheelhouse was only twenty-five feet away.

"It's not about *that*," he said, tracking Rosalie's eyes. "I just wondered why you're being so nasty to Naomi. I agree she doesn't belong here, but—"

The boat rolled. Rosalie reached out a hand and Tye grabbed it. They stood like that in the wind and rain, and she pulled him closer, her dark eyes gleaming.

"I worked hard to get where I am. Not that I think I'm going to share any of the glory of *this* jaunt. That's why when you asked me—"

"Your name will be on the research, Rosalie," Tye said, rain trickling along his nose. "You know that."

"I'm still working toward my PhD. It's your project, Tye. Yours and Kat's, and that's only right. But the idea that this undergrad is gonna get a ton of exposure for coming in here now and writing about it . . . it just makes me furious. I know it's stupid. The girl was attacked, lost her leg, and I wouldn't want to trade places with her. But it still makes my blood boil."

Another swell made Tye slip a bit on the deck, so he moved to the railing beside her, still gripping her hand. He squeezed her fingers for emphasis. Not wanting to enhance their intimacy. At least he didn't think that was what he wanted.

"I get it. You know I do. But in science, we play the long game. It's about building a legacy, and you're very firmly on the path to build yours. It's everything we've been talking about."

Her expression softened. "I know. Which is why it seems so strange hearing you say it now. Strange, and deeply hypocritical. I mean, are you seriously lecturing me on biding my time? Waiting my turn?"

Rosalie smiled. "I mean, damn."

Her hood had fallen back and her hair was slicked against her skull, but despite the misery of the storm, she seemed suddenly at ease. Her hand was still in his. Self-conscious, he released her, and Rosalie laughed silently at his sudden awkwardness.

"Relax," she said. "I'm not going to jump your bones. At least not until I'm convinced you're actually over her."

Tye held on to the railing a little tighter. "I'm over her."

"You keep saying those words and maybe eventually they'll sound true."

Tye let go of the railing, starting back toward the wheel-house. He opened his mouth to speak some nonsense words, just some happy-talk gibberish to extricate himself from the moment, and then something thumped against the side of the boat hard enough for him to feel the tremor under his feet.

"Whoa," Rosalie said, gripping the railing with both hands. "What was that?"

Tye held out his arms for balance, just in case, and slid along the deck to rejoin her at the aft railing. Together they stared at the dark, rolling sea. Tye prayed they hadn't struck a smaller boat, maybe something halfway scuttled, but he couldn't imagine what else it might be. Maybe a buoy had come unmoored and drifted.

He saw dozens of seals, their heads popping up or their backs breaking the surface, glistening wetly, but it couldn't have been a seal they'd struck. Whatever it had been was a hell of a lot bigger than that.

"Look at them all," Rosalie said.

Tye shrugged. "It's what we wanted, isn't it?"

"I figured we'd get the seals," she replied, "but I'm talk-ing about the sharks. That's a hell of a lot of fins."

Tye had seen them, of course. He'd noticed the presence of the Great Whites all through the night and knew they had been attacking some of the seals. Instinct demanded it. But with the rain and the high waves and the dark, he hadn't noticed just how many sharks there were. Squinting, he stared at the rough seas in their wake and began to count. Familiar curved shadows appeared in the mist and in the dim glow of lightning up behind the storm.

"Son of a bitch," he rasped, still tallying. "We've got more than half a dozen back there."

"That you can see," Rosalie replied. "I figure that means there are twice that many. If we keep this up long enough, there won't be any seals left to make it to Bald Cap."

She was exaggerating. Even a couple of dozen sharks weren't going to be able to eat well over a thousand seals. But Tye had not expected the sharks to react so immediately and so directly to the seal exodus. He and Kat had anticipated that the sharks would continue to move along their normal migration patterns, just a bit sooner. Luring the seals north had been a way to keep the sharks from threatening the swimmers on Cape Cod. This, though, was more than he and Kat could have hoped.

"The tourist bureau's going to be thrilled," he said.

As he spoke, there came another heavy thump against the hull. He felt the vibration in the railing and through the deck underfoot, and a deep frown creased his forehead.

"That's twice," Rosalie observed. "Is that normal? A Great White bumping a ship like that?"

"It's not unheard of. They're in a frenzy right now, losing their tiny little shark minds that there's so much food swimming around, and thanks to our signal, the seals aren't even trying to swim away."

The words were true, but he saw doubt cloud Rosalie's face, and rightly so. A Great White might bump a ship. With this much underwater traffic, it might even happen twice. But by now he figured most of the sharks had eaten their fill, and that was the thing that troubled him most. They weren't killing to eat anymore. The sharks were killing just to kill.

A terrible thought flickered at the base of his brain, a suspicion that he did not want to entertain. Tye pushed the thought away, but he stood in the rain as the boat tilted hard to port, and he started to count the fins again, reminding himself that the experiment was the important thing. The signal. And it was working. That was all that mattered.

He counted as high as eleven this time before the storm and the night and the roll of the boat made him lose count.

After that, he didn't want to count anymore.

CHAPTER 17

—◆—

Feole felt his lungs about to burst. He clawed at the water around him, tried to feel for the current, to sense the direction the gases in his body wanted to float. Which way was up? His chest burned with the need for oxygen and he had to choose, had to risk it. A ticking noise clicked again and again inside his skull, like the baseboard heat at his grandmother's house going on, and he knew that couldn't be good . . . that sound meant something bad. Salt water stung his eyes, so he kept them tightly closed, and he swam, kicked his legs . . .

And surfaced.

Gasping for air, he drew several ragged, panicked breaths and twisted around in the water. He rose on a massive wave and then slipped into a trough, but there were no breakers out here. The wind howled around him and the rain came down, but he could float awhile. Long enough to find debris, he told himself. Long enough to find something to hold on to, something that would let him ride out the storm. If only he had been alone there in the water.

But he wasn't alone.

Seals darted past him, their sleek bodies like wraiths, appearing and disappearing in an instant as they sped by. The SeaLove boat had capsized. Fifty feet away, its aft end thrust out of the water, upside-down. He could only make out the shape of it in the darkness, looming there, diminishing as it sank.

"Ash!" he screamed, his voice ripped away by the storm. "Ashleigh! Can you hear me?"

Nothing.

"Powell! Ivor! Anyone, goddammit, are you there? Are you with me?" he shouted.

He heard only the sea and the distant rumble of thunder. Seals whipped by and the frigid water sapped what little strength he had. The looming hulk of the boat vanished a little more and he knew he had to find some kind of debris, a cooler or a life vest or a chair or something, anything, to hold on to.

Pressure on his back, sliding by. Feole screamed, not once but several times as he swam away from that pressure. *Just a seal*, he told himself. But now he couldn't continue pretending to himself that the seals were the only things in the water with him. His lips trembled and he began to cry softly, and he told himself it was the cold water, the pounding of his heart, the thought of drowning. But drowning sounded almost welcoming, almost romantic.

There. He spotted something floating on the water, jutting out. Several somethings. Soaked clothes dragging him down, he tore off his coat and waited for a swell to rise and fall, and then he struck out toward that debris. Got his hand on it. A plastic deck chair, something Ivor sat in when he wanted to do a little fishing from the boat, in a lull. Would it keep floating? Would it keep him alive?

Seals glided past him, their eyes not seeing him at all. He meant nothing to them.

A larger bit of debris floated nearby, perhaps more reliable, but did he dare abandon the chair? Instead, he tried to drag it with him, but the swelling, roiling sea fought him and he had to choose. He let go, hoping he could get the chair later, and he swam to the dark thing floating on the water. Cushions from the cabin, maybe. No. Ivor's duffel, that was it. The fabric had soaked through and looked black, but it was floating, so he reached out. His fingers grazed it on the first try, and as he reached again the thing turned in the water and he saw it wasn't Ivor's duffel at all. It was Ivor. The top half of Ivor. His face shone pale and bloodless, his mouth frozen in a rictus of terror. Below the waist, there was only ragged flesh and trailing viscera.

Again, Feole screamed. He thrust away, one hand slapping at a seal passing by, and he swam back toward where he'd found the chair.

"Tony? Is that you? Oh my God, help me! Tony!"

Ashleigh.

He called out for her, shouted her name, more grateful than he'd ever been in his entire life just to know that he was not alone.

But when she cried out again, it was not to him. It was to God.

Feole considered it a blessing that he could not see her, that he could only listen to her ragged shrieks as the sharks came for her. Perhaps she was beyond the sinking boat, hidden by its diminishing shape on the water. That didn't matter. All that mattered was that he did not have to watch her being torn apart.

Worse than her shrieks, though, was the silence that came after.

Breathless, floating, Feole watched as one of the sharks came around the sinking boat, that single fin gliding so calmly through the rolling sea. He had no screams left inside him. Numb and cold, he watched the shark approach, but that wasn't the shark that killed him. He felt the impact from behind, down on his left thigh, like a car had struck him under the water. Flailing, he went under. Dragged under. The sea around him turned strangely warm, and in the last seconds of his life he understood that warmth came from the fading heat of his own blood.

By the time the shark came again, dragging him under, Feole barely felt a thing.

And then he was gone.

CHAPTER 18

Just about every fisherman Jamie knew drove a pickup or a van. Pickup was better, of course, because the bed was open to the air. His own nose might have long since quit being able to smell the stink of dead fish and their innards, but most people didn't have that advantage. A fisherman's van reeked—no two ways about it. Just riding back and forth to the harbor wearing his work clothes could get that stink into the seats, not to mention leaving his gear in the back or taking home some of the spoils of the day. So a pickup was better, but even that started to smell after a while, which was why Jamie had a different vehicle for his days off.

Walter called it the shit box, to which Jamie always replied that at least it was a *classic* shit box, but in reality he considered his spare vehicle a beauty of American engineering. The 1979 two-tone Cutlass Calais W-30 coupe had aluminum wheels trimmed with gold and a gold-over-white body hiding an Oldsmobile 350 V-8 engine. Just under 2,500 of them had been made, and of those only 537 had the T-top. Jamie had painstakingly restored the car to the point where it looked nearly new. Classic shit box indeed.

The smell of coffee filled the Cutlass as he pulled into the rutted, overgrown harbor lot. Not a lot of vehicles there this morning. The wind had howled all night and the rain had pounded his roof. When he'd turned in, the woman on NECN who always did the weather in cocktail dresses had still been saying the storm was going to turn eastward, but now morning had come and, if anything, it had grown stronger. It wasn't a hurricane or anything, no need to start battening down the hatches, but the guys who could afford a day off had stayed in bed. Jamie and Walter had planned to work today. High seas and high winds were part of the job.

Jamie parked facing the water and killed the engine. With the wind rocking the car, the interior grew cold quickly. It sure as hell didn't feel like summer. The rain sluiced down the windshield as he picked up his massive travel mug and sipped gratefully at his coffee. His thoughts drifted to Alice, though considering how often he'd been thinking of her since she'd kissed his cheek the night before, perhaps *drifted* was a poor word choice. It felt absurd, the idea that just thinking about someone could lift his spirits. But it also felt good.

The coffee mug stayed warm in his hands while he waited, but he didn't have to wait long. A familiar rumble drew his gaze to the rearview mirror and he saw Walter's red-and-white Chevy Silverado prowling across the lot. The dent on the driver's door hadn't been repaired yet. It had been plowed into by a high school girl back in December, the same day the girl had gotten her license. Walter knew plenty of auto body guys and didn't have the heart to jam the girl up with her parents or her insurance company. Jamie wondered if he regretted that on a daily basis, considering Walter had to slide over and use the passenger door any time he wanted to get into or out of the truck.

He climbed out of the car and yanked up the hood of his black-and-orange Grundens jacket. The rain gear included bib overalls, which might have seemed like overkill to anyone who hadn't been at sea on a day like today. It felt heavy, but he was warm and dry on the inside. He stood and watched Walter skid himself over to the pickup's working door and climb out. Walter reached back inside and pulled out a stained green backpack and a coffee mug even bigger than Jamie's.

"About time you showed up," Jamie said, wiping rain off his face.

Walter shot him a murderous side-eye and glanced out at the ocean. "You shitting me? Be happy I showed up at all."

"Hey, asshole, this was your idea, remember? The righteous fury of a fisherman scorned? Any of that ringing a bell?"

Walter took a gulp of his coffee and scowled, his shoulders slumping. "Yeah, it rings a bell. But it is a goddamn miserable day. Happy-go-lucky Disney sidekicks would slit their wrists on a day like today."

Jamie looked at the sky, the clouds so thick and black that it was impossible to tell if dawn had arrived. The line between night and day had been effectively erased.

"If you wanna call it off, I'm pretty sure my bed would be happy to take me back."

Walter held his coffee in both hands like a priest about

to offer up the cup of Christ's blood for a blessing. He took another long gulp and sighed.

"Nah, fuck that. I kicked Micah out of bed and sent him home. I'm already up and half-caffeinated. And now that that caffeine is kicking in and I've started thinking about those pricks out there leading seal herds up here to eat fish we oughta be catching to earn our living I'm getting pissed off all over again."

"So we're going?"

"So we're going," Walter replied.

Neither of them was happy about it, but they started toward the dock.

CHAPTER 19

The only way Naomi could tell morning had arrived was from the number of seals she could make out in the water. The sharks were still with them, and in greater numbers. Fins zipped across their wake, and her stump ached inside her prosthetic leg as if trying to remind her that sharks were the enemy. As if she needed a reminder. Still, as the first hour after dawn wore on she found herself growing numb to their presence. They were just there, following their instincts, doing what sharks did. As long as they stayed in the water and she stayed on the boat, all was well. And unless they sprouted wings, there was no chances she and the sharks would meet.

She'd propped herself against the crane, not trusting her legs—the real one or the replacement part—to hold her up as the boat rose and fell. The rain meant she had to keep the camera hooded, but since the storm showed no sign of letting up, she wasn't going to wait for better weather. Captain N'Dour had given her a spare coat from his locker and Naomi had been stunned by how much warmer and drier it kept her than the thing she'd brought. She huddled gratefully inside the coat and snapped a couple of pictures of the captain, catching his dark features in profile against the bleached background of the storm. N'Dour had been kind to her, and welcoming, but these images would cast him as grim and austere. A man determined to do his job. They would be great photos, but she wondered if they did him justice.

The thought troubled her, but she reminded herself that the paper would want the best story, the most striking images. They weren't paying her for personality profiles.

"Is there a chance you could not be in my way?"

Naomi took her eye away from the camera, but she didn't have to look to know the voice belonged to Rosalie. The woman had a camera of her own—to take video for their research, Naomi figured—but there was plenty of room for her to go around. Rosalie shook her head in exasperation, but Naomi said nothing. Just stood a bit straighter and pressed herself against the crane to give the other woman more room to pass by.

"Thanks," Rosalie muttered as she moved past, scuttling carefully toward the aft railing as the boat tilted.

Naomi didn't know what Rosalie's problem was. For half a second she wondered if there might be some weird attraction there, if Rosalie had been putting up a front to avoid anyone figuring her out, but Naomi shook the idea out of her head. She'd had her heart broken, but she didn't think she'd lost all ability to tell the difference between a girl who was interested in her and one who was just a total bitch. Though to be fair, there had been times when the two were one and the same.

Bergting had the wheel while Captain N'Dour made a

circuit of the boat, doing what Naomi assumed was some kind of inspection, to make sure the storm hadn't taken any serious toll. Kat and Wolchko were in the wheelhouse, going over data or something. She'd have to learn more about all of that on the return trip, make sure that whatever she wrote for *The Globe* didn't come off as woefully unscientific.

She took photos of the team, but there were only so many shots of their faces and the herding seals that she could manage. They were off the coast of Maine now, and had begun to pass islands small and large. Some were thickly forested, almost primeval looking, while others were dotted with small homes and cottages and had small harbors with a few boats. They kept their distance, but her camera's zoom lens saw it all. Naomi spotted a small island with several large homes poking up through the trees and thought it would make an excellent contrast to have some shots with the island as background. Kat and Wolchko were still at the bow, and she decided to join them there, get them in the foreground.

The wind shifted direction for a moment and she heard Tye's voice behind her.

"This is fucking crazy."

He sounded worried. Naomi turned and raised her camera at the same time, zoomed in on Tye and Rosalie. Both were staring at the seal herd.

"I count twenty-two," Rosalie said, the wind carrying her words as it had Tye's.

She said something else, but the wind had shifted. Naomi snapped a couple of photos and frowned when she saw the way Rosalie put her hand on Tye's arm. Not to keep herself balanced or to steady him. It was a reassuring touch, the sort of *I'm right here* reminder that suggested something more between them.

"Twenty-two what?" Naomi asked.

Rosalie turned, saw her taking photos, and pulled her hand away. "Did I *say* you could take my picture?"

"It's my job," Naomi replied.

"Bullshit. It's a sick publicity stunt by a fading newspaper happy to pimp your mother's image and your personal tragedy to get more clicks on their Web site, and you seem just as happy to whore it out, make a few bucks on almost dying."

Tye stared openmouthed. "Rosalie, Jesus."

The boat tipped and he stumbled a bit, so distracted that he'd forgotten his sea legs for a moment. Naomi snapped a picture. Her cheeks burned with shame and with anger that she had been made to feel guilt she hadn't earned. She steadied her breath and said nothing, letting her heartbeat slow.

"Stop taking my picture, for fuck's sake!" Rosalie barked.

This time Naomi did lower the camera. She turned to Tye, pretending Rosalie had vanished from her presence.

"Twenty-two what?" she asked again.

Tye blinked, as if trying to remember what she was talking about. He wiped rain from his face. "She was out of line," he said. "I apologize for that, Naomi. I want you to know that you're welcome here. Obviously Rosalie has her own issues to work out, but I don't want you to think we all—"

"I can speak for myself," Rosalie snapped.

"Maybe you've done enough of that," Tye said coldly.

"And maybe you should be careful who you take that

tone with, Dr. Ashmore. I know where the bodies are buried, remember?"

Rosalie shot him a death glare and then made her way forward. Naomi didn't bother to turn and watch her go.

"I guess you're not likely to tell me what she meant by that crack?" she asked.

Tye looked like he'd had the wind knocked out of him. He tried to brush it off, but Naomi could see that whatever Rosalie had been referring to, he really wished she hadn't mentioned it in front of her.

"No idea," he said. Revealing himself to be a terrible liar.

"Okay, then . . . back to my original question. Twenty-two what?"

"Sharks," Tye replied. "Which means there are, I'd guess, maybe forty strung back there with the seal herd. Possibly more."

Naomi felt the blood go out of her face. She'd been feeling safe, quite distant from the threat the sharks represented. Now they felt a bit closer than before.

"And they're behaving oddly," Tye added.

"Oddly how?"

Something thudded against the hull. Naomi fumbled with her camera, managed to catch it, but not before her prosthetic leg slid out from under her and she fell hard on her ass. She saved the camera, but pain shot through her tailbone and she groaned, lying back on the deck.

"Oddly like that," Tye said.

Naomi frowned, the pain fading. She propped herself up on one hand. "That was a shark?"

Tye nodded, his brow creased. "This is not normal behavior."

Naomi reached for his hand. "Help me up. And then you and Kat can tell me what the hell is going on."

CHAPTER 20

Jim Talbot felt the rain in every one of his joints. He groaned softly as he crawled out of the tent and into the storm, angry with himself and not at all looking forward to a long day of gritting his teeth behind a fake smile and trying to pretend everything was all right. He stood up straight, fists against the small of his back, and felt a series of pops rattle along his spine. Rotating his neck, he stretched and sighed, hating the rain but relieved to breathe fresh air. The inside of the tent had become claustrophobic overnight, the air too close, the atmosphere full of the tension between himself and Lorena. All he wanted was to get the hell off Deeley Island, but they had nowhere to go. Not yet.

It'll be fine, he'd told her. *The storm's headed out to sea. It'll blow over and we'll start back the day after.*

"Moron," he muttered now.

In the rain.

Jim glanced back at the tent he'd shared with his

girlfriend, Lorena Santalarsci. *Fiancée*, he reminded himself. Although after this trip, he wasn't quite sure if that would hold. She hadn't slept well last night and, thanks to her tossing and turning, neither had he. Now either she had fallen into a deep sleep at last—just after dawn—or she was pretending to be sound asleep to avoid having to talk to him just yet. Either was fine with him. He wasn't ready to face her, either.

The second tent stood a dozen feet away. The wind billowed its sides, but nothing moved within. Jim's sons were asleep inside that tent, but those two could sleep through anything. Kyle was seventeen and Dorian twenty-one. This trip had been intended as a way for them to get to know their future stepmother, and it had started out beautifully. The three Talbot men had plenty of experience sea kayaking, and Jim had taken Lorena out on shorter jaunts before. They had left Boothbay Harbor four days earlier, paddling out to Squirrel Island and then to the White Islands. They'd taken each stretch with care, but the day before yesterday they'd left Pumpkin Island and made for Deeley against Lorena's wishes. She'd wanted to go back, at least get closer to the mainland before the storm arrived in earnest. Jim had insisted the storm would veer off, and Lorena—aware that her future stepsons were paying close attention—had gone along with it.

Now they'd been on Deeley Island for a full twenty-four hours longer than they'd intended, with no sign that the storm had begun to abate. They had enough supplies to add an additional day or two to their return trip, so Jim wasn't much worried about food. But if the storm kept them stranded here much beyond tomorrow morning, freshwater would be a problem, which meant he ought to find a way to capture as much of the rain as he could.

But he had more pressing business to take care of first. The trees around their campsite bent a little in the wind, branches swaying as Jim weaved through them, moving toward the rocky shore of the island. Even at low tide, the waves were crashing on the rocks, the storm driving them above the usual waterline. In the distance, a buoy clanged. He pushed down the band of his rain pants and exhaled loudly as he pissed onto the pine needles matted onto the ground. The rain washed it away in seconds.

Despite the storm, Jim took a moment to enjoy the peace as he covered himself up. He'd be apologizing for this decision for the rest of his life, but right now he was more concerned about making it through the day without getting into a real argument with Lorena. He knew there was also the possibility that she would see the absurdity in it, that she would see past the misery of these couple of days to a time in the future when they could joke about it, but if her frustration last night was any indication, that was a pipe dream.

The rain had started to soak his hair and he tugged up his hood, feeling a bit claustrophobic even out there near the shore. If it warmed up at all, he thought he might strip down completely just to be out of the suffocating rain gear. The boys would shout at him and Lorena would be embarrassed, but the temptation was strong.

He glanced around to make sure the kayaks were secure, spotted them under the trees, and went to check on them, just to give himself something to do.

A throaty barking noise made him turn back toward the open ocean, and he spotted the seal immediately. The dark-gray beasts had slipped up onto the rocks and now laid its head back and barked again, this time a sort of ululating sound that reminded him of some kind of marine mammal battle cry. It made him smile, and some of the anxiety that had been clutching at his heart dispersed. Jim saw movement and took a step toward shore, realizing the seal wasn't alone. There were three, four, five others there as well, and now two more joined in a chorus of that croaking bark.

Jim frowned and took several more steps, wondering at the weird echo that seemed to accompany the voices of the seals. It seemed to come right off the water. He squinted against the rain, walking toward the rocks, and then stopped to stare at the crashing waves and the rough sea beyond. At the glistening gray bodies slipping through the water. Those answering barks had come from there, but only a few. Most of the seals swimming past Deeley Island were silent. Jim stared, openmouthed, as the churning mass of seals rippled by.

"Holy shit," he whispered.

He turned to follow their progress, see if they had a destination in mind, and only then did he see the boat plying the waters, rising and falling like a plastic ship in a child's bathtub. There were seals by the hundreds—by the thousands—that seemed to be following the boat, and now he saw a tall, curved fin in the water and realized there were sharks as well.

Beyond the boat, six hundred yards from the rocky shore of Deeley Island, the rusting signal tower on Bald Cap stood stark against the gray, rain-blotted sky.

As Jim Talbot watched, the boat's skipper throttled down as it slid toward Bald Cap, and the seals and the sharks began to gather around it.

CHAPTER 21

Kat stood on the prow of the *Thaumas* as Captain N'Dour navigated straight for Bald Cap. The rocky sprawl barely earned the right to be called an island. Maybe forty feet across at its widest breadth, Bald Cap was not much more than a fist of stone thrust up from the sea, likely an extension of Deeley Island, despite the distance involved. During the Second World War, the U.S. Army had built a metal watchtower on that stony outpost and bolted it to the rock. Sentries would be assigned watch duty in pairs, sleeping in shifts in the small enclosure atop the tower—not much more than a box. Now the watchtower had rusted badly and three sides of the enclosure had fallen away or been removed for safety. As N'Dour eased down the throttle and they began to glide toward Bald Cap, Kat could make out the rusted signs all around the base of the watchtower, warning boaters to keep off. The view from the small platform, more than thirty feet above the rocks, would be a natural temptation.

Not in this weather, she thought, wiping rain from her face.

There would have been stairs in the original construction, maybe bolted to the side like a fire escape. It appeared they had been removed to discourage boaters even further, just in case the signs weren't enough.

Slowing, the boat surrendered more easily to the undulations of the sea. Kat kept one hand on the railing as she turned to look at the seal herds. The wind raged, but it seemed to her that the clouds had lightened just a bit, so that it no longer felt like the middle of the night at the end of the world. Rain still poured down, but she could make out the seals a bit more clearly. She spotted a fin but barely noticed it. The sharks weren't her focus.

A shiver of pleasure ran up her spine and she found herself grinning. The grin turned to a laugh and she raised a hand to mask it. The others were moving about, or tending to their tasks, or watching the seals just as she was. Tension had been coiled inside her ever since they had set out from Woods Hole nearly twenty-four hours earlier, stress she had refused to recognize or address. This project had required countless hours of research, late nights writing grant applications, dozens of phone calls, hundreds of e-mails, not to mention all the time she had spent romancing potential donors. Kat might not be as tone-deaf as Wolchko, but she had never been very good at the social element of her job, pitching herself and her research. It made her impatient, having to smile on cue, made her want to retreat to her lab or her office. Her safe space.

Today, though, the lab would have felt like a prison. Laughter bubbled up inside her again and she threw her head back, welcoming the rain that pelted her face. It had been too long since she'd had a straight-up win in her life.

Performing for donors could be exhausting, but hiding in her lab had started to cause her soul to atrophy, so much that she'd begun to forget what it was all for. Her relationship with Tye had contributed to that spiritual withering, she knew. The support and alliance had been almost as great as the wonderfully filthy sex, but she liked simple clarity in her personal interactions and the thing with Tye had become muddied so fast. Every moment at the lab had turned into a negotiation, and the work had suffered. Breaking it off with Tye had begun to clarify things for her, but the need to navigate around the wreckage of the relationship had kept her preoccupied.

Now, though . . . now. In the midst of this storm, farther than she'd been from her lab in more than two years, her mind felt uncluttered at last. The donors would not need romancing after this. Success was its own aphrodisiac where research funding was concerned. And things would become cleaner with Tye. He might be her junior on the project, but his name would be on it—if he wanted to, he could leave Woods Hole entirely or maybe get his own project going at WHOI, with his own funding.

The weather notwithstanding, it was Kat's best day in years.

Tye had gone to the starboard side, looking down as the seal herds began to gather around the boat. Now he glanced up, spotted her, and started toward her with his arms out to either side as if he were walking a balance beam.

"You look happy," he said as the boat rocked beneath them.

"Happy? I'm absolutely *delighted*."

They grinned at each other like a pair of fools. Kat couldn't help herself—she dragged him into an embrace. It started awkwardly, all strange elbows, and then they settled into it, fitting together as comfortably as they once had. She knew she shouldn't have hugged him, feared sending the wrong signals after all they'd been through, but this moment belonged to them both.

Kat pushed back from him, held him at arm's length, and beamed. "It feels like a victory."

"Screw *feels like*. It *is* a victory. For us and for Wolchko, especially," Tye said, and they both glanced back toward the wheelhouse to see the acoustics specialist at his computer, scanning through data. "The real breakthroughs always create more questions than they answer. You told me that, Kat, and if this doesn't fit the bill, nothing does."

Her brow furrowed. "There's no way of knowing how long they'll stay here. If they'll change their patterns. If we can influence them enough to get them to start nesting here somewhere down the line. I mean, we can broadcast the signal from Bald Cap, but we don't know the effects it will—"

Tye grabbed her shoulder, bent down to stare into her eyes. "Stop. Enjoy it for an hour, at least, before you start tearing yourself apart with what comes next."

Kat laughed again. Together, comfortable at last, they turned and looked back out at the seal herd. The boat dipped hard to port, the waves pushing them too close to the rocks, and Kat felt a moment of trepidation before Captain N'Dour throttled up a bit, the engine coughing as they started to circumvent the tiny island.

"Picture time!" Naomi said, making her way carefully across the slippery deck. The storm whipped at her, but her hair had been plastered to her head by the rain and she looked like something hauled up from the deep in a net.

Tye put his arm around Kat and she allowed it. They

smiled for Naomi's camera. Then Kat extricated herself from that arm.

"Now a professional one," she said, hoping he took the gentle admonition well.

"Like this?" Tye asked, dropping into a double-thumbs-up pose worthy of a college frat boy.

"Exactly," Kat said, mimicking his pose.

Even Naomi laughed.

Wolchko remained in the wheelhouse with the captain, but Bergting stood with Rosalie at the starboard railing. Naomi turned and took a shot of them both, which caused Kat to focus on them in that moment. Bergting was the silent type by nature, kept his head down and did his job, and though they wouldn't be out here on the water without him and Captain N'Dour, he wasn't a part of this project. Rosalie, however, had a lot invested in their success. She was working toward her PhD and being a part of this project would certainly elevate her in comparison to other job candidates once she'd received her doctorate. But as she stared down at the seals and looked across the water to see them nesting on the shores of Deeley Island, Rosalie seemed unimpressed and less than enthused.

Kat called to her. Beckoned for her to join them. "You should be in these pictures!"

Rosalie stood twenty feet away, almost unrecognizable in her rain gear. A lock of wet hair striped her face.

"Come on, Rosalie!" Naomi echoed.

Tye threw his arm around Kat again. "You worked hard to get here. You should be in these shots."

"I'm good," Rosalie said, her words barely audible over the wind and the engine and the barking of the seals. "This day belongs to the two of you."

Something about the way she said it tweaked Kat's thoughts, and suddenly she felt so stupid. She might not be as perceptive as some women, but she would never have thought herself dense enough to miss this. Now the note of resignation and jealousy in Rosalie's voice gave her away, and Kat wondered how long their doctoral candidate had been holding a torch for Tye. Kat had been so wrapped up in her own complications that she'd entirely failed to see it. Arm around Tye, she let Naomi take their picture before pulling away, not wanting to make anyone uncomfortable. But when Kat glanced at Tye, she realized that he knew Rosalie was interested. Somehow this guy who'd never really been great at understanding Kat's feelings had recognized Rosalie's before Kat had.

She smiled again, this time at how blind she'd been. Kat wanted to tell Rosalie that there might be obstacles impeding a potential romance with Tye, but that she wasn't one of them. But Kat would not have that conversation today. It would wait until they were back at WHOI, not all stuck together, unable to retreat to their corners to sulk or ruminate or fume.

Naomi took a couple of more subdued shots, more professional, and in that quiet moment Kat realized that she herself might be just a little bit jealous. Silly, she knew. She had been the one to end things with Tye, but there had been a lot to cherish about their time together. She rolled her eyes at the absurdity of the feeling and exhaled, letting it go.

"That'll make a great shot, you rolling your eyes," Tye said. "What did I do this time?"

Kat barely heard him. Naomi had lowered her camera and moved toward the railing, face blank with uneasiness, and Kat walked toward her, following her gaze to see what had frightened her. Side by side, they looked out at the water, and Kat understood immediately. The sharks had become almost invisible to her, given her focus on the seal herds. But there were a lot of sharks out there, prowling the water and attacking seals. Enough seals had died that Kat thought she could smell their blood mingling with the salt air.

"Hey," Kat said, touching Naomi's arm.

Naomi flinched and glanced at her, gave a wan smile, pretending to be all right.

"You're good. We'll be here an hour or two and then we head for home, signal off. If you've been fighting your fear to be out here with us, I'm pretty sure you've won that battle. And if you want to go below—"

"They don't make you nervous?" Naomi asked, turning her head to keep an eye on a cluster of three fins as the boat kept churning the water. "It's not freaking you out that there are so many?"

"It's natural they'd follow the seals. And there aren't *that* many."

Tye had scuffed carefully across the deck to join them. "But there are," he said. "Dozens of them."

The boat tipped hard to port and they all staggered back a few steps. Naomi grabbed Kat by the arm, unsteady on her prosthetic or simply not used to the sea. Suddenly Kat wanted to go below, to have the distraction of raw data as they made their way home, asking all of the questions that would be born of this journey.

"You're suggesting the signal's had a similar effect on the sharks as it has on the seals? That we've lured them with something other than the movement of their food source?"

"Maybe," Tye said. "Rosalie and I have been monitoring them and we're sure they're exhibiting unusual behavior."

Rosalie and I. Kat frowned, not in jealousy but with a flicker of uneasiness. Why hadn't they brought this up to her?

Kat turned to Naomi. "It bears study, of course. We'll have to investigate all of this. But there could be fifty Great Whites out there and it wouldn't matter. We're just observers here. We won't be engaging with the sharks at all. Nobody's diving, and we won't be hauling one onto the deck for study. Not this trip. You're fine."

Naomi shook her head, embarrassed. "I know it's stupid—"

"It's not stupid," Kat said. "Not after what you've been through. But we'll be home by this time tomorrow. *The Globe* is going to love this story. We're all going to come out winners from this. And if you get really freaked out, you tell me, and I'll ask N'Dour to bring us into port and you can go ashore, make your way home from there. Your job is done. The rest of us have a ton of work to do now, but we'll have plenty of funding to do it. Even Wolchko has to be happy about that."

Naomi hesitated a moment before meeting Kat's eyes, her own face full of surprise and gratitude. "Thank you. I'm going to stick it out, but I didn't expect . . . I mean, I really appreciate you being so kind."

"Don't get used to it," Tye muttered, but his smirk said he was only teasing, and that was okay with Kat. They could tease. It was whatever else she now thought might be simmering underneath the teasing that worried her.

When Bergting raised his voice, Kat frowned at first. He talked so little that for a second she had wondered who was speaking. Then he raised a hand and pointed, a troubled expression on his face, and he spoke again.

"Dr. Cheong," he said. "What do you make of that?"

Kat walked to the railing and watched as two fins carved the water off the starboard side. They were fifty yards out and swimming straight for the boat. There were seals all around them and she was sure the sharks would break off, chase something to eat, but instead the fins kept arrowing toward the boat. Ten yards out, the sharks went deeper, the fins beginning to submerge.

"Hold on to something," Bergting snapped.

Rosalie swore as she gripped the railing. "What the fuck is *this*?"

They felt the boom against the hull, a tremor through the whole boat. Kat froze for several heartbeats, trying to make sense of it. This wasn't right. Sharks had been known to attack a kayak or small boat, but behavioral analysis usually provided some explanation. But something like this . . .

Her thoughts derailed. She stared out at the water as she saw the sharks circling around as if to make another pass.

This is not happening.

Off to her left, she heard Tye call out, but the words were nothing but noise. She scanned the water, taking a mental count of the fins, and then she felt a hard bump against the hull before the boat began to tilt into a trough. Another heavy thump and she fought the tilting deck to grab the railing, to look down into the storm-black water, where she saw a fifteen-foot-long Great White skidding its two-and-a-half-ton bulk along the side of the boat.

A crest swelled beneath the boat and it began to tilt in the other direction. The first pair of sharks returned, two of them booming into the hull together. Kat felt herself filled with a sort of awe, both of these monsters and of the signal Wolchko had been broadcasting for her. Whatever they had done to the seals, it had struck a very different chord in the sharks.

Another thump. Then a heavier boom. The boat tilted again. The sharks battered against the hull, and more were circling. Swarming. Kat didn't recognize the flutter in her chest at first, but after a few moments she realized this was what it meant to feel real fear.

She blinked as the biggest Great White bashed against the hull again, and for the first time she realized someone was screaming. *Had been* screaming for a while.

Kat turned to see Naomi sitting on the deck, hugging her knees to her chest, her camera forgotten beside her. The screams belonged to her.

CHAPTER 22

———

Naomi tried just to breathe. The rain felt like punishment, the wind like mockery. She wrapped her arms around her knees and squeezed tighter. Trying to breathe, finding it difficult . . . that was how she realized she had been screaming. Now she snapped her jaws shut and took long breaths through her nose, running mental calculations about how far it might be to Bald Cap or to Deeley Island, or for that matter to the mainland.

The mainland. What the hell were they doing out here?

A hand touched her shoulder and she slapped it away, twisting to see it had been Eddie Wolchko's. He offered that hand to her as if to help her up, but she ignored it, shooting to her feet. The stump of her missing leg ached so badly it felt like the bone had been exposed. It had been aching all day and most of the day before thanks to the rain and the cold and spending so much time standing, but she hadn't wanted to bitch about it, hadn't wanted anyone to think she sought their sympathy. Now they all stared at her as if she had lost her mind and she stared back, thinking the same of them. Why weren't they panicking? Why weren't they doing something?

"Naomi," Wolchko gently prodded. "You're all right. I know you must be—"

The deck slanted to port, but she kept her footing as she spun to glare at Kat. "What are you doing just standing there? Even I know this isn't normal."

Boom, on the hull. *Boom. Boom.*

A haunting sound. A nightmare sound.

Boom.

Her heart beat a frantic rhythm as they began to talk to her—Kat and Wolckho—trying to calm her down, as if any of this were rational.

"Are you not listening?" she cried over the rain. "You've done something to them. Shut it down. You've got to . . ."

Her words trailed off. She saw from their eyes, the way they studied her, that they weren't going to listen to her. Why should they? They were the brains here, the brilliant scientists, and who was she? A girl who should've died off the Cape Cod shore last summer instead of the surfer who'd saved her.

She caught the look on Rosalie's face and something clicked in her head. A conversation between the research assistant and Tye, talk of a secret.

"What are you hiding?" she asked.

Rosalie scowled. "I don't know what—"

"You told Tye you knew his secret. That you knew where the bodies were buried. What were you talking about, then? Did you two do something to cause this? Did you want to tear Kat down for some reason, or did you—"

"Whoa, now, hold the fuck on!" Rosalie snapped. "I get

that you're freaking out, girl, but you can't just go accusing people of sabotage!"

Tye paled. Looked like he was biting his tongue.

"Then what did I hear? What's this secret—"

"Maybe you need to look up the definition of *secret*," Rosalie sneered.

Kat stepped between them. "That's enough." She took a breath. The way her gaze shifted, Naomi could see that the argument had gotten under her skin. But then Kat turned to focus on her. "Rosalie's right. Accusing a scientist of sabotaging a project . . . you've got to be very careful. You could ruin careers that way."

"But—"

"Naomi, listen to me. You're not thinking straight," Kat said. "Neither Tye nor Rosalie would do anything to purposely undermine this experiment. It wouldn't just make *me* look bad. It would taint the efforts of the whole team and seriously impact our ability to get funding. It wouldn't make any sense."

Boom.

Wolchko cleared his throat. "You think I'm in on this conspiracy, too?"

"Of course not," Naomi replied.

"I'd have to be," he said. "I programmed the signal. I built the array. No way could anyone make changes to it without my knowing." A frown of guilt creased his forehead. "If something's gone wrong, it's my fault."

"It's not that simple, Eddie," Kat said.

Naomi shook her head. "Fine. Maybe nobody did it on purpose. But you're wrong if you think it's not simple."

She turned and marched toward the wheelhouse. Rosalie and Bergting saw where she was headed and went to intercept her.

Boom. Boom.

"What the fuck are you doing?" Rosalie snapped.

Naomi cocked her head back. "Turning it off. Which is what you should be doing."

Boom.

She went to push past, but Rosalie grabbed her wrist. "Whoa, whoa. Dial it down, honey. You're out of your depth here. Nobody touches the equipment without—"

Naomi hit her. Hard. Closed fist. She knew how to throw a punch. Rosalie staggered and went down on one knee. *Boom. Boom.* Voices called out. Bergting swore and tried talking to Naomi as she rushed by, headed into the wheelhouse.

Captain N'Dour blocked her way. "Mr. Bergting, please take the wheel," he said, though he never took his eyes off Naomi.

Bergting slipped by them both, took control of the boat, and Captain N'Dour held a hand up as if to forestall any argument from Naomi.

Boom.

"I know you're frightened," N'Dour said, his voice so gentle.

From behind, Naomi heard Rosalie shouting. "Get your hands off me, Kat. I'm done with this bitch."

Naomi glanced back and saw Kat and Tye both holding Rosalie back. The woman's nose had started to bleed. Naomi wasn't sorry, but the sight of that blood gave her pause.

Bump. Tilt.

She stumbled a bit and Captain N'Dour grabbed her, bringing them closer together. His eyes searched hers.

"Do not fear," N'Dour said.

Naomi laughed at that, staring at him as panic drained out of her. *Boom*. She flinched at this new impact, fought back the tears that fear threatened to wring from her.

"We're fine," Captain N'Dour said, taking her hand in both of his. His skin felt leathery, somehow dry despite the water all around them. "You must listen to me and try to think. Just hear me. A hundred sharks could pound on this ship all day and night and we would be fine. The hull is too strong for them to hurt us."

His confidence soothed her. "Still. We should shut it off."

Boom. Boom. Boom. The frenzy in the water had grown more chaotic, the thunder of the sharks smashing at the hull even louder.

Captain N'Dour looked past her to Kat, who stepped up beside Naomi now.

"We'll be done here in a couple of hours," Kat said. "Then we shut it all down and go home. If you want to wait below or something, we won't object. But we need to record this behavior from the sharks. It's part of the research now and we can't ignore—"

Boom.

Rosalie shuffled up beside Kat. Tye tried to stop her, but she shook him off. She wiped at her bloody nose.

"We've got the data on the seals," Rosalie said. "All of that we can post-game later. But if the sharks are reacting to the signal, we have to know that, and understand how. Which means we still have a job to do."

Boom. Boom.

"Go below if you want. Or you can put that fear aside and do the job *you* came here to do."

Naomi breathed. Felt the rain. Glanced at the faces

around her, each of them breaking away once they saw that she'd gotten herself under control. Tye went below, muttering something about the data. Rosalie and Bergting started making a circuit of the deck, talking quietly, maybe counting fins again. Wolchko seemed reluctant to leave Naomi alone, but after a moment's hesitation he went into the wheelhouse.

"You going to be all right?" Kat asked.

Boom.

Naomi glanced at Captain N'Dour and nodded. He knew his boat. He said they were safe.

"I'm sorry," she said. "For making such a scene. I'm an ass."

"You're scared. We get it," Kat replied. "Look, I don't know what you overheard."

Naomi met her gaze and realized Kat was curious. Even troubled. "You said they had as much to lose as you do. That they'd never—"

"They wouldn't. But I do wonder what that's about."

Naomi got the sense there might be a hint of jealousy in Kat's voice, but hadn't she heard the part about Rosalie knowing where the bodies were buried? Whatever secret she had with Tye, it had to do with something more than sex or romance.

Boom. Boom. Boom.

Kat gave Naomi's arm a reassuring grip and then joined Wolchko, talking about how sharks hear, something about their brains, and wondering about the effects of modulating the existing signal. Wolchko started to argue, and that was the point when Naomi actually believed they might be all right.

She leaned against the wheelhouse, the glass windows slick with rain. Three strikes in quick succession. The whole thing was insane, but if these scientists felt so at ease that they could stand there and debate marine acoustics she thought they really must be safe.

A dozen feet away, her camera lay on the deck, shielded by the rain hood she'd been using. How hard had she dropped it? She started toward the camera, but Rosalie beat her to it. She'd been at the railing but now picked up the camera and turned it over in her hands, tugging at the hood.

"Don't," Naomi said.

Rosalie shot her a curious look. "Don't what?"

Naomi waited for her to smash it or throw it overboard. Instead, Rosalie handed the camera and hood to her.

"Focus on the sharks. Get shots where we can gauge their size. This isn't for *The Globe*; it's for the project. Every bit of detail helps."

Naomi knitted her brows, not bothering to hide her surprise.

Rosalie touched the darkening bruise on her face. "Oh, you're worried about this? Don't worry; you've got one coming. Let's just say I owe you, and I'll save it for later, when you're done being useful."

She went to rejoin Bergting. Naomi watched them for a moment, saw the quiet approval on the first mate's features, and then gave her camera a quick examination. Snapped a couple of photos. Wiped some rain off the casing, happy that the lens was clear.

Boom.

Unsteady on her feet, careful as the boat dipped and rolled, she moved around the railing. Naomi had no expertise in sharks, but they all had a sameness about them, so she thought they must all be Great Whites. They ranged in length from eight feet to as long as what must have been fifteen or sixteen feet, the latter of which was enormous. She photographed as many as she could, got the clearest shots that the storm and the sea and the rocking boat would allow.

Working, thinking with her camera, she began to calm even further. The sharks were down there. She was up here.

Boom. Boom. She snapped away, while nearby Tye and Kat had come out onto the deck and were talking about hyperaggression and primal triggers.

With her camera, Naomi tracked one of the largest sharks, following it with her lens and moving down the railing to the rear of the boat. As the fin turned toward her, she forced herself to breathe, to watch it through her camera, to remember Captain N'Dour's soothing words.

The fin rushed straight for the rear of the boat. *The stern*, she reminded herself, leaning against the railing as she snapped photos of the shark knifing toward her. *You call it the—*

The impact jolted her much harder than the others. It felt as if the deck had shifted beneath her, as if the shark had moved the boat. But as Naomi stumbled and grabbed hold of the railing it was the sound echoing in her head that scared her. Not a *boom* this time. This time, the collision had been a crash. Something had cracked and broken, giving way, and suddenly all of Captain N'Dour's reassurances seemed like the worst lies.

The stern dipped hard. Something came skittering along the deck and she saw it was an empty soda can. It rolled right under the railing and vanished into the churning water below. Naomi ratcheted herself up, hung the camera on its strap around her neck, and looked over the side . . . knowing what she would see. Dreading it. Needing to confirm it with her own eyes.

Wolchko and Rosalie came running. The stern dipped again, hard, and Rosalie lost her footing. She slipped on the rain-slick deck and careened into the railing. Her elbow came down hard, something cracked, and when she hit the railing she cried out in pain. Naomi ignored her. They had bigger problems.

A hole had opened at the back of the boat, deep under the waterline. Ocean poured in through a breach in the hull. Naomi saw it for a moment, the water rushing in, but the boat tipped farther, the ballast of the floodwater dragging the stern down harder. Deeper.

"No, no. It can't be!" Captain N'Dour said as he skidded along the deck toward them.

The boat dipped into a trough, tipped hard to starboard, and the ocean splashed up onto the aft deck. For a moment the water seemed to drag on it, as if it wanted nothing more than to claim the *Thaumas*. N'Dour held on to the crane and the others to the railing. Up by the wheelhouse, Kat shouted as she fell, sliding across the deck before the next swell righted the boat. Naomi caught a glimpse of Bergting and Tye in the wheelhouse, shouting at each other.

"How do we stop it?" Wolchko said, glaring at N'Dour even as he crouched to help Rosalie.

Naomi felt numb. "You said this couldn't happen."

N'Dour held on to the crane as the boat dipped farther. "The propeller shaft . . . it must've—"

Another collision, a cracking sound beneath them, and Naomi felt something other than fear. As the boat tilted hard to stern and another trough came, the ocean crashed up onto the deck and washed over Rosalie, Naomi knew they were done, and what she felt was fury. Venom burned through her, a hatred of the sharks and of this project that had fueled their aggression.

Wolchko dragged Rosalie to her feet as she cradled her left arm against her chest, possibly broken.

"We have to shut it off," Captain N'Dour said, beginning to turn toward the wheelhouse.

Naomi barely heard the words. She pushed off the railing, climbing the slick incline of the deck, reckoning they had half a minute or less before the pitch would be too steep. She grabbed N'Dour, used him to pull forward, passed the crane, and shouted for Bergting. For Kat. For Tye.

"Get closer!" Naomi called. "We've got to reach—"

The rest of the sentence was swallowed by a loud crack belowdecks. Not a collision, not this time. Just the result of something else giving way, the settling of water in the belly of the boat. They listed hard to port again, the stern sinking deeper. She slipped, fell to her knees, stump hurting even more than her real knee.

"Go, go, go!" Kat roared, waving her arm as she held on to the open door of the wheelhouse.

For a moment Naomi thought she'd had the same thought, that Kat was calling for Bergting to aim the *Thaumas* at Bald Cap. But that wasn't it at all. Kat pointed toward Bald Cap, gesturing violently so the rest of them would understand. Then she reached into the wheelhouse and grabbed the back of Tye's raincoat, dragged him out onto the deck and toward the port side.

Only then did Naomi really get it. The propeller had been staved in. Bergting could do nothing to get them closer. They were slowing down, sinking, listing hard, and subject to the whims of the storm and sea. They were foundering.

They were going into the water one way or another. If they wanted to live, they were going to have to swim for it. And once they were in the water, they wouldn't be alone.

CHAPTER 23

———

Hands gripped Naomi from behind, powerful hands that hoisted her to her feet on the canted deck. She felt as if she couldn't breathe.

"Swim," Captain N'Dour said in her ear. "You must go."

Naomi took his hand, grasped it tight. "We go together."

Wolchko tried moving past them with Rosalie. He shouted to Bergting to shut down the signal, but that seemed such a small thing now. The ship would go down, the power would short, and it would be over. Naomi tried to tell him that.

The ocean fell away beneath them, the trough so deep. She heard a pair of thudding impacts on the hull and then the stern slid beneath the water and the rising crest hurled itself against the starboard and they were all sliding. Falling. Naomi saw the railing rushing up toward her and knew bones would break, and she shouted at Captain N'Dour to jump.

Together they launched themselves from the deck, fell over the side. Her camera flew beside her and clipped the railing, shattering on impact.

Then she plunged into the sea and the water stole Captain N'Dour away, his fingers torn from her grasp. The breathless cold seized her, so sharp and sudden that it shut down her panic, drove conscious thought away so that she relied only on instinct. In the water, the prosthetic felt lighter than the rest of her, but it moved at her command as she kicked upward and breached the surface.

Naomi looked up, expecting to see the *Thaumas* crashing down on top of her, but the ocean had changed its mind. The boat hadn't capsized. Another massive wave threatened to topple it, but now the water concentrated on dragging it down from behind. Half the boat had vanished now, the crane gone below the surface.

She heard screams and turned to see Wolchko swimming toward Rosalie.

Seals barked from the rocky edge of Bald Cap, thirty feet away. Farther out, past the sinking boat, Naomi saw fins, and then she stopped thinking. Her brain blotted them out. Her eyes refused to see them. Shouts and barks and screams filled the air and the wind howled through the rusted lattice of the tower on Bald Cap, but she saw nothing more. She only swam, head down, salt water up her nose, body remembering early-morning swim meets in middle school, prosthetic leg not cooperating, slowing her pace. But she swam, heart thundering, and hating that leg. She swam.

Behind her, a voice screamed itself ragged.

Her good knee scraped stone. Her hand reached up, closed on a sharp edge, and then her foot found purchase under the water. The new leg couldn't feel properly, but she jammed it forward, scraped against rocks until her boot caught and she had leverage with both legs. She climbed, dragged herself up onto the edges of Bald Cap, and turned as the shark surfaced, jaws wide, rows of yellow teeth smeared with torn bits of seal skin and flesh.

Naomi screamed and tucked her legs up against her chest, twisted away, and the shark careened against the rocks as it passed. She couldn't breathe as she watched it. Only nine feet long. *One of the small ones*, she thought, and then laughed at the insanity of the thought. Laughed and then started to cry, one hand flying up to cover her mouth. To contain a sob. She mustered her strength, told herself crying would not help them, and felt a chill seize her insides again.

Naomi heard shouts, whipped around, and saw Kat dragging Tye from the water. His pants were torn and Naomi saw blood on the stark white flesh of his right leg, but the leg remained. Captain N'Dour climbed out of the water after him, scrambling quickly, glancing over his shoulder at two fins that were slashing toward the tiny island.

Several dozen seals had found rest on the rocky edges of the island. Naomi picked a path that would keep her as far from them as possible as she crept farther inland, onto the smooth stone that gave Bald Cap its name, and stood to scan the water. There, a quarter way round the island, Wolchko and Rosalie were clambering onto the rocks, avoiding more seals. Naomi exhaled. Rosalie still held her arm to her chest, but beyond that she and Wolchko were whole. Each alive and in one piece.

A tremor went through Naomi.

All except Bergting.

"Peter!" N'Dour was shouting, stumbling as he moved to the edge of the island.

Angry seals barked at him, but he moved between them, stood on the rocks where waves crashed and soaked him with their spray. Other seals crawled out of the water as the sharks swarmed around the sinking boat. Only the bow of the *Thaumas* still showed above water, from the wheelhouse to the prow.

Bergting crouched on what would have been the wheelhouse's windshield. One window had been shattered and he had something in his hand. A radio or a phone. Naomi's heart leapt. Of all of them, only he had kept his focus on keeping everyone alive. They needed help, needed a rescue. Her own phone would be ruined, down in the pocket inside her pants, soaked in ocean water.

"Peter, swim!" the captain called to him.

The others began to shout as well, urging the man to abandon the ship, to swim before it was too late. But Naomi kept silent. She watched the sharks as they circled, focused now on the last of the ship as it slid under, vanishing by the foot. The time for Bergting to swim had passed.

"Oh my God," she whispered.

Bergting turned to gaze across fifty feet of churning ocean, and from the look in his eyes Naomi knew that he understood the choice he'd made. Maybe he hadn't known when he was making that choice, but he recognized the cost of it now. He held up the black thing in his hand and she saw that it was a phone after all. But he held it in his palm like an offering, then slowly shrugged his shoulders, the apology written on his face. His efforts had been for nothing. His sacrifice.

The first mate of the *Thaumas* flipped his phone into the roiling sea. The wheelhouse sank deeper. A shark struck the boat and it jerked to one side, nearly toppling Bergting over. He caught himself, then tried to reach the railing, perhaps thinking he could climb to the bow, buy himself a little more time.

A moment later the ocean claimed the wheelhouse, rose to the level of the steps down into the cabin, and the water must have flooded down into that hole, for the last of the *Thaumas* went down like the Atlantic had gripped it in rigid fingers and dragged it under.

Bergting went under with it, for a moment. Then his head poked out, for just a second, and he tried to swim. Naomi watched in silent hope, sharing his change of heart, thinking that anything was possible, that the sharks might not notice him for a few seconds, maybe long enough.

He jerked to a stop as if he'd collided with something. A gasp came from his throat, like he'd had the wind knocked out of him, and then he went down just as abruptly as the boat had, lost beneath the churning waves.

Had that been the last they'd seen of him, it would have been a blessing for them all. But the sharks were there, the fins rising to cut the surface, and one of them had Bergting in its jaws. Others wanted him, tried to take him away, and together they tore him apart. Naomi glimpsed one scything spray of blood and then turned away, unable to watch.

The others cried out. Turned to comfort one another. Like her, they turned their faces away from death.

The wind whistled through the rusted tower and whispered across Bald Cap. In three directions, they could see only the storm and the raging sea. To the west, though, there was Deeley Island. Larger than Bald Cap, but just as abandoned. Six hundred impossible yards away, but no point in even trying.

A wave crashed on the rocks and splashed much higher than the last one.

They were stranded.

CHAPTER 24

Jim Talbot stood at the edge of the tree line on the eastern edge of Deeley Island and watched the boat go down. He couldn't fathom what had gone wrong, how they'd managed to scuttle such a boat, but it sank so quickly that it had to have been something major. The sharks had been circling, at least from what he'd seen at this distance, but he had no idea what had sunk the boat.

The rocks, he thought. They'd sailed too close to Bald Cap, staved in the hull on that side. A colossal fuckup on the captain's part, but the only thing that made sense. Of course it had been the rocks.

A strange calm enveloped Jim, but it took time before he recognized it as helplessness. He breathed evenly, one hand on the bark of a huge skinny old pine that bent and swayed in the storm. Rain pattered his face, stuck to his eyelashes, and he blinked it away. Otherwise, he could only watch, mouth slightly parted, brain barely able to process the truth of what he saw.

Footfalls pounded the ground behind him, branches snapped, and he whipped around with his hands raised in defense, as if the sharks out there might've come for him here on land.

"Dad," his son Kyle said, grinning ear to ear. "Did you see the seals on the rocks? There's so many of them. They're almost up to the kayaks. It's crazy. You have to come and . . ." He let his words trail off, studying his father. "What's the matter? What's that look for? Wait, did you and Lorena already have a fight today?"

Jim's thoughts were so fuzzy that it took him an extra couple of seconds to process. "Lorena's still in the tent. She's . . . I don't know if she's sleeping or not. And don't hold it against her if she's not happy out here. Turns out she was right about the storm. In her shoes, I'd be pretty pissed off. All things considered, she's being—"

A good sport, he almost said. But in the midst of this defense of Lorena, he realized how absurd it was to even be having that conversation.

"Shit," he said, shaking his head. It felt like waking up from a nightmare. "Kyle, where's your brother?"

Kyle shifted his weight from foot to foot. "He's right behind me. Or he was. What is it, Dad? What aren't you saying?"

Seventeen, skinny, Kyle still looked like a kid even though he'd be a high school senior this fall. His hair needed cutting and he thought the peach fuzz on his chin might manage to be a beard if he let it grow. Still Jim's boy. But Kyle had a core of maturity that his older brother lacked, and he was the smartest of the three Talbot men.

"Have a look," Jim said, and stepped aside to give Kyle a better view of the water to the east.

A second later Dorian came through the trees. He held

his fishing pole at his side, his bait box and kit slung on straps over his shoulder. With his rain gear on, the whole ensemble seemed unwieldy as hell, but Dorian barely seemed to notice any of that.

"Gonna have to find a different spot to catch breakfast," Jim's older son said. "The fuckin' seals don't look like they want company."

Lorena would have chided him for the language, and for her Dorian would have cleaned it up. As strange as it still was for Jim's sons to see him with someone new, Dorian, at least, seemed to have taken a liking to her. Tall and lean, tattooed and scruffy, he'd set his heart on a life making music. Jim believed in his son's talent, but he knew the odds and they terrified him. Dorian saw that as his dad not supporting him, not having faith. Lorena, though, had quickly and genuinely become Dorian's number one fan.

Kyle pushed past Jim. "Holy shit, Dor . . . come and see this!" He darted back toward the rocks.

Dorian cocked an eyebrow at his father. "What's his deal?"

Jim felt his face flush with heat, despite the wind and the chilly rain. The image of the boat sinking replayed in his mind. Even at this distance, he had been able to see the man standing on the prow of the boat as it had gone down. With the waves and the rain and at this range, Jim hadn't witnessed what came next, but he could imagine.

"We've got some people in trouble," Jim said.

"Dor, check it out!" Kyle called. "It's not just seals. There're a ton of sharks out there, too!"

Dorian stepped past his father, still laden with his fishing gear. "What are you talking about?"

Jim listened to them talking, but he was less interested in the sharks than he was in the rest of the people who'd been on that boat. He had convinced his sons to leave their phones at home, to make this trip about the family, but his own phone was back at the tent. Service out here had proved to be spotty at best and in the storm, so far out, he didn't expect much, but he knew he had to try to call for help. The phone had another use, too . . . the camera's zoom would give him a better idea of the situation out on Bald Cap.

"Kyle, go and get my phone. It's zipped into my pack. And ask Lorena to come back with you, and to bring her phone."

He was a smart kid and didn't need it explained to him. Zipping off into the trees, he left Jim and Dorian standing at the tree line. For long moments, father and son stood and watched the small figures moving on Bald Cap. One of them had begun to climb the old metal tower.

"They're gonna be okay now," Dorian said, sounding sure. "We'll call the Coast Guard."

"Absolutely," Jim replied.

"It's crazy, though. I've never seen so many sharks in one place. Or so many seals. Is it, like, some kind of migration?"

Jim pondered that a moment, then gave his son the tiniest of shrugs. "Not like any I've ever heard of."

Over the roar of the storm and the waves crashing on the rocks, the movements of the people on Bald Cap seemed like a grim pantomime. Jim and Dorian kept glancing back through the trees until at last they heard Kyle crashing through the branches and he returned, breathing hard, with his father's phone clutched in his hand. As he handed it over, Lorena appeared behind him, making her way much more carefully along the path.

"Kyle said to bring my phone," she announced, her

words clipped and precise as always, as if she were talking to a patient. Lorena had a sense of humor that seemed to sneak up on her constantly, but her default position was seriousness. "Something about . . ."

Her words trailed off when she spotted the seals. Her eyes scanned the storm-tossed sea and she must have noticed the fins as well. Then she squinted, staring across at Bald Cap.

"There are people out there."

"Their boat sank," Jim said, tapping in the code to open his phone. "We've gotta call nine-one-one. Get somebody out here."

Lorena started asking about the seals. Dorian began to fill her in, but Jim hardly paid attention. He walked a few paces north, held up his phone, hoping to get any kind of signal. At the moment he had zero bars, so he turned south again and wandered a dozen paces.

"Shit. I've got zero signal." He looked at Lorena. "Try yours."

Her eyes narrowed further as she stared out at Bald Cap for a second, then held up her own phone, just the way Jim had.

"One bar," she said.

"Better than nothing," Kyle said hopefully.

Dorian just stood there with his fishing pole, watching the churning sea. Watching the sharks.

Lorena tried the call, waving the phone ahead of her in the rain like it was a Geiger counter hunting for trace radioactivity. When the call failed, she swore under her breath. The rain slicked the phone's face and Jim knew she shouldn't keep it exposed like that for very long, not in this soaking. He studied her face as she tried the call again. Her black hair tied back, she wore a touristy-looking rain hat that wasn't suited to the weather at all. Lorena had been through physical and emotional ordeals in her life that had honed her body and spirit into those of a formidable woman. She was already miserable about them being temporarily stranded on Deeley Island in this weather. He wasn't about to make it worse by saying a word about her hat.

She'd put the phone on speaker. They all heard a crackle of static on the line before it started to ring.

Halfway through the second ring, it cut out.

Lorena cursed and tried again.

CHAPTER 25

⟨—

Wolchko stood a dozen feet from the nearest of the seals. The beasts had been barking at the human arrivals ever since they'd dragged themselves onto Bald Cap, but as he and the others had congregated nearer to the rusty tower the bellowing had calmed down. The alpha males continued to bark now and again, just to remind the humans that they'd claimed the barren rock first, but the seals didn't seem inclined to attack. Wolchko spotted another seal humping its bulk up onto the rocky edge of Bald Cap, eluding the sharks for the moment. The seals would be exhausted now. They'd been drawn on by his acoustic lure, the signal keeping them moving long after they'd have otherwise stopped to rest. For the first time, it occurred to him that it might have been cruel, but that small doubt—that hesitant regret—seemed just a flicker compared to the mass of other emotions he struggled to decipher.

Captain N'Dour knelt beside Tye, inspecting the shark bite on his right leg. In the rain and the gray storm light, it was hard to be sure from his vantage, but Wolchko didn't think the wound looked too bad. Tye's pants had already been torn, so N'Dour ripped off strips of fabric and bandaged the wound as best he could while Rosalie looked on, trying to persuade Tye he was going to be all right.

Kat had sprung onto the watchtower almost immediately after they'd come ashore. It creaked as she climbed. Large flakes of damp rust fell from the metal and were swept away on the wind. Wolchko didn't want to look too closely at the orange-crusted joints on the tower, but it made him nervous as hell, having Kat up there.

Seals barked loudly. He glanced over and saw Naomi walking toward him with something in her hand. It didn't surprise him at all to see that it was her cell phone.

"It's useless," she said, pushing a knot of wet hair away from her face. "It was supposed to be waterproof."

Her face had gone pale, features slack. Her eyes were a little too wide, and he knew shock had begun to set in. Shock over the sharks attacking, over the boat sinking, and over Bergting's death.

Wolchko took the phone from her hand, shook it, and saw droplets of water squeeze out around the small thumb button on the bottom of the screen. "Water-resistant, not waterproof," he said. "It's not meant to be submerged and sure as hell not in seawater. Salt water. The phone's fucked."

Naomi shuddered as she drew a breath. "*We're* fucked."

Wolchko handed back her phone. She took it and hurled it into the water, skipping it once on a rising wave before it plunked into the Atlantic.

"My phone was in my pack, on the boat," he said. "I figure everyone else's phones are just as useless."

Naomi hugged herself against the rain. Her gaze

twitched toward Tye and she looked quickly away. He figured she didn't want to think too much about the shark bite on his leg.

"Oh, Jesus," she rasped, lowering her head. "Oh, shit."

Wolchko lifted her chin, startling them both with the uninvited contact. He pulled his hand away fast, but he had her attention.

"I need you with me, Naomi. We're all smart people, out here, but the only way this turns out right is if we stay smart. If we fall apart, it's not going to go well."

"Go well?" She stared at him. "You think it's going well for Bergting?"

"That story's done," Wolchko said. "It doesn't matter now—"

"Doesn't matter? What's wrong with you? Don't you think it matters to the guy's family? To the people who cared—"

Wolchko held up his hands in surrender, but he kept his gaze locked on hers. "I can't figure out the right way to say things, but you need to start thinking about what I mean, not whether or not I've chosen the nicest way to say it. Focus on what happens next, to us."

Naomi took a breath and he saw her eyes clear, saw the glint of something hard there, something he knew was inside her. You couldn't go through what she'd gone through and come out swinging at life without developing some steel, down inside.

"All right," she said. "What *does* happen next?"

Wolchko glanced around, then up at Kat. Rain spattered his face. Soaking wet, cold, already exhausted, he had gone numb. But they couldn't afford numbness, not any of them.

"Kat saw it even quicker than I did," Wolchko said.

"Saw what?"

"We're even more screwed than you think, and I need you to hold it together, Naomi. You listening to me?"

Captain N'Dour started toward them. Rosalie helped Tye hobble toward the tower. Wolchko ignored them, focused on Naomi.

"I'm listening," she said.

"Look at the rocks where you climbed ashore."

Naomi did, and he saw it click on her face. The truth of their situation. Just how screwed they were.

"They're almost gone." Naomi put a hand on her forehead, bent over, looking like she might be sick. Then she straightened up and stared at him. "The tide's coming in fast. But it can't cover the island or Kat would never have picked this spot to try to get the seals to nest."

"It was always Bald Cap and Deeley both," Wolchko said. "But you're right. Normally this rock stays above the high-tide line—"

"Storm surge," Naomi said, looking out to sea.

"Bald Cap's gonna be underwater in a couple of hours," he confirmed.

Naomi turned to gauge the distance to Deeley Island. Wolchko could practically read her thoughts, because he'd already had them all.

"Too far to swim in this storm—maybe without the storm—and that's not even accounting for the sharks." Wolchko glanced upward. "That's why Kat's testing out the tower, seeing how sturdy it is."

Naomi's expression hardened. "Someone will come looking for us. They'll be expecting word. When they don't get it they'll try to contact us, and when they don't get an answer they'll come."

Wolchko didn't reply. She'd figured it out, but he could

see her working through the timetable, sorting out how long it would take for anyone to come searching for them, particularly in this weather.

She looked up at the tower. Kat had reached the platform and paused to rest where the remaining wall fragment provided some protection from the gusting wind.

"How sturdy is it, do you think?" Naomi asked without looking at him.

"Sturdy enough," Wolchko said.

But he watched the tower sway slightly in the wind and the way rusty rainwater ran down from its joints, and he tried to mentally calculate the combined weight of the six people who had survived the sinking of the *Thaumas*.

"Sturdy enough," he said again, but this time he was trying to convince himself.

CHAPTER 26

Walter had the helm. Jamie had one hand pressed against the ceiling of the wheelhouse as they rode the slow rising of a rippling crest. It wasn't a *Perfect Storm* sort of wave, none of that Hollywood stuff, but it certainly qualified as rough seas. The kind of seas that would have kept wiser men—guys who didn't make their decisions in bars over pints of beer—from venturing out.

"We are goddamn idiots," Walter said. But he laughed when he said it.

Jamie wanted another coffee, but the last time he'd tried to pour something from the thermos he'd spilled half of it onto his pants.

"Don't shit your pants," he said. "You been out in worse than this."

Walter scoffed. "That I have. And I've seen every episode of *Deadliest Catch*. But those guys go out and freeze their balls off and risk their lives because it's their livelihood. This is our day off, James. Our day off. And here we are, when at least half of the guys we know who were supposed to be out here working today probably decided to stay home."

"But only half. Which means half of 'em are out here with us."

Walter shot him a dark look. "Those guys are getting paid to be out here."

Jamie grinned. "Those guys are gonna be buying us drinks for years if we make a stand against Woods Hole on this. Massholes comin' up to Maine for the summer are bad enough, but now they wanna send their Masshole marine life up here, too?"

"Did you just say that?"

"I said it. Okay, I know the seals and sharks are both migratory, Walter. I know that. But they're screwing with the natural order of things and . . . look, we've been through this. You want to turn the boat around, go on and do it. But we're already out here, so we might as well see if we can mess up their day."

Walter glanced sidelong at him. "We haven't really talked about how we're gonna do that. How far we're willing to go."

"Yeah. I've been thinkin' about that. I don't really have an answer," Jamie confessed. "If there's some way to disrupt the seals, confuse them, I'm for it. But obviously we're not doing anything we can go to jail for."

"We may be idiots, but we're not stupid," Walter said with half a smile.

"Even if all we do is block their way, yell at them for a few minutes, shoot off a flare, we'll still be heroes as far as I'm concerned. At least we gave enough of a damn to stand up for the rights of Maine fishermen."

"More than most of these assholes can say."

"I don't see any other boats going our way," Jamie agreed.

They fell into a familiar companionable silence. They talked plenty, but there were also long stretches of quiet between them, particularly when they were on the water. Being out there, especially in the wind and rain, the tang of salt in the air, the spray of the ocean coating everything, made them feel more at home than either of them ever felt on land. If the Atlantic had been calmer and they'd had the time to cast a couple of lines out, maybe they would have had a couple of beers, damn the hour of the morning. Deeper into summer, maybe they'd have had a couple of pitchers of mai tais or something. But they had a job to do today, which made it a coffee day. Still, they didn't need to talk. Their friendship didn't require them to fill the silence.

That was Jamie's train of thought, anyway. Right before Walter broke the silence.

"So what's the story with Alice?"

Jamie glanced at him. "What do you mean?"

"Just what I said. You've been mooning over her since your momma ejected you from her womb, but now all of a sudden you grew the balls to ask her out?"

"I told you what happened, Walt. She kinda let me know she wouldn't hate the idea of us going out for dinner some-time—"

"And you didn't faint?"

"And I didn't faint," Jamie confirmed. "You were there. Just in case you forgot, given it happened as long ago as last night."

Seconds passed. The rain hit the windshield and the boat rode the swells, Walter guiding it masterfully. The engine moaned in conflict with the wind.

Walter shot him that same studious, dubious glance. "So you're gonna take her out?"

"I said as much." Jamie wished desperately that he hadn't decided it was a coffee morning. "Y'know, I don't stick my nose so deep into your business."

"Mostly because if we talk too long about my love life you've gotta contend with mental images of me sucking a dick or doing something even more exciting."

"So you like picturing me and Alice doing exciting things?"

"Jesus. Forget I asked."

Silence again. Jamie decided to make another attempt at getting some more coffee, and this time he managed it without spilling any on himself. As he screwed the cap back on the thermos, kneeling in the wheelhouse, making sure his travel mug didn't topple over, he saw Walter scrutinizing him further.

"Okay, enough," he said, rising to his feet just as the boat nosed through a swell. He stumbled a bit, caught himself, and nearly dropped his coffee. "Either you've finally realized just how deeply you love me or you've got something you want to say."

"Could be both," Walter said, turning his attention back to the wheel and the churning sea. "But I'm familiar with the stench of you taking your boots off, which is a powerful argument against any romantic interest. Even if big hairy fishermen were my type. I like my men smarter and prettier than you."

"So you do have something you want to say."

"Guess I do."

Jamie didn't reply, just sighed and rolled his eyes, sipped his coffee, and waited.

"Be careful, that's all," Walter said at last.

"Careful of what? If you're telling me to wear protection—"

"I'm being serious here, James."

"Okay."

"No joke. Alice is broken. I don't mean she isn't strong—most of the time broken people are the strongest. But her husband dying smashed her into little pieces. She's brushed off every guy who's shown an interest since, and you know there have been plenty."

Jamie stiffened. Tightened his hand on the coffee mug. "And now that she's maybe ready for something new, you're worried I'm gonna hurt her, break her some more?"

Walter smiled, but there wasn't any humor in it. "Naw, man. I mean, yes, of course, because Alice is a sweet woman and I'm fond of her. But you're so in love with her that your heart's been breaking a little bit every day since you met her, and now you've got a chance at making something with her. And I pray to every god that's ever spurned my prayers that it works out. I'd love to see that. It'd be a beautiful thing. But a woman who's hurt as long as she's hurt, who's finally starting to rebuild . . . she's out of practice and liable to break a few things herself. She may decide she's not ready after all, may decide she'll never be ready, or maybe you'll be her test drive, just see if she can handle it, and then someone else'll come along. You're my best friend, man. I don't want to see *you* broken."

Jamie felt the air go out of him. He glanced at the floor, sipped his coffee.

"Thanks, Walter."

"Sweet of me, I know, to give a damn."

"Yep."

Silence again, save for the engine and the wind and the rain and the sea.

"We could go back to talking about me sucking dick."

"Not sure which conversation makes me more uncomfortable, but I do appreciate it."

Walter laughed softly. A couple of minutes passed without another word. They scanned the horizon ahead, watched the coasts of distant islands, expecting the Woods Hole boat to appear around one of them any moment.

"Y'know," Walter said, "there's probably some beer in the cooler under the bench over there."

"Thank God."

CHAPTER 27

Kat rested. She lay on her back on top of the watchtower, hating her closeness to the rusted surface but too exhausted to move. The rust made her feel dirty, even though it hadn't touched any part of her skin except her hands. There were often spiderwebs hanging from the ceiling in her basement, and she had accidentally walked through them a dozen times. Invariably, she'd bat at the air around her head, bend, and shake out her hair, push her fingers through it, just to make sure she didn't have a spider on her. Even when she had done all of that, her skin would crawl and she'd haunt herself with the conviction that somehow a spider had gotten inside her clothes, that it was on her, right now, and that it would bite her after she'd gone to bed or crawl into her mouth while she was sleeping. The closeness of the rust gave her the same creeping feeling. She felt dirty, like she needed to strip off her clothes and shower.

On her back, face turned to the rain, she uttered a soft and humorless laugh. A shower.

"Good one, Kat," she whispered to herself. Rain fell into her mouth as she spoke. The tiny drops of contact in that inviolable space made her think of spider's legs, and she shuddered.

Enough of that, she thought. Exhausted, she rolled over onto her knees and studied the platform. One partial wall remained. No roof—no real shelter, except a bit of a windbreak. The edges of that remaining wall had sharp corners, plenty of things to cut herself on. But Kat knew they were lucky to have this.

She glanced over the side of the platform. From here, the broad swath of marine life made her breath catch in her throat. It was one thing to have seen all of these seals from the deck of the *Thaumas*, but from above, the extent of the herd seemed even more breathtaking. Based on the number of heads she saw, there were well over a thousand of them filling the channel between Bald Cap and Deeley Island and smaller numbers spreading around the rock the team had been stranded on.

Kat tried not to see the fins. Instead, she stared at the spot where their boat had gone down, where Bergting had died, and wondered how deep it was. If not for the watchtower, that question would have been much more important, but still she tried to do some quick guesswork. Deep enough that the boat had vanished beneath the swells, but not very deep, she was sure. The middle of the channel would run deeper, but here at the edge of Bald Cap the boat couldn't have sunk too far before it settled. Unless the current had dragged it, moved it.

It doesn't matter, she told herself. *They're going to come looking. And you've got the tower.*

She stood, the weight of her clothes nearly dragging her back to her knees. It had been foolish to climb wearing them. The weather gear had done a fine job keeping her dry when all they had to worry about was rain, but in the water, drowning, swimming for her life, it had nearly been her shroud. Soaked through, she'd come ashore so stunned that it hadn't occurred to her to divest herself of the heavy things before she'd climbed up here. But now she could breathe. Now she had a moment to think.

The coat came off first, so heavy that it felt like she'd grown an inch the moment she slid out of it. Her Woods Hole sweatshirt was already soaked, so the rain didn't bother her at all. She started to unsnap her pants, but as she scuffed her foot across the platform and bits of rust flaked and smeared wetly under her heel she decided the protection provided by the durable fabric was worth the weight. She wore black yoga pants under the all-weather gear, and she didn't want to climb down and back up in those.

Huffing out a weary breath, she moved to the edge and knelt again, lay on her belly, and slid her legs off the platform. The smell of rust filled her nostrils. She grabbed the sharp edge of the broken wall, carefully. So carefully. This was the hard part. Her sweatshirt was soaked with rusty rainwater and she realized she'd been hasty in taking off her coat.

Too late now.

Kat jammed one knee in a space between the platform and its support beams, searching for purchase with her hanging foot. Her body began to slide. The toe of her boot scraped off something and panic thundered in her chest for a moment that felt like eternity. Then her boot slipped into the latticed trestlework beneath the platform and she exhaled. For a few seconds she stayed just where she was, happy not to be falling, but then she got moving again. The tide was coming in and they didn't have time for her to freeze.

Careful with her handholds, not wanting to cut herself on the rusted metal, she clambered down the tower. The structure seemed narrow, with very few places to rest comfortably before reaching the top, but they would have to figure it out. The wind gusted and she felt the tower swaying. It creaked and groaned with her weight and with the force of the wind. The remaining wall above her shook and rattled in the storm, but Kat told herself that this was not a new development. The thing looked ancient and fragile—even brittle—but it had stood out here for decades. It would be safe. It had to be safe.

Kat forced herself to breathe evenly as she descended. The tower reminded her of the kind of thing she'd seen in state forests, where rangers would be stationed. Maybe forty feet high, it had horizontal beams at ten-foot intervals, holding the whole thing together. Each section—each layer of the trestlework cake—was a honeycomb of rusted latticework that made for uncomfortable footholds, but at least the crossbeams were there.

The wind battered her, tried to push her off the tower, but she resisted even as the rain plastered her ponytail against her neck. One step at a time. One handhold at a time. Then her right foot came down on a slippery diagonal and her boot skidded to one side. She tightened her grip at the same moment the bar shifted, cracked, and gave way under her weight.

She slammed against the tower, left foot finding a toehold just a moment later. Her fingers were so tight on the lattice above that she felt rust crunching into her skin.

Someone down below called up to her, the first indication
she had that they were watching her. She counted to five
before she sagged backward and looked down. The diagonal hadn't snapped—the bolts on one end had rusted
through and it had given way.

Fifteen feet from the ground, she clambered sideways
until she reached a perch that seemed more reliable and
then continued her descent. It seemed only a minute later
that she reached the bottom, but before she could find comfort in the solid rock underfoot a wave crashed against
Bald Cap. A thin inch of water foamed all the way to the
base of the tower, washing against her boots.

Kat looked up at Wolchko and Naomi and Captain
N'Dour. She saw the grim certainty in their eyes, reflect-
ing her own, and she turned away from them. They would
be okay, she felt sure. She would make certain of it. Even
Naomi, with her prosthetic, should be able to climb without assistance. It was Tye she worried about.

Rosalie and Tye had been sitting together a couple of
yards away. When the wave crashed over Bald Cap, the
layer of surf rippling around them, Rosalie shot to her feet
and turned in a circle, maybe thinking the sharks could
come ashore in two inches of water. She knew better, of
course, but Kat understood the kind of irrationality that
fear could produce.

"How's it look up there?" Tye asked, glancing up at the
platform.

"Room for three on the platform. Maybe four, if they're
all standing."

Tye gave a tight nod, getting the message. Room for three,
not four, because he wasn't going to be able to cling to
the side of the watchtower with a shark bite in his leg.
Rosalie had wrapped it well enough to slow the bleeding,

maybe even stop it, but if he made the climb to the platform there was no way he could dangle off the side of the
tower. The angle and the pressure would keep him bleeding or start him bleeding again eventually. That's if he even
had the strength to hold on.

"It's all right," Rosalie told him, crouching to squeeze
his shoulder. "Three on the platform and three wedged into
the trestle under it. The rest of us will takes turns on top.
It'll be fine. All we have to do is wait until someone comes
to get us."

Kat narrowed her eyes. "Can you give me and Tye a
minute?"

Rosalie hesitated visibly. She worked for Kat, worked
for the project, but she didn't like being dismissed. Kat
knew that and didn't care. The protocol of the lab had gone
down with the ship. Rosalie nodded once, then walked
away without another word. Between the seals and the
tower, she couldn't go very far, but she crossed to the other
side of the watchtower and found a bare few yards that the
seals seemed to be avoiding. Rosalie stood and looked out
at the dark, turbulent sea.

"You didn't have to do that," Tye said.

Kat knelt by him. Another wave crashed up, surf sliding across Bald Cap.

"They will send someone to check on us," she said. "It'll
be hours yet. And when that someone comes, the sharks
might attack their boat."

Tye cocked his head. "Come on. They could have gone
on smashing at our hull for days and nothing would've
happened. If that one hadn't smashed in the propeller shaft,
we'd still be afloat."

"I know you're right. I just . . . the malice—"

"Sharks don't feel malice," Tye said. "That's a human trait."

"How can we really know that?"

"It's what we do. We're supposed to know."

Kat shrugged. "We think we know. But we're also the geniuses who worked out a way to use acoustics like catnip on seal herds and never bothered to consider that it might alter other marine life. We turned every shark in range of that signal into a hyperaggressive monster. We did this, Tye. The two of us and Eddie. Now Bergting's dead because we didn't think it through."

"It was an experiment," Tye said, shuddering. "We were rushing, yeah, but even if we hadn't been under pressure we might still have made the same mistake, never considered it. That's cold comfort, I know, but let's worry about recriminations after we get home."

Kat smiled sadly. "Thank you."

"For what?"

"For not telling me it isn't my fault."

Tye reached out—wincing as he moved his bandaged leg—and took her hand. "You think everything is your fault. I'm not going to waste my breath arguing. I have to save my strength for climbing the goddamned watchtower."

Kat's smile went cold. She couldn't help it as she drew her hand away.

"Sorry," Tye said quickly. "I didn't mean to . . ."

The wind howled around them and the rain pattered the rocks and the waves crashed, but it was awkwardness they were drowning in.

"I need to ask you something," she said.

Tye's face went slack, his eyes cold, as if he'd drawn a

curtain to hide whatever might be in his heart. "You want to know what Naomi was talking about, the stuff about Rosalie having a secret."

"About *you* having a secret," she corrected. "And Rosalie knowing where the bodies are buried. I believe in secrets, but not if they're going to hurt me. Is this going to hurt me, Tye?"

He reached both hands up to wipe the rain from his face and let out a huff of air before focusing his gaze on hers again.

"We had something good going, Kat," Tye said, his eyes narrowing. "At least I thought we did. But you treated me outside the lab the same way you treated me inside it . . . like I was just another useful tool you could keep in a box and only take out when you needed it."

"That's not fair—"

Tye replied with a humorless smile. "The truth isn't fair?" He shrugged. "Look, it's fine. I'm over it. I had feelings for you, but I'm past it—"

"You and Rosalie?"

"In a way, yeah. But you said you didn't need to know secrets. You asked if mine will hurt you. The answer is 'not physically.'"

Not physically? Did he think she was jealous of him and Rosalie?

"What does that mean?"

Tye put a hand on her shoulder and gave it a squeeze. "Look, we're in this together. Let's get the hell out of here and when we're back at Woods Hole I'll put all my cards on the table. For now, it's just gonna have to be enough for you to know I was in love with you, even if you never wanted me to be."

Kat hesitated, wanting to know more. But he'd made it

clear the conversation was over, and they had more important things to focus on right now than hurt feelings and
recriminations.

She offered him her hand. "Come on, let's get you up.
We've got a while before we need to worry about getting
off the ground, but you're not going to get any stronger
than you are right now. Best to start climbing, get you up
to the platform."

Tye groaned as she helped him to stand. He put an arm
around her shoulders and together they shuffled toward the
watchtower. When Wolchko and Captain N'Dour realized
what was going on, they hurried to be of assistance. Past
the tower, Rosalie had turned to watch them all. They all
stared up at the platform. Nobody mentioned how difficult
it was going to be for Tye to get up there without being able
to put much weight on his wounded leg. They all knew.

"What are you going to do?" Kat asked.

"For starters, I'm gonna try not to bleed to death," he
said.

And then he started climbing.

CHAPTER 28

————

Lorena had to remind herself how she had ended up on Deeley Island in the middle of a nor'easter. Not just how, but why. Her husband, Luciano, had been unfaithful from the day of their first date until the day, nearly seven years ago, they finalized their divorce. On their wedding day, he'd sent his own sister around to visit several of his more serious girlfriends to tell them he was getting married. Most of them continued to sleep with him, as did many others over the years of their marriage. Luciano had been handsome and charismatic and a liar of Olympic skill levels.

Seventeen months after their divorce, he'd been struck by an MBTA bus and killed, just after leaving church. Even his friends had said it was karma. She'd grown up in a strict Italian Catholic household, where *divorce* had been a dirty word, so her mother had been relieved when Luciano died. It meant she could pretend her daughter was a widow instead of a divorcée. Lorena herself had felt no vindication, no justice. Instead, she'd felt more cheated than ever. Once upon a time they'd had the potential for such happiness, and he'd squandered it. Thrown it away.

In spite of her mother, Lorena had built herself a happy single life, full of music and coffee and friends. Not long before the accident that took her ex-husband's life, she had been named to a position on the Board of Directors for the Portland Symphony Orchestra. Her therapy patients fulfilled the needs of her mind, but the symphony made her spirit soar. The only thing that gave her more peace was the sight and sound of the ocean, especially at night or in winter, when the coast would be abandoned by everyone but the lonely and the hopelessly romantic.

Her friends had gently nudged her to try dating, but she had refused to be set up—didn't want to risk a disaster that might interfere with those friendships. It had been her friend Sarah's nineteen-year-old daughter, Angie, who'd persuaded her, with the aid of an excellent bottle of Merlot, to try online dating. *You don't have to even reply to them if they don't appeal to you*, Angie had said. Sarah had cheered Lorena on. Reluctantly and a bit drunkenly, Lorena had gone along with the plan. In the morning she had nursed a headache and promptly forgotten all about it, until two weeks later when she'd had dinner with Sarah and Angie again and the girl had logged back into Lorena's profile to find dozens of messages. After the first obscenity, Angie had taken over, deleting the filthy propositions before Lorena could see them and only showing her the ones that seemed decent and sincere. The whole thing had made her skin crawl. She hadn't been able to trust the man she'd married, so how could she trust a man she met on the Internet? It felt wrong to her, inappropriate, and she certainly had no intention of telling her mother. At seventy-nine, the old woman hadn't softened her judgmental nature one iota.

Then Angie had smiled. *Aww, this guy seems sweet. Cute smile for a dad-type.*

Playing along so as not to disappoint the girl, Lorena had read through the gentlemanly message she'd received from the dad-type, who seemed athletic and adventurous and, yes, was handsome. But it was when she'd clicked on his profile that something had woken up in the back of her mind. The photo featured him standing at the edge of a dock, with gray skies and a rough ocean behind. Beneath the photo had been a quote from a song by Van Morrison— one of her favorites.

"Let your soul and spirit fly / Into the mystic."

The moment had felt electric. She'd always believed in kismet, in serendipity, though she had rarely felt it in her own life.

Lorena and Jim had their first date the following Wednesday night. Without her ever mentioning that electric moment, they had finished the date by walking along the beach after dark. She hadn't waited for him to kiss her, though she'd promised herself there would be no kiss. No kiss and no anything else. But he had been so kind and so smart, so open, and so obviously devoted to his sons that she had dared to imagine there might be something there.

Seventeen months later, he'd asked her to marry him. They had their differences, but she believed that was important in a marriage. Her only hesitation had been that she wanted to make sure Dorian and Kyle felt included, that they supported their father's choice. She wanted them to feel like she was family. Meeting Jim, beginning a life with him, had felt like climbing the steps to a dream she had never imagined might be possible for her again.

Now they were inside a nightmare.

She stood at the tree line at the edge of Deeley Island, staring out at Bald Cap. This was the spot where Jim and Dorian had been standing when Kyle had come to get her. Lorena had been hiding out in the tent, fighting the depression and anxiety that had threatened to overwhelm her. Better for her to stay in the tent and have Jim and the boys think she was unwell than to let them see her at her worst, angry and emotional. She knew that was the wrong approach—hell, she was the therapist, wasn't she? But just because she knew better, that didn't mean she had to be rational all the time. Nobody was.

Yes, Jim had been foolish not to cancel their trip when the weather threatened to turn against them. He had gambled on the forecast being accurate, but this was New England—the forecast was never much better than an educated guess. And, after all, he'd made the wrong choice for the right reason; he wanted them to have this adventure together, to bring them closer.

But he never imagined this, she thought now. *How could he*?

Lorena blew out a breath. Sometimes the rain made her feel as if she were suffocating. Her raincoat had a duck bill on the hood. It seemed silly now and it didn't provide much real protection, but under the trees and with her duck bill she could hold her phone up and use the camera zoom to get a closer look at what transpired over on Bald Cap. She'd watched one figure clamber down from the watchtower there, and now she saw another begin to climb.

She tried not to look at the sharks. Tried not to think about the kayaks. The storm would pass eventually, and so would this bizarre gathering of sea creatures.

Quietly, her own whispered voice drowned out by the

rain and wind, Lorena prayed to God for the safety of the people stranded on Bald Cap. Her mother had always told her that God heard your prayers even if they were only in your heart, so she wasn't worried about the noise drowning her out. What worried her was that in her whole life she had never had a prayer answered. Not demonstrably. It comforted her to pray, to talk to God, and she always told her patients that this sort of comfort had real value to their state of mind, even when they wondered if God was actually there to hear them.

Today, she really hoped he was listening.

"Lorena," a voice said, and she nearly jumped out of her skin as she spun to see that Jim had come up behind her.

"Don't do that! You'll scare the life out of me!" She smiled, but her heart, as her mother would have said, was going to beat the band.

Jim apologized, but he didn't smile in return. Tree branches moved and the boys appeared. Dorian might be twenty-one, but Lorena couldn't stop thinking of the two of them as boys because they were Jim's boys and might one day be hers, if they could make this work.

"Look," Jim said, fidgeting on his feet, not wanting to meet her eyes. "Things are going to get worse over there before too long, and—"

"I know," she interrupted, unpleasant thoughts tumbling through her head. "The storm surge is going to overtop them by at least a couple of feet. They'll be safe on the tower, though. They can ride it out."

"Probably. But we can't be sure of that. And there isn't room up top for all of them, not to mention the one guy is obviously injured."

"The guy climbing the tower right now?" It felt to her like she knew where this was going, and she wanted to cut it off before Jim got there. "We're all going to ride this out, honey. Just like you told me about the storm. We'll take our gear uphill and wait the storm out, and so will they."

Jim exhaled, then turned toward his sons. Dorian glanced away, not helping, but Kyle's eyes were excited. To him, this was all part of the adventure.

"Dad thinks the surge might be way more than two feet above the rock over there," Kyle said. "And the tower's old, maybe not very sturdy. Those folks are in trouble and we wanna help them."

Lorena slipped her phone into her coat pocket and forced herself to breathe, angry with Jim for putting her in this position. What was she supposed to say to them now? She wasn't his wife or the boys' mother. If she used her role here to undermine their courage, they would resent her for it.

"How will you do that?" she asked, glancing at Dorian, hoping to appeal to his logical mind and sense of self-preservation. "There's nothing we can do for those people except keep trying to call for help."

Jim frowned. "We have the kayaks."

Lorena wondered how much of her horror showed on her face. "You want to put a kayak in the water now, in this storm, with all of those sharks out there?"

Kyle brightened. "Sharks aren't a natural enemy for people. They wouldn't attack the kayaks or even us if we were in the water—"

"Unless they confused us for seals," Dorian said. "And there are a hell of a lot of seals out there."

Jim glanced at him. "Dor, I told you, we don't have to do this. I'm not going unless you're sure."

Dorian shrugged. "I'm fine. As long as we stay out of the water, we'll be all right. Though I'd like to give the sharks as wide a berth as we can, so we oughta strike out to the south first, come up on Bald Cap from the other side, away from the main bulk of the seal herd."

"I'm coming," Kyle said darkly.

"Absolutely not. We're not leaving Lorena here by herself," Jim said, "and anyway, we need the room. As it is, we're only going to bring back one person at a time per kayak, and there are six people over there."

He caught himself then, seemed to realize that the three Talbot men had been talking as if she'd suddenly vanished. Jim turned toward her, apology written on his face. Lorena stepped toward him and put her right hand on his cheek, the scruff of his beard rough on her palm.

"Have you thought this through?"

Jim nodded. "Promise."

"Tell me why this is necessary."

"For me," he said instantly. "I think there's a damn good chance some of those folks are going to die if we don't get them off Bald Cap. You didn't see the sharks kill the one guy—"

"You're not helping your case, Dad," Dorian put in.

Jim shot him a dark look, then faced Lorena again. "The seals are everywhere. The guy was in the water. We'll do just what Dorian said, give them as much space as we can. I swear to you, we'll be careful. But honey, listen, if I do nothing . . . if we could have helped them, and anyone else dies over there, I'll never forgive myself."

Lorena studied his eyes, but she knew this man so well that she'd heard the truth in his voice. Known it before he'd expressed it. The waves were one thing, the churning ocean bad enough, but she knew he had the skill to manage it. Dorian she felt less certain of, but if Jim had that much confidence how could she doubt it? He wouldn't risk his own son. Not knowingly.

"You know how dangerous this is," she said almost as quietly as she'd said her prayer. "But I understand what you feel, and I wouldn't want you haunted like that. I don't have the experience you have, so maybe this is even crazier than I think it is. Just in case, you need to make me a promise. If you get out there and you go over, even once, you both paddle back here as fast as you can. If the sharks seem too interested, if one of them so much as comes near you, then you come back here immediately. If you can't make those promises, and you go anyway, then the Talbot men and I are going to have a conflict."

Lorena glanced at the boys. She didn't want to tell their father what to do, to diminish him in their eyes and make her seem like their enemy somehow, but she couldn't let them go without speaking up.

"I promise," Jim said, no trace of a smile. He meant it. "I swear to God."

"Me, too," Dorian added, though she hadn't asked him to. He stood up straight, respectful, not treating her like an enemy or an outsider.

"Go," she said. "Kyle and I will move our gear up the hill. Don't forget what you promised, and don't do anything stupid."

She felt sick to her stomach as Jim kissed her. When he stepped back, Dorian gave her a quick, awkward hug, the first one ever. As he and Jim hurried back through the trees, headed for the spot where they'd dragged the kayaks ashore, Kyle slid his arm through hers as if he were her escort.

"They've got this, Lorena. They know what they're

doing." He still sounded excited, even proud, as if the danger weren't real.

She knew it was. Very real indeed. She snaked her hand into her coat pocket and pulled out her phone, tapping her screen to redial 911. If she had to call a thousand times, she would. Jim and Dorian were courageous and confident in their skill, but in this storm, with all of those sharks, she would rather have relied on the watchtower sustaining the weight of those six people than on Jim's and Dorian's skill with kayaks.

"Let's go," Kyle said, trying to guide her through the trees, to watch them push off.

Lorena resisted him. "We can watch from here. They'll pass right by."

The call didn't go through, so she dialed again. On the third try she had crackling static and a single ring. Separating from Kyle, she walked down onto the shore, ocean spray blasting up from the rocks as the tide swallowed more and more of Deeley Island. A few seals were nearby, but they ignored her.

"Anything?" Kyle called to her.

She shook her head and called again.

By the time she stood watching Jim and Dorian paddle by, navigating the swells so perfectly it was as if the kayaks were a part of them, she had tried 911 fourteen times.

On the nineteenth try, it rang through. Lorena froze, thinking the call would be cut off, but then it rang again. And clicked over.

"Nine-one-one, what is your emergency?"

"Oh, thank God!" she said, spinning around to stare at Kyle, who watched her in disbelief. "Call them back. Get your father back!"

"Ma'am?" the operator said. "I'm sorry, can you repeat that? What is your emergency?"

"No, no, I was talking to my . . . Sorry I—"

"Ma'am, calm down. Where are you?"

Lorena took a breath. There was plenty of static on the line, but the voice came through crisply. Kyle raced past her, out onto the rocks. A seal barked at him, bellowed at him, but he ignored the beast and began shouting for his father and brother. Out on the water, Jim and Dorian were flashing their paddles up and in, slicing the water, gliding up a swell and down again.

"Ma'am?"

"Deeley Island. We're on Deeley Island on a kayaking trip and there are thousands of seals and all these sharks, oh my God, dozens of sharks, and there are these people on Bald Cap and they're trapped there and the storm surge is going to—"

"You're *hsssss* kayaking trip right now? You kayaked *hsssss* Deeley *hsssss* this storm?"

The static cut in and out, but Lorena could make out enough. "Not today—"

"Tell me about the sharks again?" The woman's voice was dry and flat. Bored. Maybe even a little angry.

Calm down, Lorena told herself. *Breathe.*

"Listen to me!" she snapped. "Don't do that. Don't brush me off."

"You said *hsssss* people *hsssss* Bald Cap?"

"Yes! They're climbing the tower because the tide's coming in and the sharks are—"

"How did *hsssss hsssss* they kayak, too?"

"They had a boat, but it sank! The sharks—"

"Ma'am, did you *hsssss* fined up to five thou—*hsssss*

misuse of the emergency call system. We've got real emergencies to—"

"Goddammit, this is a real fucking emergency. Listen, I get it. I know how crazy this must sound, but do I seem like a crank to you? I'm not some kid screwing around. A man is dead and others are in danger! My fiancé and his son are in danger right now. They just took kayaks over from Deeley to try to get the people off Bald Cap and—"

"They're kayaking *hsssss* now? Off Bald Cap?"

"Yes!"

"Nice weather for it," the woman said. The one thing she'd said that had come through with perfect clarity, not a hint of static.

And the line went dead.

Lorena let out a scream of frustration and turned back toward Kyle. He shouted one last time for his father and Dorian, but already he had a slump to his shoulders. Over the storm, there was no chance they might hear him. Lorena slipped her phone back into her pocket and joined him there on the rocks. A wave crashed and soaked the two of them, but they didn't back up. Not yet. Instead, they watched the two kayaks cutting across the swirling water to the south of the island, already out of the channel. There were seals around them, but she didn't see any sharks in their vicinity. Not yet.

"Are they coming?" Kyle asked. "You were yelling at them."

"I think I got through to her," Lorena lied. "Yeah, for sure. Help is coming."

CHAPTER 29

Naomi knew they were safe, but she certainly didn't *feel* safe. The past twenty-eight or so hours had caught up to her and her bones felt weary. Her thoughts seemed slightly askew, diffused like light passing through a dirty window. The rain had soaked her so thoroughly that she had no desire to move, her clothes so stiff that it was almost as if she could not have moved even if she'd wanted to. Nearly drowning hadn't helped, either. If not for the crisp, cutting chill of the wind she'd have been tempted to strip down.

She stood with her arms folded, watching the water, willfully ignoring the way some of the outlying rocks had vanished beneath the rising tide. They were safe, after all, so what difference did the tide make?

Safe.

It occurred to her just how long it had been since she had really felt safe. An image swam into her mind of herself tucked into the crook of Kayla's arm, head resting on her breast. Her skin had been so soft and always so much warmer than Naomi's. They had showered together in the dormitory, daring and not caring if anyone overheard. They'd left a trail of sudsy water as they'd hurried back to Kayla's room, barely wrapped in their towels, and fallen into bed together. Later, so warm and soft, wrapped in flannel sheets, Naomi had lain her head on Kayla's breast and listened to her heart beating.

Naomi had felt whole, then—all parts of her intact—and she'd been in love. The smell of sex and shampoo and the candles Kayla had lit had lingered in Naomi's memory for weeks, maybe months. It rose up inside her now, as vivid a sensory memory as she'd ever had, and she caught her breath, eyes fluttering closed. The rain pelted her and the wind raked her, but for a moment she was back there in that third-floor room in Lewis Hall.

Memory is agony, she thought. The epiphany knocked her back a step. Memory could be the greatest treasure of her life, she knew. But now she understood that it was also this other thing. Standing on the slick rock face of Bald Cap, cold and full of dread, watching the angry black sky and the malignant killers circling the island, she thought memory had the capacity to be not only agony but hell itself. If she had no memory of that moment, of being warm and contented and in love, this place would not have had so much power over her.

Kayla had called her the day before yesterday, wanting to fix her mistakes. Naomi had hung up on her. Now she thought that when she finally got back to the mainland and got her hands on a phone, she might give Kayla the chance she was looking for. The woman wanted to fix her mistakes. The least Naomi could do was let her try.

"You all right?"

Naomi felt herself turn slowly, a delayed reaction, as if

she were moving underwater or in a dream. Wolchko had come up behind her and she wondered how long he had been standing there, watching her stare at the sea and the storm.

"I'm not Bergting," she said, "so I guess that makes me all right."

Only the sight of Wolchko wincing made her recognize the hardness of her words.

"Shit, I'm sorry," she went on. "I didn't mean that to sound disrespectful or . . . cold. It's just that I figure as long as we're not in the water, we're okay. He seemed like a nice guy—"

"He was," Wolchko agreed, brows knitted.

"That was really awful of me. I'm sorry."

"You said that."

"I know, but it was pretty bad."

Wolchko smiled. "If it made me flinch, it had to be. Normally I don't notice . . ."

"Insensitivity?"

Wolchko stood next to her and looked out at the undulations of the dark, surging sea. "Why don't we start this part again? Are you all right?"

Grateful, Naomi linked her arm with his and leaned her head onto his shoulder. "Yeah. Weirdly, I am." She never felt so comfortable with people this fast, but Wolchko wasn't like most people. His Asperger's—or whatever it was—stripped him of all pretense.

He gave her a sidelong glance. "I'm glad to hear it. On the boat you seemed like you were kind of falling apart."

"Kind of?"

Wolchko shrugged.

"Panic attack," Naomi said. "I had to do breathing exercises yesterday morning just to psych myself up to get on the boat, knowing there would be sharks in the water. When sharks started smashing themselves against our hull . . . yeah, I fell apart. But the boat fucking sank, Eddie, and I'm still here. I'm standing on solid rock and I'm alive."

Wolchko glanced away, head darting around, almost bird-like. He stared at his boots for a few seconds.

"What?" she asked.

He pressed his lips together. Scratched at the back of his head.

"Eddie, what?"

Wolchko did that bird thing again, then gave a sharp sigh. "I'm trying to figure out how to say this without freaking you out."

"We're not going to have solid rock to stand on for very long," Naomi said. "I know."

"But you're so calm."

"The tower's on top of the rock. Help will come. The storm will pass. We're okay. Cold and wet and wishing we were anywhere but here. I lost my camera and all the photos and you guys lost a ton of equipment and data, but Bergting lost his life and we're okay. As long as the sharks are in the water and we're up on the tower, I'll be fine."

Wolchko exhaled with obvious relief. He nudged her. "So do you want to get climbing?"

Naomi turned to look up. Tye and Kat and Rosalie were already on the wreckage of the platform up top, but Captain N'Dour hadn't started climbing yet and Wolchko didn't seem to be in a rush. She imagined wedging herself into the tower's crossbeams.

"I think I'll hang out down here until time runs out," she said. "You'll let me know when that is?"

Wolchko's expression turned solemn. "Of course."

Naomi thanked him and turned to look back out at the storm. At the sea. At the dark bodies of the seals and the fins among them, at the way the largest of the sharks displaced water above as they moved just under the surface.

She remembered that night in the dorm after showering with Kayla, the warmth of her skin and the sound of her beating heart. It had been the first time anyone other than her mother had told Naomi they loved her and meant it. Kayla *had* meant it, at least back then. She'd been loved, for a little while. It had been worth the pain that came later.

Breathing deeply, she tried to conjure up that sense memory, the sex and the soap and the burning candle, but she had lost it. She wondered if she could ever get it back.

CHAPTER 30

Jamie had fallen silent, just watching the wipers fight the rain on the windshield. Behind the fishing boat, back toward the mainland, the sky had begun to lighten. The wind kept battering them and the black sea rolled, and Walter kept the throttle up, charging through the rough water. Jamie knew better than to think the lightening of the sky at home meant the storm would clear off quickly, but it was a reminder that the rain wouldn't last forever. The sun would come back eventually. Until then, they would just be miserable as hell.

He'd turned the music on in the wheelhouse, but with the engine and the storm he could barely hear anything except the bass line and drums.

"You look pretty grim," Walter said.

Jamie shook his empty coffee cup, as if that explained it. What was he supposed to do, tell the truth? *Sorry, Walter, just thinking maybe this was a really stupid idea and a total waste of our day off?* Yeah, that'd go over well.

"You know we can turn around, right?" Walter said. "No shame in it. Only one who knows why we came out here today is Alice, and she wasn't too thrilled with the idea to begin with. Plus she thinks you're cute, so if you're having second thoughts . . ."

More than once, Jamie had admitted that Walter usually knew him better than he knew himself.

"It's tempting," he admitted, raising his voice to be heard.

"But?"

The wipers swiped shrilly against the windshield, working dry in a momentary lull in the storm. Then the rain hit again, full blast.

"But all that talk about being pissed at these scientists and their Cape Cod benefactors wasn't just talk," Jamie said. "People from Massachusetts act like just 'cause they've got Harvard University down there in Cambridge it makes every one of 'em a goddamn genius, like they're somehow better, and folks in Maine aren't much better than inbred hillbillies. Maybe they cleared their little experiment with the governor, but nobody cleared it with the people it might affect, and that's just not right."

Walter twisted the wheel, pointed them right into a wave. The fishing boat crashed up and over—nothing they couldn't handle. They'd been through much worse.

"You gonna say anything?" Jamie asked. "Or did you just wanna hear me wax poetic?"

"Just trying to recover from hearing you use a big word like *benefactors*."

"Fuck off."

Walter smiled. "Excellent riposte, my good man. Happy to know you sounding smart and thoughtful was a glitch and we're back to *fuck off*."

"Fuck off."

He laughed at that, and Jamie grinned.

"Seriously," Walter said, "you wanna go back?"

Jamie braced his hands against the ceiling and stared out at the Atlantic. Today would have been an excellent day for a nap, maybe an old movie in his threadbare recliner. The dark shape of one of the many harbor islands loomed off to port. He felt torn.

The radio crackled. "*Little Martha*, this is Boothbay Harbor Harbor Master. Come in."

Walter burst out laughing for a second or two, then just shook his head and gave the radio a sidelong glance. "Go on."

Jamie smiled and reached for the mic. It crackled loudly.

"*Little Martha*—" the harbor master began again.

"All right, Bronski, you don't have to repeat yourself," Jamie said into the mic.

Static, then a muttered profanity. "I hate radioing you two assholes."

"We do get a special joy out of hearing you say 'Boothbay Harbor Harbor Master,'" Jamie admitted. "It's like no matter how many times you do it, you don't hear yourself repeating the word *harbor*."

"I'm not the harbor master of Boothbay—"

"I know. You're the harbor master of Boothbay Harbor," Jamie said.

Walter snickered. "Still sounds stupid."

"Still sounds stupid," Jamie echoed on the radio, making sure Brodski got the message.

Crackle. Static. "—told Delia you guys would be useless. I don't even know why I—"

Jamie went cold. "What does Delia want with us?" He exchanged a worried glance with Walter.

Water slapped the starboard side and the boat slewed to port. Walter swore loudly and adjusted their bearing. Just a moment of distraction, but Jamie understood completely. When the harbor master calls with a message from the area's emergency dispatcher, you start to worry your house is burning down or your mother's dropped dead in her kitchen.

More static and then— "She got a crazy call from a woman, said she was on a kayaking trip out to Deeley Island and a boat went down. Some folks were trapped on Bald Cap. There was something about sharks in there, too."

Walter frowned at the radio. "Nobody's kayaking in this storm."

Jamie repeated as much into the mic, then released the button and listened to a few seconds of static before the harbor master came back on.

"Said the same thing myself. I figure it's a crank, and that's what Delia figured, but she also said the lady sounded really upset. Like she meant every word."

"Crazies usually do," Jamie observed.

Static. Jamie hesitated. The kayaking thing did sound like a load of bullshit, some high school kid's idea of a big joke. It just didn't make sense. Not unless you remembered that Bald Cap had been the Woods Hole research team's destination and that it wouldn't be any surprise if they had sharks swimming around, considering the seal population they were trying to move.

If their damn experiment worked, Jamie thought.

"You guys know Delia." Brodski's voice filled the wheelhouse suddenly, strangely loud and clear, crisp and static-free. "She doesn't hit the panic button for nothing. Maybe it's a hoax, but she's worried."

Jamie glanced at Walter as he raised the mic to his lips. "We'll go check it out."

He didn't mention that Brodski had just sent them to the very spot where they'd been headed. The harbor master thanked him and signed off.

"Guess we're not going home yet," Walter said.

Jamie zipped his jacket a little higher, shivering a bit from the wind. "Who said anything about going home?"

CHAPTER 31

———

Naomi hooked an arm through the latticed bars of the watchtower's trestlework and rested her weight against the creaking metal, heart thumping in her chest. Down on the solid rock of Bald Cap she had heard the creaking and seen the tower swaying slightly, but now that she'd climbed nearly two-thirds of the damn thing the swaying seemed anything but slight. The wind wailed around her and she clung more tightly to the metal, fear fluttering inside her chest like some demon butterfly, determined to break out.

Her face felt flushed and warm—the only part of her not numb with cold. *Not true*, she thought. *You can feel the leg.* That was the weirdest part, the way she could still feel her missing leg. In books and movies people talked about phantom leg pain—the nurses had even talked to her about it in the hospital, after the attack—but what they didn't talk about was just *feeling* it. Sometimes even without phantom pains, the leg seemed as if it were still her own instead of a prosthetic, leading to odd sensations like this one, when the rest of her body had been chilled to the bone, but her face and her ghost leg felt warm. Alive.

It creeped her the hell out. She'd worked hard to come to terms with the loss of a limb, taken a hard road to reach a point where she could think of herself as a whole person, but those little extra reminders didn't help.

Naomi reached up and to the right, climbing another couple of feet, and planted her good foot into a V where two rusting beams met. There were only a few horizontal crossbeams on the tower. The rest of the climb involved jamming her feet into those V joints, squeezing her feet inside her boots. The prosthetic didn't hurt at all, but the other foot felt much worse for the beating it was taking. Her fingers were worse. The bars were slippery with rain and she'd lost her grip twice, hands sliding hard as they tried to regain a grip. Rust sloughed off the bars like peeling paint. Her palms and fingers were scraped and bruised and she had already accepted that she'd need a gorilla-sized tetanus shot when this was over.

Over. That had suddenly become her favorite word.

"You all right?" Wolchko yelled.

Naomi pulled her face away from the beam where she'd rested it. Wolchko had been climbing the opposite side of the tower, with N'Dour to her left, on what she gauged must be the north side of the tower. The captain had already reached the third crossbeam and he rested there now, just below the platform.

Wolchko had paused halfway up. Naomi moved her head, trying to get a view of him through the trestlework. When she got a glimpse of his face, she gave him a thumbs-up, pressing her body against the metal to make sure she didn't topple backward.

She reached up and to her left, raising her left knee at the same time. When she planted her foot, the bar gave way instantly. Her left hand missed its hold and she pitched forward, smashed her forehead against rusted metal, scrambled for a handhold, foot pumping in dead air. Her right hand slipped, most of her weight dragging her down. She must have shouted, because she heard the others calling to her.

The tower swayed. The wind raged so hard against it that for a moment she felt as if she were dipping backward, as if the tower wanted to pitch her into the ocean. Then the gust died and the tower straightened and she thrust her left arm through the lattice in front of her, hooked it to the right, and let the V joint catch her. Her shoulder wrenched a little, but she brought her left foot over on top of her right, and she could breathe again.

"Naomi!" Wolchko called.

Her head jerked back. For a few seconds she had forgotten that she wasn't alone up here. Her heart did a hummingbird buzz as she spotted Wolchko again. He was climbing, moving fast, trying to get around the corner onto the south side of the tower—to get to her.

"Stay where you are!" she said. "I'm okay. Watch your step. Some of these bars are rusted through!"

Naomi thought she sounded okay. Not nearly as terrified as she felt. Flushed and shaking, she glanced down at Bald Cap, thinking about the fall she'd almost taken. The view stole her breath again.

Waves rippled across Bald Cap, white lines of frothing water. Between them she could still make out some of the more jagged rocks, but the tide had already hidden the island under at least three or four inches of water and it was still rising.

With new strength, she climbed another half-dozen feet, shoulder and back muscles aching badly. On the third crossbeam, thirty feet above the water—maybe twenty-nine now—she dragged herself up and tucked into a tri-angular space. Wary of the beam giving way, she sat rigidly for several long seconds, waiting for the worst to come. When it didn't, she still held on to the bar that angled down in front of her, forming the top of the triangle.

The tower swayed. The creaking of its joints sounded like a hundred tiny voices.

Down below, the seals were abandoning Bald Cap. It offered no haven to them now. They slid through shallow water and vanished into the deep, resurfacing with their sleek backs gliding swiftly away. Some would head for Deeley Island, but the signal from the sunken boat would keep them coming back despite the danger here. Their in-stincts should have kept them away, scattered them to many of the islands nearer to the mainland, but those in-stincts had been rewired. They wouldn't go far, even if it meant their deaths.

Naomi watched the fins, saw one of them cut toward a seal. For a few seconds the fin submerged, lost in the depths. The shark came up jaws first, and it bit the thrash-ing seal in two before it plunged into the water again.

The tide kept rolling in.

Naomi glanced down and saw Wolchko struggling to make the climb, looked over, and saw Captain N'Dour watching her in silence. Overhead, Kat and Tye and Rosà-lie were resting, and the rain pattered the metal platform almost gently. The smell of rust and salt filled the air. Naomi told herself again that they would be all right.

But whoever might be coming to check on them, she wished they'd hurry.

CHAPTER 32

Jim's kayak cut diagonally over a wave. His shoulders ached a bit, but he knew it was only the beginning. By the time he reached the end of the day, his back and neck would be burning.

He had paddled rougher waters than this. Near the island, the swells turned into waves and crashed onto the shore, but out here to the south of Deeley there wasn't as much whitewater. Some of the surges and swells frothed at the top or started to break, but he knew his way around them, knew how to stop them and avoid them. Dorian might not have quite as much experience, but he had enough. He'd been ocean kayaking since the age of seven. They'd be fine. But the people on the watchtower over on Bald Cap were going to owe them many, many beers.

Jim lifted the paddle, swiped it into the water, and started to turn north. They'd kayaked south and then out to sea. The extent of the seal herd had astonished him and filled him with wonder. Their numbers made the moment surreal, as if he and Dorian had found themselves in an impossible dream. The storm and the ocean and the dark skies fed into that sense of detachment. But now they had gotten clear of the densest gathering of seals and it was time to approach Bald Cap from the east.

Jim scanned the water for sharks, counting fins, gauging their patterns. They seemed to be staying mostly in the channel between Deeley and Bald Cap, circling out and then returning to one spot in particular, where they would dive and vanish for a while before emerging. That worked fine for him. He had spotted some outliers and now that the water had swept across Bald Cap many had drifted beyond the tower, but he could work with that. The sharks would focus on the seals, and if there were a few nearby when he and Dorian approached the tower he wasn't concerned. They weren't seals, after all. The kayaks were bright yellow, even in this grim weather. Though it occurred to him that he had no idea if sharks saw color.

He craned his neck around to check on his son. Dorian paddled smoothly, keeping up with his dad seemingly without effort. Jim grimaced. He had a lot of pride in his sons, but he wouldn't have minded if it had been a little difficult for Dorian to keep up with him.

Jim kept his palms open as he swept the paddle forward and the kayak glided over the water. Even in the midst of the storm, he couldn't help enjoying himself just a little. If not for the specter of what he'd seen, that one man being killed by the sharks, this would have been one of his great adventures.

He dipped the paddle into the water to port and the kayak rode a large swell.

Something struck the paddle, thumped against the kayak hard enough to jostle him. The tug on the paddle nearly dragged it from his grasp. The kayak slewed sideways and tilted, out of his control for a moment. Jim swore as an enormous gulp of ocean water spilled into the kayak. He'd have been safer in a single, but then there'd have been no way to evacuate anyone off the watchtower.

Dorian shouted his name. Jim ignored him, paddling hard to get himself at the correct angle to the next swell. A frisson of fear prickled his skin and he remembered the man in the channel and the way the sharks had torn at him, but then he saw an enormous seal, and a second, and then a third and fourth, not quite so large, and he realized it had been them he'd struck.

He whispered a prayer of thanks, grinned into the salt spray and the rain, and paddled toward the watchtower, which was the only sign now that Bald Cap had ever been there.

Jim turned to look back at Dorian. "I'm all right!" he called.

His son was gone. The kayak drifted, upside-down in the undulating sea. Jim shouted Dorian's name, paddled hard, turning himself around and scanning the water. When Dorian's head burst from the sea, the kid whipping his head back and forth to get his hair out of his face, the relief Jim felt nearly brought him to tears.

"It's there!" he said, pointing to the overturned kayak. "Swim, and I'll find the—"

He'd been about to say *paddle*. Dorian needed his paddle. But Jim saw two things at once that silenced him. One was the fear in his son's eyes and the other was the dark, narrow shape just beyond the overturned kayak, the tall fin that zipped toward them both.

"Swim, Dorian!" Jim screamed. "Jesus, please swim!"

He paddled straight for his son. For his boy. Twenty-one

now, pierced and tattooed, but still the toddler who hadn't liked to walk up their street without holding his daddy's hand. Still the sweet boy who'd loved Winnie the Pooh well into elementary school and who'd written his mother the most profoundly sincere get-well notes ever scrawled in crayon. Jim had no memory of tears now, only a dark, primal strength that welled up from some ancient place inside him.

Dorian fought the pull of the sea and the weight of his clothes, swimming to meet his father. The shark glided just below the surface, breaking the water around it. The kayak flipped backward and to one side as the shark passed by. Jim swept the paddle down, firing his own kayak into the space between Dorian and the shark. He shouted to his son, not even hearing his own words as he planted his paddle into the water, dragging to a stop, prow pivoting. He lifted the paddle and swung it around with all of his strength as the fin came toward him—toward his boy.

The paddle struck even as Jim's kayak rose on the water displaced by the shark's arrival. The impact jarred him, lifted the kayak off the water. The prow went up and up and Jim paddled at the air for a heartbeat before he understood that he was flipping over backward. He heard Dorian scream for him as he plunged into the cold Atlantic, the deep current seizing him.

He kicked toward the surface, lungs already clamoring for air. He hadn't had a moment to hold his breath and now he exploded from the water, gasping, terrified, and freezing. The water surged around him and he caught a mouthful of it as he floated, scanning for his kayak . . . for Dorian . . . for the shark. He spotted Dorian, but then he saw bright yellow fifteen feet farther out. He called for his son to follow and he started to swim.

For a second he thought he saw a flicker of light, just south of Deeley Island. His wrist batted something hard and he saw it was his paddle. Triumphant, he grabbed it and kept swimming, one-handed, for the kayak. Shouting again, he glanced back to make sure Dorian was following, and when he turned again toward the kayak he saw nothing but teeth. Teeth and the yawning darkness of the shark's gullet. It hit him so fast that he didn't have time to scream, taking his left arm, head, and shoulders all in one snap of its jaws.

CHAPTER 33

———

Dorian saw his father die, saw the shark thrashing back and forth so hard it sawed him apart. The horror of it froze Dorian, grief pouring into him even as he saw a second fin circling out by his father's kayak. Dorian had been bitten already, the snap of something smaller than these sharks, and he could feel the warm cloud of his own blood around him in the water. The sea swelled ahead of him and he saw something dark and ragged and awful bob up to the surface. He understood that he was seeing what remained of his father, but he couldn't accept it, couldn't allow himself to really see. Not with the fins nearby.

Swim! his father had screamed. And now Dorian did. His own kayak was behind him. He turned in the water, forcing himself not to think about how close the sharks were, how quickly they could reach him. Forcing himself not to admit that his only chance was if they paused to eat the rest of his father. Hating himself for wishing they would. Screams bubbled up inside him, but he forced them away and just swam, arm over arm, roiling water swamping him, dragging at him, making him hold his breath.

He glanced up, searching for the yellow of his kayak even as he realized it would not save him. Of course it wouldn't save him. *So stupid*, he thought even as he spotted that yellow plastic bobbing on the water and struck out toward it. If he managed to flip it, to climb aboard, he'd only be buying himself a little time.

Dorian slowed. He felt tired. The cold water and the blood seeping from his leg and the leaden weight of grief tugged at him. He almost gave up, then, but his father's voice still echoed around in his skull. *Swim, Dorian!*

Determined, he kicked hard and pressed on toward the glimpse of yellow again. The rain fell, made him blink his eyes. A wave rose beneath him and his heart stopped a moment, as he thought a shark had caught up to him.

A noise blared into the storm and he jerked up short in the water. For half a second he thought it might be the bark of a seal, but it was so loud, so long and baleful, and then he recognized it as something that simply couldn't be. Dorian spun in the water and saw the fishing boat churning through the water, on a course to pass right by him. A big, bearded man stood at the rail, trying to call to him over the blare of the horn.

Dorian saw the sharks, still back where his father had died, where even now his blood was spreading, vanishing into the endless ocean. One of the fins struck out toward Dorian.

The horn went silent. The wind and rain replaced it, along with a voice, the fisherman shouting at him. Dorian shook himself from the daze of grief and shock and looked up to see the man tossing a life preserver toward him, the rope on it unraveling as it plunked into the water. Again he heard his father's echo in his head, shouting at him to swim, only this time it merged with the voice of the fisherman.

Bleeding, numb, mourning, fatherless, Dorian swam.

His hands closed on the life preserver, held on while the fisherman dragged him toward the boat. Moments after the big, bearded guy hauled him into the back of the boat a shark bumped against it hard enough to rock the whole vessel.

"Hey, man," the fisherman said, "you're okay. We got you, all right? You're okay."

Dorian's vision dulled and he blinked as black dots blotted out the corners of his eyes. Lying on his back, he looked up at the fisherman and at the storm high above them.

"Bit me," Dorian said. "I'm . . . I'm bleeding."

The fisherman glanced down at Dorian's leg—Dorian himself didn't bother looking, didn't have the energy. But he saw the bearded guy's brow wrinkle and the cloud that passed across his rescuer's eyes.

"Ah, shit," the fisherman growled. "This ain't good."

CHAPTER 34

Jamie got the young guy's name out of him—Dorian—
but nothing else. He ripped apart the guy's pant leg to
check out the wound and let out a huff of air. The shark
hadn't torn a chunk out of him, but the punctures from
the bastard's teeth were deep and ragged and bleeding
badly.

"Oh, Jesus," Dorian said blearily, on the verge of passing out. Which would be a better option for him than staring at that wound.

"I got this, buddy," Jamie said. "Don't sweat it. You're
gonna be all right."

Dorian gave him a doubtful look, full of despair, too
smart for his own good. Jamie turned and called for Walter, shouting to be heard over the engine. They'd been
powering farther out, away from the sharks and seals
they'd seen. One of the sharks—maybe the same one that
had bitten Dorian but maybe not—bumped them a couple

more times on the way, but a few minutes had passed since then. Now Walter throttled down and when Jamie looked up to shout for him again he was already there with the first-aid kit in his hands.

"That ain't good," Walter said, staring at the guy's torn-up leg as he handed over the kit.

"Exactly what I said." Jamie pulled a plastic bag from the kit, tore it open, and tugged out a thick roll of gauze, started wrapping it tightly around the leg. Blood began to seep through a moment or two later. "I'm gonna need something more than this. A sweatshirt or something."

Walter dug around in a cabinet and pulled out a stained Red Sox hoodie, unsheathed his fishing knife, and started cutting the sweatshirt into strips.

"I saw two kayaks out there," Walter said.

"Two kayaks, maybe," Jamie replied, "but this guy was alone. Anyone else with him is already gone."

Dorian had turned deathly pale. Now he slumped to the deck, the last of the fight going out of him. Unconscious, for now, and mercifully so.

"You think he'll make it?" Walter asked.

Jamie turned to him, grim determination forming inside him. "Fuck if I know, brother. But we're not done yet. Maybe it's just so many seals being around, but those sharks were in a feedin' frenzy or something. Let's check out Bald Cap, make sure nobody else is in danger. It'll add five minutes, and then we get this guy to a hospital."

"Harbor master said there are people on Deeley Island, too. This kid's family, right?"

Jamie thought of the two kayaks. "Or what's left of his family. But if they're on Deeley, they're safe enough." He looked down at the blood soaking through the bandages on the young man's leg. "This guy ain't."

"All right," Walter said. "Bald Cap, then home."

But the way Dorian was bleeding, Jamie wasn't sure the guy was ever getting home.

CHAPTER 35

———————

Tye's head throbbed. He lay on one side of the platform with Rosalie and Kat sitting face-to-face, occupying the other. The rain had soaked him through and the wind made the last, partial wall on top of the platform creak and squeal as it held in place, uselessly. The bleeding had stopped on his leg, at least according to Kat, which explained why he hadn't just fallen unconscious or bled to death at this point, but a part of him wished he'd bled just a little bit more—enough to put him out. Instead, he gritted his teeth and lay on his side as the pain thumped against the inside of his skull and throbbed in his temples. His leg had gone mostly numb, and what pain remained felt minuscule in comparison to the thudding in his head.

A hand shook him gently.

His eyes popped open and he realized with some surprise that he'd drifted off, in spite of it all. A groan escaped him. His neck and shoulder muscles burned and his spine felt like he'd been kicked by an elephant. With only one useful leg, the climb had messed up his back.

"Hey," Kat said, forcing him to focus on her.

He blinked against the rain. "Tell me we're rescued."

She shook her head, too miserable for the joke to make a dent. "Rosalie and I are swapping places with Wolchko and Naomi for a little while. Give them a rest. I just wanted you to know."

Tye watched Rosalie wave to him before she climbed over the side of the tower. Wincing at the renewed throb in his skull, he gave the tiniest of nods.

"Listen . . . about that secret—"

"Tye."

Kat's tone said it all. He frowned, blinked away the raindrops, and tried to focus on her face.

"I've been thinking about it," she said. "I guess I was so convinced this was about you being in love with me, and feeling weird about starting something with Rosalie—"

"It's not."

Kat nodded. "I know. It's about The Persimmon Foundation. Why they pulled their funding from my lab. They're funding you instead."

Tye shivered in the cold rain. His whole body throbbed with the pain in his leg and he wondered how much blood he'd lost, how long before infection set in. Gangrene. But he forced himself to focus.

"You knew?"

"For months," she assured him. "Dashawn at Persimmon told me you'd done an end run, pitched them your own projects. I'm not going to say I wasn't pissed, but you were always going to end up with your own lab."

Tye stared at her. "I stabbed you in the back and you knew, but you kept me on your team."

Kat shrugged. "For me to be really angry, I'd have to see you as competition. You're smart, Dr. Ashmore. But you're not smart enough to really be a threat to my funding." She glanced around. "Of course, after all of this, I'd say we're both going to have some lean times, funding-wise. I guess my only question is, what's the deal with Rosalie? I thought you two had a thing."

Tired, Tye closed his eyes. His lips felt chapped and dry, despite the rain. "She's . . . Rosalie's coming to work for me."

"Ah. Now it makes sense." Kat bent to whisper in his ear. "Watch yourself. That one's even more needy and conniving than you are."

She moved to the edge of the platform and started to carefully slip over the edge. Tye dragged himself a few inches so that he could see over the side. He flinched back as Wolchko's face came into view.

"Jesus," Tye muttered.

"Sorry. I didn't mean to spook you," Wolchko said.

Tye grumbled and slid himself over to let Wolchko onto the platform. His thoughts cleared for a few seconds and he registered what Kat had told him about them all taking turns on top of the platform.

"I should . . . ," he began. But really, what should he do? What could he do? Take his turn down below, bleed into the water, risk going up and down and taking turns until help arrived? Maybe that would be the noble thing, but it would also be the stupid thing.

Shivering, head throbbing, the wind howling, he looked over the side again. Captain N'dour was down there, on the second crossbeam. It should've put him twenty feet above the water, but instead he was barely ten and when a swell rolled around the watchtower the captain clung only half a dozen feet above the wave. The tower swayed with the passing of the swell and the urgency of the wind and Tye heard the metal groan. It wasn't a reassuring sound.

"Kat?" he said, turning in search of her, only to remember that she'd already gone over the side.

Wolchko knelt on the other side of the platform, giving Naomi a hand up.

The wind roared and the tower tilted so hard that Tye gripped the edge of the platform. He felt stupid—they weren't going over. The thing had been built to give a little bit. But with the water pushing at it, the way it leaned and the groaning of the metal made his heart race. The pounding in his skull increased and he tried to breathe more evenly, calm himself down. For the first time, he realized just how thirsty he was. The idea of becoming dehydrated out here surrounded by the ocean, with rain pouring down from the sky, felt like the sickest joke ever. *Water, water everywhere* . . . Wasn't that how that old poem or whatever it was had gone? *And not a drop to drink.*

Not funny. Not funny at all.

"Tye? You all right?"

He glanced up to see Wolchko and Naomi kneeling on the platform, watching him as if they thought he might grow a second head. Or a fin. Watching him the way he'd spent his life watching cultures and beakers and computers screens in his lab. If anyone else had asked, studying him like that, he might have told them to go to hell. But Naomi's gaze shifted to the bloodstained cloth wrapped around his calf, and he remembered that she hadn't been so lucky.

Lucky? You think you're lucky? a cruel, sneering

voice—his own voice—asked in the back of his mind. But he didn't like that version of himself, and he had an answer. *Luckier than Naomi.*

"I'll be all right. Just get some rest. It won't be long till you have to swap places again." Tye gestured at the rusted wind-and-rain-swept platform. "Four-star luxury up here. Enjoy it."

Wolchko and Naomi both frowned, apparently trying to figure out if he was being a cynic, a dick, or a cynical dick. Simmering with misery, he turned away from them and looked down into the water again. The next swell rolled beneath and around the tower, even higher than before, but this time as it passed, Tye saw a fin break the surface.

He shot a glance down at N'Dour, directly below him. "Hey, Captain?"

"I—" N'Dour began to reply.

What would he have said? *I see it*? *I want a cigarette*? *I wish I'd never met you fucking people*?

The shark struck the base of the tower so hard that huge flakes of rust fell like dirty snow. The impact reverberated through the bars, all the way up to the platform. Tye heard a voice cry out, figured it was Rosalie because Kat wouldn't, would she? No. Kat wouldn't show her fear like that.

The shark hesitated a second, perhaps a bit dazed, and then slid along over the now-invisible rocks of Bald Cap and vanished into the dark.

"—shit, oh shit, oh shit," Naomi had begun to chant, behind Tye on the platform.

Wolchko tried to comfort her. "It's okay, kid. We're up here and they're—"

But the acoustics man, Chill Eddie Wolchko—which

Tye had sometimes called the guy when he and Kat were alone in the lab—sounded entirely unconvincing. Whether that was Asperger's syndrome or pure uncertainty Tye didn't know. Maybe Wolchko was remembering the thudding against the hull of the *Thaumas* and how that had ended. The signal they'd been broadcasting would still be going, even now, emanating from the sunken wreck of their boat. This wouldn't be the last time one of these hyperaggressive fuckers bashed itself against the tower.

Tye brushed rain from his eyes. The pain in his skull had ebbed a bit, which was a merciful relief, but in its absence the wounds on his leg had begun to remind him quite fervently that he'd been bitten by a shark. He shifted again on the platform, sucking air in through his bared teeth, and started to scan the water. Had the seals begun to settle? How many had gone up onto Deeley Island, unsure what to do now that the signal that had lured them had stopped moving? How many had been eaten? Would they adjust to the signal over time? Would the sharks?

"Hey, Eddie," he began, realizing Wolchko was the one to ask.

Below, he heard Kat shout to Captain N'Dour. Tye looked down just in time to see a Great White thrust itself up out of a massive swell, jaws gaping wide as it aimed straight for N'Dour. The captain gave a shout and grabbed the lattice over his head, pulled his legs up to hang like some kind of marsupial. The shark missed him by just a couple of feet, then crashed bodily against the tower with a crunch of rending metal and a slamming impact that gave the whole structure a violent shake.

Rosalie screamed as she fell; Tye saw her arms flailing as she tumbled toward the water. Kat made not a sound as she lost her balance. Tye could only watch as she grabbed at a bar, scraped her palm and fingers on jagged rust, and then—as she saw that she wasn't going to hold on—thrust herself away from the tower.

Tye heard a roar and thought it must be the wind or the ocean, but it was his own voice. Why had Kat done that, pushed away like that? He thought he knew, figured she feared she might strike the tower on the way down and break some bones, maybe her spine, maybe her skull. When she hit the water, she plunged into the rushing, roiling current a dozen feet from the base.

"Tye, no!" Wolchko barked.

He wasn't even sure what Chill Eddie had objected to at first. Then he had already slipped over the side of the platform and he realized it was this. Hand over hand, feet dropping down, leg wounds splitting open again, ignoring it all, he descended the tower as fast as he could. Voices rode the wind, cries of fear from the water below and warnings from above, but they were nothing more than noise to him, just like the pain in his leg had become a distant thing, the heat of his freshly flowing blood no more a factor than the patter of the rain.

"Get her!" he heard N'Dour snap.

Tye hung from one hand, stood on one foot, and turned to see N'Dour already doing the same, dangling down toward a hand that waved in the air, bobbed on the swells. N'Dour caught that hand, grabbed hold of the upraised wrist, and the hand held him. The captain, this calm and aging gentleman from halfway around the world, wiry but small, hoisted Rosalie out of the water.

N'Dour swung her toward Tye, who caught her and pressed her to the metal. She clasped the trestlework, babbling in terror, thanking Tye and God and N'Dour, maybe not in that order. Tye snapped at her to climb, to get out of the way, and he saw the pain in her eyes at this dismissal and couldn't give a shit about that bit of hurt.

"Go!" he roared, mad with fear, and she climbed.

There was Kat. Right there in the water. Five feet from N'Dour and six feet below. How had she gotten there so quickly? Swimming hard against the current, against the waves? Maybe they'd been with her instead of against her; maybe they'd delivered her right back to the tower.

Shapes loomed in the corners of his eyes. He ignored them. If he turned now and saw a fin, saw a Great White the size of the one that had gone for N'Dour—had it timed its attack so that it rode that huge swell up, so that it could get the height? Could it do that?

You're the goddamned scientist, he thought.

Below, Kat swam toward the tower, whipping her head right and left in search of the death she knew was hunting her now.

"Don't look, Kat! Don't you look!" Tye cried.

He climbed down another set of latticed bars, plunged his boots into the water, planted his feet onto the lowest crossbeam. A swell rose till he was waist deep, and he and N'Dour both reached for Kat. Her eyes were wide. Tye stared into them and knew there'd been a thousand things unsaid between them, and he understood how badly he'd handled their relationship, both personally and professionally. In his mind's eye, he saw what it could've been.

"Come on, Kat!" Captain N'Dour snapped. "Reach!"

She kicked her legs, swam with one arm, lunged out for Tye and N'Dour with the other. But then the swell subsided and a trough followed it and she dropped eight feet in half a second. Tye spotted the fin behind her then. Kat hadn't seen it, but she didn't have to. Panic engraved itself upon her face and she tried reaching for them again.

"Climb!" Tye said even as he started to move lower. "Just—"

He didn't see the shark coming. It burst from the water on his left side, bleeding from its dead black eyes. Tye slammed himself against the tower and he felt the shark scrape against his back, crush him against the trestle, crack a rib or two. He heard screaming and turned to watch the shark slam back into the water, a huge splash rising around it.

Kat screamed his name, but Tye wasn't listening. He could only stare at Captain N'Dour. The man still hung from the tower with his left hand, but his right arm—the one with which he'd been reaching for Kat—was gone from above the elbow. Somehow he'd hung on, the shark's jaws shearing off the arm with razor-sharp suddenness. N'Dour stared at the ragged stump of his arm and watched blood spray from the torn blood vessels, pouring down into the water. In shock, stunned into numb confusion, Tye could only think about the fact that sharks could smell a single drop of blood in the water from a quarter mile away. There were dozens of them closer to the tower than that . . . and so much more than a single drop of blood.

N'Dour's grip on the rusty bar slipped and he tumbled into the water, vanishing under the churning waves in the very same place where the shark that had taken his arm had gone under.

Tye heard his name being screamed from above and from below.

He blinked. Focused on Kat. She'd reached the corner of the tower and grabbed hold. The water rose and floated her enough that she managed a better grip. He climbed up a few feet and began to crab-walk sideways across the narrow tower. He thought of the fact that she'd known of his betrayal and said nothing. That when the truth had come out, mere minutes ago, he hadn't even said he was sorry.

The torn and bloody fingers of Kat's left hand slipped on the bar. She slammed against the metal as the water level dropped beneath them. He saw her gaze shift and glanced back, saw a shark snatching the gory prize of N'Dour's body and then dragging it down.

A moment's distraction. The water rose again.

Kat shouted Tye's name. He reached for her, but she lost her grip and fell back into the water. His fingers missed hers by inches, and only then, as her eyes locked on his one last time, did he see the shark dragging her down, already whipping her body from side to side as it submerged, a fresh blossom of blood unfurling beneath the sea.

Up on the platform, the others were screaming for him to climb.

Slowly, his own blood dripping into the water from his wounded leg, all his strength gone, Tye reached up for the next bar. And the next.

CHAPTER 36

Lorena held her phone up, camera on, and zoomed. While she and Kyle had been gathering up their gear, she hadn't been able to keep track of Jim and Dorian on the water. Only when she and Kyle had retreated up the hill a bit and found a clearing in the trees, well back from where the storm surge would reach, had she had seen the fishing boat in the distance. Her heart had leapt and she'd turned to Kyle, let him look through her camera phone's zoom to see the boat. She had told him everything would be all right now. That the people on Bald Cap would be saved and that they could all get out of this awful storm and go home and get dry. She'd promised Kyle that she would bake brownie cookies from scratch, just the way he liked them. Lorena wasn't in any mood to bake, but she would have promised anything just to be able to be somewhere warm and dry.

Her promises had been empty.

"What is it?" Kyle asked when he heard her gasp, saw

her horrified cringe. "Did someone fall? I thought I saw someone, a minute ago. I—"

He reached for the phone and she slapped his hand away, turned her back to him. Shaking, she lifted the phone again and took a couple of steps to give herself distance from Kyle. Seventeen might be old enough these days for all sorts of things her generation thought of as the province of adulthood, but surely not for this horror.

Lorena stared at the zoomed camera image. Several sharks were in a frenzy at the base of the watchtower, the water churning around them. Bald Cap had been swallowed by the sea and the storm. A man climbed the tower, slipped, and nearly fell, then seemed to be crawling up the metal scaffolding, practically dragging himself up the side.

"Are they dead?" Kyle asked, his voice flat but clear, loud enough to be heard over the storm. "I see some heads up on top of the tower there, but the others . . . whoever fell . . . they're dead, right?"

"There's one guy climbing back up," she said, knowing there was no point in lying to Kyle. He'd be able to see well enough if he moved around a bit, just not in the same detail that the camera phone's zoom provided. "He's injured, I think, but he's okay."

"What about Dorian and my dad?"

Lorena tore her gaze away from the watchtower. Kyle might be seventeen, but in that moment she could see the little boy he must have been once upon a time. He might have been capable of great things at this age, but here with her on the island, unable to do anything but wait, he seemed so very young.

"They'll be all right," she said. "They went off in the direction that fishing boat is coming from. Your father will signal them somehow. I'm sure he and Dorian are already onboard."

"You think?"

Lorena swung the camera around and zoomed in on the fishing boat again, saw it plying the water straight for the tower. "Absolutely," she said. But then she frowned and narrowed her eyes, took a step down the hill, and raised the camera, tried to get as focused a picture as possible. Out there to the southeast, amidst the gray skies and indigo swells, through the trees around the hill, hadn't she just caught a glimpse of yellow bobbing on the water? Urgent yellow. Kayak yellow.

She stared at the image on the camera. Kyle called her name.

There, she thought. Another flicker of yellow, visible for a moment and then hidden again by the rough seas. She strained her eyes to see.

The camera winked off. Lorena swore softly— something she almost never did—and started tapping the screen, thumbing the main control button. She unleashed a stream of profanity in her parents' native Italian, the language of her youth, but the phone didn't respond to cursing.

"It's dead," Kyle said quietly.

Lorena wanted to hurl the phone down the hill. Tensed to throw it. But then she took a breath and just gripped it in her fist, unable to stop thinking about the people who'd fallen off the tower and the man and woman she'd watched die through her camera phone's zoom.

Kyle told her it would be all right. It seemed they were taking turns at the reassurance game. She put an arm around him, still clutching the phone with her free hand, and stared out at the fishing boat as it made its way toward the watchtower, looking past the boat, searching the water for a splotch of yellow. Urgent yellow.

Whatever had happened, at least it was over now. The men on the fishing boat would help them. She forced herself to stop looking for that flash of urgent yellow on the water and told herself that all she wanted was to go home. That was part of it, certainly, but it wasn't the whole truth. She did want to go home, to leave this awful place and never return . . . but she didn't want to go home alone.

CHAPTER 37

———

Naomi had a handful of Rosalie's coat, helping her up onto the platform, when she spotted the fishing boat churning toward them through the storm. She'd felt so isolated, so impossibly alone out here, that as she shifted aside to make room for Rosalie she watched the boat rise and fall on the sea and half-thought it was a daydream.

"Boat," she said, strangely calm. In shock.

Kat and N'Dour were dead. A shark had struck the tower so hard that at least one rusted crossbeam had snapped and the tower seemed canted slightly northward now. Naomi's skin had become so gray and sodden with constant rain that she could barely feel anything, and that numbness lent an impossible nightmarish quality to the world around her. The air shimmered, the rain fell, and it all felt unreal. A dream. Or the fevered imaginings of one who had already died.

But then she shifted again, making sure Rosalie and Wolchko had room on the platform, and her prosthetic leg

made a low hum, something to which she'd become so ac-
customed that she barely heard it anymore. But she heard
it now, and it was real and tangible, connected to the vis-
ceral memory of the hard tug on her leg when the shark
had bitten into her. Her shark, a summer ago. Somehow
the missing leg and its unreal replacement were the things
that reminded her that all of this must be real. In shock,
numb, drowning in grief and fear, locked in nightmare . . .
she woke up.

"A boat," Naomi said.

Wolchko had been comforting Rosalie, who'd been
shivering and crying and couldn't stop talking about Kat
being dead and N'Dour being dead and Tye still being
down there on the side of the tower. Somewhere in the
back of her mind Naomi realized it must have been rude of
her to ignore Rosalie so completely, to blank out the
other woman's terror and shock, but they all had their own
terror and shock, didn't they? Rosalie's terror and shock
might be fresher, but only a little. Naomi had been looking down from the platform and seen N'Dour's arm torn
off, seen the captain fall in, seen Kat dragged under and the
bloody frothing water as the sharks savaged them, there
at the base of the tower. There in the place where they'd
all been safe just a couple of hours before. Though they
hadn't all been safe, had they? Bergting had already been
dead by then. So to hell with Rosalie's terror and shock.
Naomi had her own.

"Boat!" she barked, glaring at Rosalie and Wolchko.

Rosalie fell silent. She and Wolchko both turned to stare
at the thirty-foot fishing boat coming their way. Naomi
heard a grunt and glanced over to see Tye clawing at the
top of the platform.

"Shit," she said, grabbing his hand, then reaching out

to help haul him up. When she saw how much blood had soaked through the rags tied around his torn-up leg she felt that hideous dreamlike unreality envelop her again.

"There's a boat coming," she told him.

Tye blinked, his face alight with urgency. He looked more alive than she felt, despite his wound, the blood he'd lost, and the fact that he'd just seen a woman he'd once loved die ugly. Savage and bloody. Somehow he still had hope blazing in his eyes.

"Careful," Naomi said. And maybe she meant it more than just one way. Yeah, the platform didn't really have room for all four of them and Tye had to perch right on the edge and she had to shift over much closer to the ragged, sharp metal of the remaining wall and they all had to be damned careful up here. But in the back of her mind, in the flicker of something that tried to spark inside her, she felt sure she also meant something else.

"Do you see it, Tye?" Rosalie asked. "Oh my God, do you see it?"

The light in Tye's eyes didn't go out, but Naomi watched it diminish, watched his strength flag when he finally had a good look at the boat that was headed straight for them.

"I see it," Tye said. "Question is, do any of you? That's an old boat, private fishing. Maybe a Merritt or a Lyman. It's got a wooden hull."

Naomi felt her heart sink.

She turned and watched the boat, wondering who might be onboard. Wondering how they had known to come out here to Bald Cap. They were good people; she knew that. Whoever they were, they were coming to the rescue.

It seemed a terrible shame that she could only perch there on the tower and watch them die.

CHAPTER 38

⟨⟩

Jamie crashed into the instrument panel, coffee cup flying. The windshield cracked from the impact on the hull. Walter throttled up, engine roaring to cover his swearing. Sitting in the corner off the wheelhouse, young Dorian hung his head, halfway between praying and hyperventilating.

"What the hell kinda shark hits like that?" Jamie snapped, feeling his forehead. His fingers came away sticky red and he realized it hadn't been the shark smashing against the hull that had cracked the windshield—it had been his skull. "God damn—"

The next impact shifted the whole boat sideways, raised it up off the water like a car riding on two wheels. He heard a crash and the snap and splinter of rending wood and knew the shark had just stove in the side of the hull. Shuddering, thumping down on top of the shark itself, the fishing boat settled into the water, and immediately Jamie felt the drag below them, like Neptune had gotten his fingers up inside the wood and begun to slowly pull. Water had started pouring in, fighting their momentum, the ocean merciless. They didn't belong out here, not as far as the sea was concerned. All the shark had done was strip them down, expose their frailty. Without a solid hull beneath them . . .

Jamie braced himself. "Hard to port, Walter. Hard to fucking port!"

"Got it—"

"I'm not ending up on that Tinkertoy tower, man. We've gotta make Deeley Island! We've gotta—"

Walter roared, nostrils flaring, lips curled back in rage. "I'm going, goddammit! You see me turning the wheel here? I've got the fucking helm and it's under control, man. It's under control!"

Jamie snapped his jaws shut. He tasted his own blood on his lips. He braced himself and nodded. "Sorry, brother."

He saw the apology in Walter's eyes, too. Regret and fear. What the hell had they gotten themselves into? When had sharks ever behaved this way? This was just not normal. What had stirred them up like this?

Off the starboard bow Jamie saw the tower, saw the people up on the platform, watching as the fishing boat began to turn toward Deeley, and all the air went out of him.

"Walter," he said quietly, thinking he knew after all, thinking he had a damn good idea what had triggered the sharks to all turn psychotic.

The engine whined and choked and the boat hove lower in the water, the drag worsening. But he could see the trees of Deeley Island through the storm, a dark welcome, only four hundred yards or so away. He turned to look at Dorian, saw that the kid had given up praying, just hung his head and stared at the floor, braced against the wall, maybe trying to come to terms with his father being gone, maybe just patiently waiting to find out if they were all going to join the old man.

The next impact tore the hull wide open, smashing in planking, breaking boards in two. The shark shook its huge body, whipped its tail, trying to force itself inside the belly of the boat. Walter hung on as he went to his knees. His forehead bounced off the wheel, but he kept his grip. Jamie sprawled onto the floor of the wheelhouse and rolled half-way out onto the deck. Dorian had gone back to praying, but no longer silently. The kid was screaming to God now. Maybe God couldn't hear him over the whining, coughing, dying engine and the further splintering of wood, or maybe God just didn't give a shit.

"Oh, Jesus," Jamie whispered to himself, maybe doing a little praying of his own. He dragged himself into the wheelhouse, the boat listing hard to starboard, the nose dipping so much that the next wave washed over the bow. The cracked half of the windshield shattered, water and glass sweeping around them.

Jamie tried to stand, but Dorian beat him to it. On his one good leg, the kid stood beside Walter at the helm, dragged Walt up to his feet, and threw the throttle all the way up. The engine screamed, moments away from its dying breath, choked with water. Jamie shouted at the kid, confused, but then he saw the way Walter perked up and nodded and took the wheel with determination.

They'd changed course again. The boat kept sinking, but now they were aimed back at the watchtower on Bald Cap. The shark kept thrusting itself into the boat's guts. Jamie knew if he looked below he'd see it, and he didn't dare for fear he'd piss himself.

He grabbed the radio, started barking into it, shouting

for the harbor master—for anyone—to answer. They had to tell someone what the hell was going on here. He heard only static. Rain blew in through the shattered windshield and he looked out at the watchtower where Bald Cap used to be, thinking it looked almost as if it was leaning.

"We'll never make it," he said. "It's too far!"

Dorian whipped around toward him. "Then we'll get as close as we can!"

A hundred yards away. Eighty. Sixty.

A fresh rending of wood came from below and the boat suddenly bobbed up a few feet. Jamie turned to Walter, thoughts so chaotic and upside-down that for half a second he thought some miracle had taken place.

"There!" Dorian shouted, pointing.

The huge fin cruised right past them, around the fishing boat's stern. There were others out there, much too close, but somehow Jamie understood then. The boat had bobbed upward because the shark had withdrawn. But it had been a plug in the side of the boat, and now that momentary bob of release from the shark's weight was countered by the inrush of thousands of gallons of seawater.

Forty yards, and going down.

The prow went under. The engine choked out. A wave crashed over them and the boat nosed down in the water so fast Jamie thought he could feel the Atlantic swallowing them. A memory flickered through his mind, some kind of Greek myth he'd read in high school about a monster and a whirlpool. Another wave swamped them and water poured into the wheelhouse and then it shocked him to find that he was drowning. The ocean crashed onto him, filled his throat, stung his eyes, and Jamie felt his brain screaming denial. He lashed out, clawed his way upward even as the boat's sinking dragged at him. His left arm struck someone and he latched on, dragging, making sure that if he made it to the surface he wouldn't be alone.

Gasping, pissed off, lungs burning, he burst from the water to discover he'd only been a few feet under. The aft railing of the boat had somehow reappeared above him. Walter's precious wooden lady was going straight down— *not supposed to happen this way*—and Jamie saw the rear portion of the deck just a few feet in front of him. The railing sank toward him and for a second he just treaded water, too stunned to get out of the way.

A hand grabbed the back of his jacket and tugged hard, and he turned to see it was Walter. "Swim, you dumb son of a bitch!"

Jamie did, anger stoking higher within him. Walter's fucking boat, his pride and joy, was going down right in front of their eyes, and for what? How did sharks do something like this?

Someone cried out and Jamie glanced over to see Dorian, hair plastered to his face, looking like a drowned rat. The kid was only a few feet from him and Jamie realized it had been Dorian whose arm he'd grabbed as he swam up out of the wheelhouse. Now the guy turned and started to swim toward the listing, rusting watchtower, which seemed like a damned good idea. Walter tugged Jamie, wanting him to do the same, but for a second all he could do was watch the boat vanishing into the water.

Then he heard what the kid was shouting. "They're coming!" Over and over.

Of course they were. *Oh shit, oh fuck, oh shit.* Of course they were.

Walter shouted at Jamie, tried to drag at him again, but Jamie knocked his hands away. Jamie's clothes were soaked through and weighing him down, dragging at him, and he sloughed off his jacket as he started swimming harder. Walter saw him moving and gave him a thumbs-up. Behind them, the last few feet of the fishing boat slipped into water and Jamie felt the pull of its sinking as water rushed in to fill the void where it had been. He ignored it, kept swimming. Rain whipped down at his eyes. Walter had gotten a little ways ahead of him, but the watchtower loomed closer, no more than twenty-five yards now.

Jamie didn't look behind him. If he saw sharks there, saw the fins slicing the water, what could he have done? Not a damn thing. And anyway, there were sharks ahead, cruising around the tower on the prowl. A low laugh burbled up inside his chest, a manic sliver of lunacy that he fought against by just swimming. Swimming harder. His boots were full of water, each one an anchor beneath him, and he slowed for a second or two to kick them off, letting them sink into the channel. When he glanced up, the largest fin slid across a rising swell no more than fifteen yards away, and that laugh escaped his lips. In all his life he had never imagined there might come a time when he would swim toward a shark instead of away. It felt more than a little like suicide.

Walter had outpaced him, a dozen feet ahead now. But Dorian had youth and grief driving him and he clearly knew how to swim a hell of a lot better than these two middle-aged fishermen. The kid went for it, Olympic-style, as if he'd never been bitten at all, as if his face hadn't gone deathly pale from losing so much blood already.

It must've been the blood that called to the sharks.

"Dorian!" Jamie roared, pulling back in the water. "Look out, kid; they're—"

But what was he supposed to say? *They're coming*? Dorian had been screaming that for the past minute. And where was he supposed to go? The only route they had to survival meant moving through the paths of the sharks orbiting the watchtower. Dorian's leg had been bitten already, and he was still bleeding. A burst of rage flared inside Jamie and he struck out toward the kid, swimming on an intercept line, wondering if Dorian had yet seen the fin coming around from his right, almost stealthily, a silent killer. Walter shouted after Jamie, but he kept going. He'd been nineteen when his father had died and he'd never been the same again. Now this kid had seen his father torn apart, had survived being in the water and been dragged out to safety, scarred forever, grieving forever. And now this other shark was going to make forever turn into a quarter of an hour? Not on Jamie Counihan's watch.

But the shark that took Dorian didn't come from the kid's right . . . it came from below. Jamie saw him jerk to a halt. Saw the kid's eyes widen with realization and the crestfallen expression on his face, the disappointment when he understood that his life had ended so soon. So young. His lips moved and he mumbled something, some refusal or prayer or plea, but he didn't scream. Then he was yanked down under the water, arms flailing over his head, and he was gone. One hand broke the surface again, but only for a moment, after which there was only blood.

Jamie stared at the spot where Dorian's hand had reappeared.

Then Walter grabbed him by the hair and yanked his head back, twisted him around so they were eye to eye. "Are you deaf? Look!"

The shark he'd been trying to intercept, the one he thought would kill Dorian, had altered course, straight toward them. Jamie heard voices, understood they must be coming from the people on top of the watchtower, but he

didn't take the time to look. He turned and started swimming, wanted to scream at Walter, who'd backtracked a
few yards to reach him. *I'm bleeding*, he would have said.
*My head is bleeding and it's coming for me and what the
hell is wrong with you?* But he knew what Walter would
have said. Even as his body remembered high school swim
team, even as he put his face in the water and picked up
the rhythm he needed, he could practically hear the words
in Walter's own voice. *You're my brother*, he would've said,
and that would be the truth.

Thirty feet from the tower, another fin surfaced, right
in front of them. Jamie stopped swimming, turned in the
water, he and Walter rising on a swell that crashed right
through the tower's trestlework and rolled toward Deeley
Island. The shark that had been behind them, the one he
knew would kill him, had vanished.

The fin ahead of them submerged again, sinking with
the swell.

"Where did it go?" Jamie snapped.

Walter twisted himself around, trying to look down into
the water, but with the storm and the dark sea there was
no way he could have seen anything at all. And yet Jamie
saw a terrible wisdom in that rough, familiar face.

"Come on, damn it!" Walter growled. "We're almost
there!"

The people on the tower urged them on, shouting for
them to swim, to climb, and Jamie determined not to look
around again. Several seals darted just beneath the surface,
almost if they were getting out of his way. Whitewater
rippled around the legs of the tower, fifteen feet away. Ten
feet. Five feet. When he heard Walter cry out, Jamie turned
to his left and saw the shark breach, surging toward him
fast . . . so much faster than he'd imagined it would be. Its

jaws opened and he saw blood and torn strips of dark flesh, strings of sealskin, and he couldn't help himself. He screamed. The thought of Dorian's silent sadness broke his heart, but terror erupted from within, and he screamed.

Then Walter was there, again. There, as he'd always been.

But this time, he was too late.

Jamie roared in pain as the shark gripped his torso, dragging him sideways, ripping at him as it plunged him deeper. As he went under, his eyes locked on Walter's.

"Swim, goddamn—" he tried to say.

Then there were no more words.

Alone in the sea, Walter kicked his legs and lunged up with a rising wave to grab hold of rusty diagonal bars. He had his fishing knife sheathed at his hip and all he could think about was what would have happened if he'd tried to use it, thought of it sooner. There were a lot of goddamn sharks and only one knife, but maybe it would have made the difference. Given Jamie that crucial minute.

Walter would always wonder. The knife felt like it weighed a hundred pounds.

Walter hauled himself out, cursing every beer he'd ever drunk, every order of French fries Jamie hadn't finished, leaving him to pluck fries off of his best friend's plate. He climbed, knowing just a few feet wouldn't be enough, not with the swells and the rough seas, not with whatever had been done to these sharks to make them like this. Even as he climbed, one of the things rose from the water and seemed to reach for him. It scraped its hide against the rusty tower and Walter took one more step up, holding on for his life, staring at the crashing sea as the monster slid away.

"Fuck you!" he screamed at the shark. At the seals. At the ocean and the storm and the people stranded with him on the tower. "Fuck you!"

He held the last word, listened to his own fury rolling out over the waves, carried by the wind, and he knew it was a lie. That it wasn't fury at all, but agony.

His strength gave out and he hung there on the side of the tower, unable to climb. Eyes wide, he draped himself against the bars and stared at nothing. The last shark had come for him, and Jamie had put himself in the way. He'd chosen to put himself in the way.

"Oh, you asshole," Walter whispered to himself, eyes filling with tears. "What the hell did you just do? My God, James. What did you do?"

From the ocean, there was no answer.

CHAPTER 39

Naomi lay on her belly on the platform and watched the fins gliding through the maelstrom. The seals were still there, all around Bald Cap, but the sharks seemed less interested in them now. Maybe their bellies were full to bursting, but she couldn't stop the grim, insinuating voice that whispered in the back of her skull, telling her that the sharks were bored with seals. That the signal had done something to their brains besides making them hyperaggressive. That they were spiteful and pissed off and determined to get the people who'd eluded them so far. Naomi knew that was bullshit, that whatever Wolchko's acoustic broadcast might be doing to them, it couldn't make them any smarter. But it didn't *feel* like bullshit. She couldn't escape the sense of the sharks' awareness of her, the certainty that they knew she and the others were still up here.

Malice, she thought. *That's the word*. She felt their malice. Which was impossible, but as she watched the fins, the inexorable circling, the malignant intent of their presence, it simply felt true.

She shifted, boot scraping rust off the platform, and wondered why she wasn't crying. Earlier, on the boat, she'd been a broken thing, a pile of shattered glass in the shape of a person. But she felt whole now, not shattered at all. And she damn sure didn't feel like glass.

About the others she could not say the same.

Wolchko clung to the side of the tower, on the topmost crossbeam. Rosalie and Naomi had dragged Tye back up onto the platform and now the other woman was sitting with him, trying to rewrap the wounds on his leg. Rosalie's attachment to him was clear, but she wisely kept silent about her feelings. Tye lay on his side on the platform, his back up against the fragment of wall that remained. His eyes were dull hollows. Rain accumulated in those hollows and slid across his nose, ran across his forehead, and sluiced along his lips. Tye didn't bother to wipe it away, remained so still that it almost appeared that his wounds had finished him, that it had been him the sharks had just killed, instead of Kat. Her death had shut him down. Whatever their relationship had become, he'd obviously still loved her.

Rosalie touched his face with her fingers, brushed the rain away from his eyes. Naomi thought she had venom in her, a poison that worked both directions, touching those around her even as it was working in her gut, but she saw the pain on Rosalie's face now and couldn't stop herself from feeling sympathy.

"He'll be all right," Naomi said.

When Rosalie turned, it was as if she'd forgotten she and Tye weren't alone up on the platform.

"He'll live," she said. "That's not the same thing."

Naomi popped her head over the edge of the tower again. Wolchko clung there, just a few feet below. Another ten feet below him was the other guy, their new arrival, this massively tall fisherman to whom only Wolchko had yet spoken. This guy seemed like a wreck, too, unraveled by the horrors he'd just seen. He kept muttering to himself, and Naomi thought he might be praying or swearing or a little of both.

"Eddie?" she said, just loud enough to be heard over the storm.

Wolchko hooked an arm around a crossbar and leaned out to look up at her. He seemed exhausted, stubble on his cheeks and dark puffy circles under his eyes. His pupils were little pinpoints, almost like he might be high, but she figured the slack expression on his face was its own sort of shock.

"Do you—" she began.

A shark thumped into one of the legs of the tower. Naomi flinched and held her breath. She thought her heart even stopped for a few seconds as she listened for the sound of damage, the grating crunch of rusty joints giving way. Of things getting worse.

Down below them, the fisherman ratcheted up the volume on his stream of profanity. No prayers there, it seemed. Only curses.

"You did this!" the fisherman said, glaring up at them. "Just had to fucking play God!"

Naomi saw the way Wolchko's face went ashen. Even in the storm and at his age, he'd never looked so wan. So old. She didn't ask if he was all right because she knew the answer— How could he be? The fisherman was right. All of this was Wolchko's fault. His and the rest of Kat's team. They rushed the research. They'd been too eager, too cocky.

"Eddie," Naomi said again, "I don't think the water's getting any higher."

Wolchko nestled himself back into the crook of metal above the thirty-foot beam. "Agreed. The tide's in, and the surge might have subsided a little. The wind's dropped some, too. But it's not the water I'm worried about."

Naomi nodded slowly. "I know."

The problem wasn't the tide or the surge. Not now. The problem lay with the tower itself. She slid along the platform, still giving Tye and Rosalie room, to the opposite side. When she hung her head over, she could make out the section of rusted metal that had been smashed apart, and it wasn't her imagination that the platform tilted slightly in that direction. Climbing up, she had noticed several pieces of latticework that had deteriorated so badly that they had rusted through, two bars hanging down at odd angles like broken spokes on a bicycle wheel.

The sharks would keep coming. With the boat, the rumble of the engine had riled them up, but even without that noise they somehow knew there were still people up here. Maybe the growl of voices resonated through the metal into the water, or maybe just the blood that had already been spilled. It didn't matter. They might not be attacking as consistently, but they were out there, and every impact on the tower vibrated the rusted joints a little more.

"The hell with this," Naomi said, scrambling back to the side of the tower where Wolchko waited.

"What are you doing?" Rosalie asked.

Naomi shot her a look, wanting to snap at her, ask her why she cared. But she saw the brokenness and fear in the other woman's eyes and any last traces of yesterday's animosity vanished.

"Not sure yet," Naomi said. "But I don't intend to die here."

Rosalie almost sneered. "Good luck with that."

Naomi ignored her. She turned around and slid over the edge, a little too fast, nearly losing her grip before her prosthetic foot found a V joint below. Then Wolchko had grabbed her legs, helping her climb down even as he asked her the same question Rosalie had asked.

Side by side with him, arms feeling somehow weary and powerful at the same time, Naomi hung from the metal lattice like it was part of the monkey bars in the schoolyard near where she grew up.

"Get up there. Take a rest," she said to Wolchko. "I may need you."

He started to protest again, but she was already moving down, sidling around the corner of the tower to avoid a section of broken bars. The fisherman looked up at her as she climbed, all of his bitterness gone. He stared like he had never seen another human being.

"What's your name?" she asked him.

"Walter Briggs."

Naomi didn't like being so close to the water, but she moved down until she hung beside Walter, the smell of rust filling her nostrils.

"I'm sorry you got into this, Walter," she said. "I'm sorry about your friends."

The guy stared at her. He had huge hands, a bunch of little scars on the backs of them, and a rounded beer belly. A strong guy, she figured, maybe used to being strong in a lot of ways. Definitely not used to the kind of horror he'd just seen.

"I didn't know the young guy, Dorian," he said. "Me

and Jamie just picked him up. He and his dad were kayaking out from Deeley to try to get you folks outta here."

Naomi widened her eyes. "Are you kidding? They tried kayaking in the middle of this?"

She didn't mean the storm, and it was clear Walter understood that.

"They didn't know, did they?" he said, voice rippling with anger. "They didn't know what you idiots did."

She could have argued, explained that she wasn't a part of the WHOI team, but she was too surprised to separate herself from the whole business.

"How do you know about that?" she asked.

Walter shifted, hoisted his body into a diamond-shaped opening in the trestle so he could rest his arms a bit. "We didn't know exactly. We read about it and got pissed off about you bringing so many seals to the waters up here, worried they'd eat all the damn fish. We wanted to stop it, or at least make some trouble, but then we got a call from the harbor master, said you folks were stranded."

A flicker of hope in her chest. "They know? Someone knows? The harbor master sent you?"

Walter scowled. "It sounded like bullshit, but we were out here anyway, so he asked us to check it out."

"But when they don't hear from you, they'll send someone," she said excitedly.

A wave of disgust crossed his face, leaving only sadness behind. "I guess they will. Maybe pretty soon."

Naomi's heart had been so frayed, her emotions so raw, that she didn't understand why Walter would be anything but happy at the prospect. Then she remembered the fishing boat, and this guy Dorian, and . . .

"Jamie," she said. "He was your friend?"

Walter looked as if he might be sick. He hung his head. "My best friend. Shit . . . maybe my only real friend."

He blinked in surprise, as if he hadn't expected to speak the thought aloud and now regretted it. Fresh grief etched itself onto his face and he looked away, out at the water, where the sharks were circling.

One of them broke away, even as Naomi and Walter watched, and started for the tower, picking up speed.

"Hold on," she said. "They're determined to knock us off."

Walter did more than hold on. He climbed another couple of feet and wrapped his arms around the sturdiest bars he could find. As the shark darted at the tower, Naomi did the same. It thumped hard at the base, down under the water. The whole structure shook and rust rained down, and all she could do was wonder how much damage it had caused down there under the water, where she couldn't see.

The tower listed northward, creaking, but she told herself it would hold. That a little rust wasn't enough to tear it apart.

"What happened to you?" Walter asked suddenly, staring at her prosthetic leg.

Naomi watched the sharks. Watched the churning sea. "They did," she said. "Last summer."

"Shit, I thought I recognized you," the fisherman replied. "You're the governor's kid."

Naomi didn't correct him. Her mind was otherwise engaged. She had escaped sharks before and she would find a way to do it again. Maybe the harbor master would send someone else, but even if that happened, unless they were in a boat sturdier than Walter and Jamie's fishing boat, it would do no good. Not while the signal kept going. Sure, the storm would subside eventually and the tide would recede and they'd have Bald Cap to themselves again.

But she didn't think the tower would last that long.

"Eddie!" she shouted up to Wolchko.

He poked his head out, looking down at them. "You okay?"

"Not even close," Naomi said. "I think we're gonna die. I think we've got maybe one chance to avoid that happening."

"You've got ideas, I'm all ears," Wolchko said.

Naomi pointed out to the spot where the *Thaumas* had gone down. "Someone has to dive on the wreck and shut the signal down. It's the only way."

Wolchko stared at her, lost for words.

"You're outta your friggin' mind," Walter said. "Anyone dives down there is dead."

Naomi shot him a dark look, then glanced up to include Wolchko in her disapproval. "Either of you have a better idea?"

Neither of them did.

CHAPTER 40

Lorena had zero skill when it came to setting up a tent, but fortunately Jim had taught his sons very well. Kyle had broken down the tents in their camp and now he set one of them up again at the edge of the clearing in the space of ten minutes. Lorena stood and watched as he finished the job, tapping a couple of anchors into the dirt. Rainwater sluiced from a branch overhead and spattered the top of the tent, but it would be dry inside, at least.

"Ready?" Kyle asked, masking his unease.

"Very much so. And grateful, too."

Kyle held back the flap so that she could slip inside. Before she did, Lorena slid out of her rain gear. She wore a sweatshirt and yoga pants underneath, which were comfortable and mostly dry. Squeezing rain out of her hair, she ducked into the tent and balled up a blanket to sit on. It wouldn't be warm inside, but at least it would block the wind and keep the rain off.

Quiet and swift, Kyle removed his own coat and hung it from a tree branch. He left the pants on and climbed in beside her. Side by side, with the flap open, they were able to see out past the edge of Deeley Island. Kyle had erected the tent to face the watchtower on Bald Cap, but if a kayak were to pass by on the way back to the point where Jim and Dorian had launched they'd see that as well.

"That was awful," she said quietly. "I'm so sorry you had to witness it."

Kyle huffed and shuddered, making a show of it. Making light of it. "Yeah, me too."

Lorena's chest tightened. The storm seemed to have subsided slightly, but the wind still screamed around them and made the walls of the tent snap like a flag in a gale. For the rest of her life, she knew that she would associate every big storm with this day. She and Kyle had watched as the fishing boat sank, blessedly unable to make out the details as sharks moved in to attack the people who'd been onboard. The boat went down so fast and all she could think was that the hole in its side must have been huge.

That's not all you thought.

The view from the mouth of the tent allowed her and Kyle to see down along the path they'd climbed. From here they could watch the waves flooding the shore of Deeley Island. The tide had risen dramatically, the storm surge covering the rocks and the steep slope down to where the water would normally have stopped.

Stop thinking about it, she told herself.

"Do you think they were on the boat?" Kyle said softly. "Dad and Dorian?"

Lorena shivered, trying to pretend it was the chill in the air. "I couldn't make out faces. Maybe if the phone was still working and we could've zoomed, but . . . Anyway, no. I don't think they were on the boat."

"That one guy . . . he looked skinny enough to be Dorian."

"You saw him for a second or two. We don't have any reason to believe that was your brother." She put a hand on his back. "We're just going to wait here, Kyle. We're just going to sit and wait for them to come back."

Her voice sounded hollow, even in her own ears.

"Those sharks," Kyle said, "the way they attacked that boat . . ."

He let the thought go unfinished, but Lorena did not need him to explain. His father and brother had gone out in kayaks. Given what had happened to that fishing boat, two men in kayaks wouldn't stand a chance, but she told herself there were plenty of things that might have drawn the sharks' attention. The engine noise or maybe a net dragging in the water with fish in it. She didn't know how likely those things were, but she needed to tell herself there were possibilities that didn't end in heartbreak.

"Just watch the tower," she told Kyle. "Your dad said they were going to head south and circle around behind Bald Cap. He and Dorian will get there. Those kayaks will show up. And once they learn what's happened, they'll have the sense to just stay there on the tower with whoever else that is over there."

Kyle shifted a little to get a better view out through the open mouth of the tent. "Okay. Yeah. We'll just watch for them."

So they sat and stared out through the open flap of the tent and Lorena wished that she had known Jim longer, that she had developed more of a relationship with his sons. She wanted very much to comfort Kyle—and to comfort

herself—by putting an arm around him. But they just
didn't know each other well enough yet. She might be engaged to his father, but she and Kyle weren't family. They
were all going to have to work on that.

She scanned the water out past the tower for any sign
of something yellow, purposely ignoring the flash of yellow she'd seen earlier, through the zoom on her camera
phone. If the phone's battery hadn't died, they might have
gotten a better look at the men on the fishing boat, including the skinny one, the one Lorena told herself wasn't
Dorian.

The seals had clustered on the shore of Deeley Island,
moving farther and farther uphill and inland as the storm
surge had driven the water higher. Now they were only
about thirty feet away, barking and shifting, unable to
settle down. She had seen seal herds before, both in real
life and in pictures, and they always seemed to mostly laze
around doing nothing, but these were agitated by something. Most came ashore, rested briefly, lumbered around,
seemed to threaten one another, and eventually slipped
back into the water.

They weren't her focus, those seals. Lorena watched
the tower and the figures clinging to it. She saw that it
tilted to one side and wondered if it had been that way
when they arrived or if the storm surge had done it. Her
attention might be diverted for a moment or two by the
fins circling the tower or swimming the channel, but it
was the people up there on that old Tinkertoy structure
who had her interest.

Then she heard the commotion in the water, down at
the shore, and glanced down just in time to see one of the
fat seals sliding up onto rock and scrub from a huge, crashing wave . . . and the shark that burst from the wave and

bit the seal in half, blood and viscera spraying the ground as the wave pulled back. The shark lay stranded, whipping its body back and forth, dinosaur brain not understanding where the water had gone, not realizing that it had doomed itself. But even then, its jaws kept gnashing. Another wave crashed down and it slid several feet down toward the water.

"Oh my God," Kyle said. "What the hell is happening to them?"

Lorena thought the ocean might reclaim the shark after a few more big waves, but she couldn't be sure and she didn't want to have to look at it. Didn't want Kyle to have to look at it. She took his hand in hers, gave a reassuring squeeze, and then leaned forward to pull the tent flaps closed.

"We'll look again in a little while, see if anything's changed," she said.

"What if it doesn't?" he asked.

Lorena squeezed his hand again but said nothing.

CHAPTER 41

—

Wolchko sat on the edge of the platform, trying to determine the exact location of the *Thaumas* and how far out he'd have to jump to make sure he wouldn't hit the rocks of Bald Cap. The storm surge hadn't gotten any higher and the tide had begun to turn. Already the highest swells were a few feet lower than they'd been at their worst.

"You are not doing this," Naomi told him.

"Who do you suggest?"

"I'll go," Naomi said.

Wolchko actually considered it for a moment and then hated himself for that hesitation. "Not a chance."

"If this is some bullshit over me being female, I swear to God—"

Wolchko crawled away from the edge and reached for her hand. Naomi helped him so that they were both standing. The tower swayed and creaked so badly that his heart pounded and the whole world felt unsure beneath him, as if they might topple right off the edge of the Earth any second.

"It's nothing to do with that," he promised.

"The truth. If you're worried about the prosthetic, don't be. It's light and waterproof. Yeah, it's awkward underwater, but more because it's too light than too heavy."

"I'm only being logical," Wolchko said. "It's what I'm best at, remember? The system that's broadcasting the signal from down there . . . I built it, Naomi. I'm the logical choice."

Wolchko could have added that he was older, that he'd lived more, and that since his wife, Antonia, had died he had felt like he was just marking time in the world, but he said none of that. His Antonia would have been so proud that for once he had recognized which thoughts should stay inside his head.

Naomi poked a finger at his chest. "How long can you hold your breath?"

Wolchko backed up a step. "I don't know."

"I was a swimmer in high school."

Wolchko nearly stepped on Tye.

"Hey!" Rosalie barked.

Naomi and Wolchko both turned to look at her. She knelt next to Tye, looking not so much angry as incredulous.

"Could you two maybe not jump around up here?" Rosalie asked. "The tower's rickety enough already."

From below them, Wolchko heard a throat clearing and a voice say, "I second that."

The fisherman. Walter. In the moment, trying to work out the next few minutes in his head, Wolchko had forgotten all about the other refugee on the tower. It brought him back to his senses, somehow, and he realized Walter and Rosalie were right.

The tower shuddered with impact as a shark crashed into the structure down below. Wolchko and Naomi braced themselves and they all held their breath for a moment or two as the platform shook and groaned. It swayed, but Wolchko told himself that was just a wave sweeping by underneath them, not that the tower had tilted farther. He told himself that, but the tight knot in his gut twisted a little tighter.

"Okay, point taken," he told Rosalie. "But I'm afraid there's going to be a little more jumping around, as you put it. If I'm going to reach the *Thaumas*, I need to land as close to it as I can. Just climbing down the tower and going for a swim would be suicide."

Naomi looked out over the edge, careful not to slip. "Do you really think you can clear the island?"

"Maybe with a running start," Wolchko replied.

"Oh, Jesus," Walter muttered below them.

"You're out of your mind," Tye said weakly. He looked pale, and Wolchko wasn't sure how much blood he had lost. Maybe too much.

Rosalie shifted to get out of the way, give Wolchko a clear path. "Do it, Eddie."

Wolchko could have spent hours dithering about it, but they didn't have hours. If he was going to take action, it had to be now. He closed his eyes a moment. The burr of voices around him vanished and he thought of Antonia, the smell of her skin when she was just out of the shower, the crinkle at the left side of her mouth when she tried not to laugh at one of his jokes. Wolchko tended to be overly serious, but around Antonia he had found his sense of humor. She liked to sing snippets of silly old pop songs while they were making dinner together, sometimes with a little dance routine to go along with them. He knew the risk he was about to take, but he also knew that Antonia would have understood.

A hand touched his arm and he opened his eyes, wishing for Antonia's smile but getting Naomi's grim worry instead.

"Eddie, please," she said.

"Time's running out," he told her.

Wolchko walked to the remaining fragment of wall. To his right, Tye and Rosalie watched hopefully. Rosalie nodded, urging him on. A bitter little voice at the back of his brain said that of course she would urge him on, as long as she wasn't the one taking the risk. But that was true of almost anyone. If someone else would put themselves in danger, in their place, most people would be happy to allow it.

Naomi, though . . . she stood directly in Wolchko's path. The platform measured only about ten feet in diameter, so he needed all the room to run that he could get.

"I'm going," Wolchko said, locking eyes with her. "If I'm forced to go through you, then we both fall, and we'll never get the distance we need to clear Bald Cap."

His head throbbed and the swaying of the tower made his stomach give a twist, but he kept his gaze steady. Naomi had turned out to be smart, formidable, and kind. He didn't want a conflict with her, especially because he knew she was trying to help.

"We're all soaked through and miserable. We're all grieving and exhausted," he said. "But my head's clear. Before anyone else tries to get close to this rock to help us, that signal's got to be shut down."

"Eddie—" she began.

A shark smashed into the tower, then another, the double impacts so hard they made Wolchko and Naomi steady themselves, arms out to keep their balance. Rosalie swore as the noise of metal under duress filled the air. To Wolchko it sounded like rusty hinges creaking, and it made them all hold their breath.

"Honey," the fisherman, Walter, said from his perch on the side of the tower. "Get out of the man's way."

Naomi deflated. She opened her mouth, gasping like a fish on a hook, but whatever she had wanted to say seemed to vanish from her head. Instead, she just nodded quickly and stepped aside. The wind kicked up, blew a strand of her soaked hair across her face.

"Whatever you're gonna do, make it quick."

Wolchko took a deep breath, then lunged forward in a long, loping run. He only had room for a few good steps, but he'd done the long jump in high school. Even went to the state track-and-field championship once. He sprang off the tower—felt it give a little too much as he pushed off, heard the creaking-hinge noise grow. His arms windmilled as he began to fall and he bicycled his legs, instinct telling him that he needed just a little more distance.

Then he saw the dark water below, the rain plinking into the sea, the white curls rolling across the rocks at the edge of Bald Cap, and he knew he hadn't gotten enough momentum. Knew he wasn't going to make it.

Wolchko hit the water, wondering how much it would hurt, how many bones would break, how long he'd be conscious as the sharks tore into him.

He plunged into the water, a little prayer in his head, and his body stiffened for the impact. But the impact didn't come. Salt water plugged his nose and he blew out a little jet of air as he began to rise again. Wolchko's eyes shot out and he fought the ascension, twisted in the water, and began to swim lower. He opened his eyes, the salt stinging. In the murk he could make out almost nothing but the bodies of fat gray seals darting around him. One brushed against his back and his heart almost exploded in fear.

Wishing himself invisible, as if just by thinking it he could draw some kind of field around him so the sharks wouldn't see him, he swam in a direction he thought was away from Bald Cap. Only now, deep in the water, cold and sodden and wondering how long he could really hold his breath, did Wolchko understand just how stupid he'd been. He'd seen their boat go down, gauged the location as best he could from above, but how accurate had he really been? He was prepared to die down here, but not if it was for nothing.

Antonia, he thought. *What have I done?*

Desperately he swam on, pulled himself deeper, whipped his head back and forth, and fought the salt sting to keep his eyes open. He saw a glimmer in the murk, the gleam of something neither seal nor shark, and his heart leapt. All his life he'd had a hard time with the concept of God, holding out hope for heaven only after he'd lost Antonia. Now his whole being sent up a prayer of thanks and he swam for the boat, not counting the seconds he'd been down there, only feeling the burn in his chest and knowing he didn't have long to get to the dish that had been mounted on the underside of the boat. Hoping the seconds remaining would be enough.

He could make out the shape of the wheelhouse and he started to circle the body of the boat. Shadows moved above him, made the murk even gloomier, and he looked up to see nearly a dozen fat seals passing overhead. In the same moment several of them broke away and swam toward him, faster than anyone on the surface would have imagined they could go.

Wolchko went numb when he saw the monster chasing them. The Great White caught one of the seals and ripped it in half with a single clack of its jaws. A cloud of blood blossomed around its enormous body as it plunged toward him, impassive and unrelenting.

CHAPTER 42

—

Naomi saw the blood in the water not far from where Wolchko had gone in. Her heart tightened in her chest, almost like a fist. All her fear shut down and she felt her face go slack as she backed up to the wall, the same way Wolchko had before he'd jumped.

"Whoa, whoa, Naomi," Tye said. "What the hell are you doing?"

"Eddie didn't make it. Someone's got to," she said, and then she lifted her gaze to study Rosalie. "What do I need to do? Smash the two broadcast dishes? I saw the one on deck, but where's the one fastened underneath?"

Tye forced himself to sit up, wincing in pain. "Don't be stupid. If Wolchko couldn't get there—"

"Shut up, Tye," Rosalie said, never taking her eyes off Naomi. "Girl's trying to save our lives."

Naomi nodded once, not in thanks but acknowledgement. She and Rosalie understood each other. Naomi was willing to risk her life because somebody had to do it. The fisherman wouldn't even know what to look for, Tye was too badly injured, and Rosalie had no intention of dying for the rest of them. That left Naomi as the only option. Of course, she also had no intention of dying . . . but that fact wouldn't keep her alive. She'd need to be fast and she'd need to be lucky. Just about the luckiest woman alive.

"So tell me," she said.

Rosalie ignored Tye's protests. "The computer's fried at this point, but that was just monitoring the signal, not broadcasting it. The broadcast unit's a small waterproof box with a bunch of cables coming out of it. Yes, it's in the wheelhouse. You go down there and you'll see it immediately because it looks like it doesn't belong there. It's gray and smooth, rubbery looking."

"I think I remember seeing it," Naomi said.

"Yank it out, cables and all. You do that and the dishes don't matter."

Naomi nodded, glancing out at the water. She could see where Wolchko had gone in, could see the patch of blood still blooming on the water, beginning to fade. How close had he gotten to the boat?

Only one way to find out.

"You don't have to do this," Tye said.

But they had all been onboard the *Thaumas* . . . all seen the fishing boat sink.

The tower shook with a fresh impact, swayed in the wind. Naomi knew they wouldn't last long enough for someone to resolve this for them. Nurturing a tiny flame of hope, she peered out across the water, scanning in every direction for a rescue that might work. She saw only the rain and the sea and islands too far to do more than taunt her with the safety of their higher ground. Her stump ached, pain throbbing in the femur above it, down in the marrow.

Naomi ran. Her right boot slipped on rain and rust but only for a moment and she hurtled forward. Tye did not shout her name—no one did. He and Rosalie only watched as Naomi launched herself out from the edge of the tower thirty-five feet above the water. A swell rose below. She saw a fin, spotted the shark as it smashed into the watchtower's base, heard a snap—a bang—that was nothing like the crunch and metal shriek they'd all heard earlier.

The water rushed up at her and she pressed her legs together, hands at her sides, and punched right through the heaving swell, wishing she'd taken a bigger breath to hold. Eyes closed, Naomi thrust out her arms and swam, dragging herself forward. Her left hand brushed against something and her eyes snapped open. Salt stung her and she had to close them again, but she knew she had no choice. If she couldn't see, her chances of surviving dropped from slim to zero, so she opened her eyes again and endured the searing pain.

Seals rushed around her, ignoring her. She saw a floating chunk of flesh and for a fearful flicker she thought it must be Wolchko. Then she caught sight of the flipper and she realized it was a seal. The sea enveloped her in murky darkness, but its effect was not total. She could see shapes, could see seals near and far, spotted a school of tiny fish . . . and there, not thirty feet away, the *Thaumas*, on its side on the bottom of the channel. Had it sunk farther out, she'd never have been able to dive deep enough. Here at the edge of Bald Cap, the water ran shallower, though even as she watched she thought the boat might be sliding in the current, shifting deeper.

Naomi didn't bother to look for the sharks. She knew they were there. Knew they would be coming. The only question now was whether or not she'd fulfill her goal before the sharks fulfilled theirs.

CHAPTER 43

—

Walter sat in a V joint in the trestlework where rusty bars met and watched the girl drop into the water. Naomi, they'd called her. And the guy . . . the one who'd gone in before her and been eaten pretty much right away . . . he'd been Eddie. Just people. Wet and cold and miserable and going-to-die-soon people. When Walter and Jamie had been sitting in the Dog, talking shit about the Woods Hole research team, they had seemed like the enemy. Even on the way out here this morning, when Jamie and Walter had gotten the call that the scientists had been stranded on Bald Cap, he had been thinking of them as somehow *other*. Like they were opposing navies, fighting for their respective homelands. His life had its share of hardships and heartaches and it had felt nice for a little while to have somewhere to point a finger, someone to blame. Jamie had needed that even more than Walter. Somehow they managed to string together a living as fishermen, taking odd jobs here and there to supplement that life. If the folks from WHOI were going to upset the balance, then all of Walter and Jamie's frustrations could be laid at their doorstep . . . even though they hadn't technically done anything harmful. Not yet.

They certainly had now.

Walter watched the water where Naomi had dropped, saw white foam rippling over the surface and the deep sea roll and churn, but he saw no blood. Not this time. He saw no sign that she'd been caught. Ten seconds underwater and apparently she had managed not to get eaten quite yet.

Up top, Tye and Rosalie were losing it. Walter listened to them freaking out and barely heard the words. Not that the words mattered much. They were gibberish expressions of the same fear that he'd felt upon hearing the massive crack just as Naomi jumped, the latest shark impact down below. This time, though . . .

Walter craned his neck to the right to get a look at the east-facing side of the tower, where he was sure the sound had originated. A swell rolled beneath them, swallowing a few extra feet of the tower, throwing that extra pressure against it—a push westward. When the swell passed, the push subsiding, Walter saw the broken beam. Rusted through, the lowest of the tower's crossbeams had given way, and now as the tidal flow of the churning sea pushed eastward again the whole tower groaned and began to lean. Trestlework connected to the broken beam strained and bolts broke and even the corner began to sag toward the broken middle.

"We're going to die," Rosalie said a dozen feet over Walter's head.

The woman had a gift for stating the obvious, but she wasn't wrong. *It's all over but the screaming*, he thought.

A sound came from below—a human sound—and Walter craned his neck a little farther, looking inside the latticed structure of the tower. He saw a face there, a swimmer bobbing in the water within the broken cage formed by the bars and beams.

Wolchko. Alive. Which meant the blood hadn't been his. Which also meant that he'd failed to shut down the signal they'd been talking about and Naomi was out there on her own, trying to save all of their asses.

Cold inside, hollowed out by grief and now by his certain fate, Walter looked back toward the place where Naomi had gone into the water, scanned for fins, and then started climbing down. Another shark slammed into the tower, this time on the southern side, and he heard something else snap. He scraped his hands raw on rusty metal, snagged his shirt on a jutting bolt, and listened to Tye calling out to him, asking him if he was out of his mind. Walter tried to reply, opened his mouth and found that he could not speak. He wanted to say that he figured staying up top might be crazier than climbing down, but the words wouldn't come.

He paused ten feet above the water and took a breath. Several fins were cutting the water out in the channel, but none of them were close by. To the north, he saw one cruising his way, but he had a little time. Seconds. If the tower fell, they were all dead within minutes, at best.

Walter thought about Jamie, knew his dearest friend would have told him that only an idiot would do what he was about to do. But he also knew that Jamie would have gone ahead and done it himself anyway. If Naomi was still alive down there, she might need help.

Better to die fighting than crying, Walter thought. But it was Jamie's voice he heard in his head.

He clapped his hand to the knife that still hung sheathed at his side and hurled himself away from the tower. The water caught him, dragged him down, twisted him in its current.

Walter began to swim.

CHAPTER 44

———

Bleeding, exhausted, too old for the panicked swim he'd just endured, Wolchko floated inside the tower and drew long gasps of air into his burning lungs. His heart pounded so loud that his skull throbbed with each beat, but at least here inside the tower he could take a few seconds to orient himself, to think. Behind him there came a splash like someone else jumping in, and he turned but couldn't make out anything beyond the crossbars of the tower.

Only when he started to turn back, to survey his surroundings, to figure out the best spot for him to begin climbing up the inside of the thing . . . only then did he see the hole in the side of the tower, the broken beam and the jutting bars that had torn away from the structure. He whispered a string of profanity spoken with such reverence that it might have been a prayer. The columns on either side of the hole had bent slightly inward and the one at the northeast corner had cracked.

Wolchko rose and fell on the churning sea, frozen with

uncertainty. If he climbed, he'd fall. If he left his position, he'd die. If he stayed where he was—

Thud.

The shout that came from his lips belonged not to the adult man, the scientist. It came from the boy he'd once been, for whom real fear had seemed so much nearer, so much more intimate, as close as the nearest shadow. Wolchko spun and stared at the shark as it strained against the lattice, its head thrusting through a hole just under the water like a dog snarling at the end of its chain.

Another thud struck the south side of the tower and the whole structure clanged. Rust drifted down from inside, falling on his head like tainted snow. That shark kept moving, the fin curving away from the tower, maybe circling around for another run. Wolchko bled into the water and the tower squealed as if it were sobbing, the high keening wail of a dying thing.

Then Wolchko saw the circling fin turn back toward the tower . . . out to the east, so that now it arrowed straight for the gaping open wound in the structure. A swell rolled past and Wolchko sank into a trough. His boots hit the rock of Bald Cap for just an instant before the water began to rise again, and in that same instant he saw the real size of the hole in the tower's eastern face. And the shark came on.

"Eddie? Eddie, get out of the water!" Rosalie shouted from above. "Is that you down there? You have to—"

Wolchko climbed. Hand over hand. Boots searching for purchase, slipping and then catching. The tower slanted inward on all sides, making him climb an angle that dragged on him, as if the ocean itself wanted to pull him off the metal. He would fall. No question of if, only when. Seconds, he thought. Wolchko flashed back to childhood jungle gyms as he dragged himself through the diamond-shaped opening, awkwardly, all elbows and knees. Even as a boy he had not been agile, and boyhood had been so long ago.

He heard the rush of water being dispersed and risked a glance back through, into the interior of the tower. The shark surfaced as it smashed through the hole, its bulk knocking aside a rusty bar that hung from one last bolt.

When Wolchko screamed it wasn't the little boy he'd been doing the screaming. It was the man. The man who'd lived and loved and struggled to understand the world but now knew, above all, that he didn't want to leave it. His upper body was on the outside of the tower, his lower body still only halfway through the lattice. He reached up, grabbed bars he couldn't even see, and slid his hips and legs free. The shark had lunged from the water and it smashed into the lattice in the very spot his legs had been a moment before. Wolchko lost his footing, lost the grip of his right hand, and hung only from his left as the shark's snout raked downward and it crashed back into the water, inside the tower. Trapped in that cage, for at least a few moments.

Wolchko regained his footing, reached up to climb.

His hand grabbed nothing but air.

The sound of rending metal enveloped him as he felt himself toppling forward. Tye and Rosalie screamed, but Wolchko didn't look up. He clung to the lattice and rode it down. The tower fell slowly, so slowly, buoyed by the water. It crashed into the sea, coming to rest on Bald Cap. The rocky island remained underwater, but only five or six feet now. Wolchko found himself on top of the metal lattice and he stood carefully, wind and rain slashing at him.

"Rosalie?" he called. "Tye?"

The platform jutted out over the edge of Bald Cap. The fallen tower slanted into the water. The remaining wall fragment had submerged completely. The bottom of the tower had been four feet wider than the top, where it supported the platform, so Wolchko retreated toward the rear of the fallen structure. Like the arm of a crane, it reached out from where he stood, narrowing, the water washing over the far end. Wolchko stood eight feet above the water, but as a swell rolled toward him his breath caught in his throat. The water washed over the entire fallen tower, covering everything to his ankles for a moment before subsiding. He glanced around, saw the circling fins, and knew. Eight feet wouldn't be nearly enough.

"Eddie?" a voice called, and then he saw Rosalie dragging herself up onto the fallen tower. Tye lay behind her in the water, holding on to the lattice. "Help me!"

Wolchko hurried as best he could, boots slipping on rust as the water washed over the tower again. He stared down, knowing not all of these bars were safe, afraid one would snap and his leg would go through. When he looked up, he found himself eye to eye with Rosalie, who pleaded with him to help.

"Come on, Tye," Wolchko said, kneeling painfully on the lattice. "Up you go."

Together, he and Rosalie maneuvered Tye out of the water and got him onto his feet. Tye mumbled thanks, but he'd lost so much blood that he could barely keep his head up and Wolchko and Rosalie had to stop him from stepping down into the open spaces underfoot.

"Eddie, what are we supposed to do?" Rosalie asked, but he knew this woman. She wasn't expecting a rescue. She just needed to know she wasn't alone.

The crash came from beneath them. Rosalie shouted more in fury than in fear, past the point of terror. Wolchko stumbled and lost his grip on Tye. He tried to hold on, tried to save the other man, but instead they both pitched forward. Wolchko smashed face-first onto the rusty lattice and found himself staring down into the dark cage of the fallen tower, where the fourteen-foot Great White had become trapped. It lunged upward, smashing itself against the lattice, fin poking up through one of the holes. It thrashed sideways and the whole tower shifted, turned, skidded along the sunken rocks of Bald Cap.

"Oh, Jesus," Rosalie said, on her hands and knees, just trying to hold on.

Tye's left arm hung down inside the cage. His right knee had bent and slid through. Wolchko didn't think. He didn't feel. He just grabbed hold of Tye and started to drag him. The other man's leg caught at a strange angle, but Wolchko kept pulling, fighting that resistance. Rosalie helped him, but this time when they pulled, Tye's eyes went wide with pain and he fought them, twisted and turned, and slipped down inside the trestlework. He fell into the water as Rosalie screamed and reached down into the fallen tower to try to grab for him. Wolchko wrapped his arms around her waist and pulled her back, forced her to walk, stumbling, up to the higher end of the tower.

Through the lattice, they could hear Tye shouting weakly. The shark thrashed harder, furious because Tye had fallen behind it and the monster had been hemmed in by the sides of the tower. It tried to turn, tried to smash the lattice on either side, but it couldn't reach Tye. Not as long as it stayed where it was. Behind it, behind Tye, was the platform, which closed off that end of the tower. But ahead of it, where the tower had been fastened to the rock face of Bald Cap, the cage yawned wide open.

The shark began to move forward, toward freedom. Toward a place where it could turn itself around. In the water, injured and disoriented and weak from blood loss, Tye began to cry out for someone to help him.

"Climb out!" Wolchko shouted. "Just pull yourself out, crawl through, and get up on top!"

Tye didn't reply at first. Rosalie started back the way they'd come, but Wolchko grabbed her firmly by the arm and yanked her back. She stumbled and slipped off the bars and her leg shot through a hole, but he stopped her, hauled her up with both hands.

"Let me go!" she snapped, knocking his hands away.

Over the wind and the sea, they heard Tye reply at last.

"Kat?" he called out, voice thin and reedy. "Is that you?"

Rosalie's eyes widened and she turned to stare at Wolchko, seeking silent confirmation that they'd both heard the voice, that they both knew what it meant. Tye had become so disoriented now that he no longer remembered that the sharks had already taken the woman he loved. Wolchko thought of his Antonia and he knew what she would have said now, knew she would have demanded that he go back down along the fallen tower and try to fish Tye up out through the lattice, get him out of the water.

"We can't just leave him," Rosalie said, eyes imploring.

Wolchko swore softly. "All right." He jabbed a finger in her direction. "But you stay here. Keep the high ground. If they hit it again, hold on for—"

Rosalie scowled. "Fuck that. I may not be brave, but I'm no little kid. He's my friend."

Wolchko glanced back to see the shark had turned and now arrowed straight for the open end of the fallen tower. For a heartbeat he closed his eyes, kissed the tips of his fingers, and offered that kiss up to the sky, to Antonia, wherever she might be. When he opened his eyes, Rosalie had already started moving quickly along the tower, picking her steps carefully. Up ahead, Tye called out for Kat again, and Wolchko wondered if Kat could hear him, if her spirit might not be far away at all, if she'd stayed, knowing Tye wouldn't be far behind. As Wolchko started after Rosalie, the thought unsettled him, but it warmed him as well, made him wonder if Antonia's spirit might also be near. Knowing her, being in love with her, was the only thing in his life that had ever made him believe there might be life after death.

His boots splashed into the water as a swell washed over the fallen tower. A glance back and he saw the huge fin rushing at the tower opening. Rosalie knelt down in the water, cried out as the current forced her to hold on to avoid being washed away. Wolchko dropped to his knees beside her and stared down into the water, knowing Tye was underwater now, that for a few seconds he would be drowning.

The swell subsided. A trough dropped the water level all the way down to bare rock. Something thrashed inside the tower and Wolchko didn't have to look back to know it would be the shark, momentarily drowning in air the same way Tye had been in the water a second ago.

"Now!" Rosalie shouted at him.

They both thrust their arms down through the openings in the lattice, shouting Tye's name. Wolchko saw him, hunched over on hands and knees, coughing up seawater. He roared the man's name again as the water level began to even out. Tye put out his arms to keep himself afloat.

"Goddammit, stand up and reach for us or you're dead!" Rosalie shouted.

To Wolchko's astonishment, Tye did precisely that. His head snapped back, his eyes clear and alert, and he rocketed to his feet, grabbed both of their hands, and let them hoist him up. He grabbed the crossbars as the water level rose inside the fallen tower. Rosalie snapped at him and at

Wolchko, and together they got Tye up inside the lattice. His head and shoulders were out, his hands and arms giving him leverage as he started to hoist himself up.

The shark took him then. Ripped him so hard on its way toward the dead end of the tower that the crisscross rusty bars caught his upper body by the armpits and his lower body was torn away. Tye didn't have time to scream. His face went slack and his eyes flat and dull. Blood and offal filled the water and Rosalie screamed and scrambled on hands and knees back the way they'd come, moving in swift horror toward the higher end of the fallen tower. Wolchko knelt there, unable even to retreat. He could only stare at Tye's dead face, knowing that below his rib cage there was nothing left of him.

Then the shark hit the platform from inside the tower, crashed into it so hard that the tower slid scraping along the rock. The shark began to thrash again, twisting and seizing in the water, trapped in that case for at least a few moments. The rusty bars jumped and shook and Wolchko started to back away, moving toward Rosalie.

He didn't see the second shark before it crashed into the platform end, turning the tower on the rocks like a compass needle. Rosalie shouted for him to hold on, but he knew that much. A swell rose and washed over the fallen tower and he saw a shark rising with it, coming toward him, and he closed his eyes as it skidded against the tower, smashing against it, passing within two feet of him but unable to get its teeth into his flesh.

Another struck the back of the tower and it shook again, scraped again, and he felt the tower begin to slide, as if it might just slide right off Bald Cap and into the channel. Rosalie cried a prayer. Wolchko held on and wondered just how close his Antonia must be now.

CHAPTER 45

Naomi's chest burned and her eyes felt as if they would burst from her skull. Everything inside her screamed at her to swim for the surface. She fought the temptation to open her mouth, to try to breathe the sea into her lungs, and yet somehow at the same time her throat felt closed, as if no air or water could ever enter there again.

The salt had stopped stinging her eyes, but even with them wide open she could see very little down in the murk. Surfaces and shapes guided her and her hands. She had hold of the lip of metal that ran around the roof of the wheelhouse and she used it to anchor herself. The cold had flayed her to the bones, but she kept moving, dragged herself down through the shattered windshield of the wheelhouse.

She felt the impact, felt the familiar tug, and air bubbled from her lips as she let out the leading edge of a scream underwater. Then she clamped her lips shut and fought. Whipping her head around even as she held on to the broken windshield frame, she saw the shark clamped

on to her leg and her eyes were wider than ever, panic searing through her, blackness eroding the edges of her vision
as her brain began to suffer from oxygen deprivation.
Again. It was happening again. The shark jerked its head
back and forth and she should have been bleeding, should
have been shrieking, should have been dying. Except this
shark hadn't been the first. Its jaws were clamped down
on her prosthetic leg, sawing at something it didn't want.

Naomi felt something give way, saw the prosthetic twist
into a mangled thing, and knew she had to fight. She tightened her grip on the windshield frame and pulled, twisted
her hips, and kicked with her good leg and tried to tear
herself loose.

Something huge filled the left side of her peripheral
vision and she knew she was about to die, that this shark
would get flesh and bone and blood from her. But then she
glanced back to see it wasn't a shark at all, but a man. The
fisherman, Walter.

And his knife.

Walter punched his blade through the shark's eye and
its jaws opened. Released, out of air, Naomi rocketed
through the shattered windshield, grabbed hold of the
wheel, and maneuvered herself around so she was facing
the control panel.

She didn't even have to look for the box Rosalie had
described. Airtight, it floated there, anchored to the panel
by long cables. Her fingers closed around it, and she pulled
with all the strength remaining in her.

The blackness at the edges of her vision closed in. Her
chest began to heave, her body to seize, and then she couldn't
stop herself. She opened her mouth and let the ocean in.

She barely felt the hand that grabbed at her shirt and
began to haul her toward the surface. Toward air.

CHAPTER 46

On his hands and knees on the fallen tower, Wolchko saw the swell rising, saw the water washing over the metalwork, and he held his breath and closed his eyes, wondering. As the current dragged at him, he felt his knees slide out from under him. His fingers clutched at the rusted bars and he counted to five, after which the swell had passed.

"Eddie, get up!" Rosalie said.

Wolchko lay on his face and belly, fully stretched out by the passing swell. But Rosalie was right. They had to be at the highest point. The tide had begun to go out, the storm surge dropping. The tower had been skidding along the rocks, but the lattice had caught on an outcropping or something, been snagged there. The sharks would smash it off; he felt confident of that. But how soon? If the tower would just stay caught on the rocks long enough for the water to recede from Bald Cap, they'd be safe. They'd live.

"Eddie!" Rosalie called. "Get up!"

But her voice was different now. Confused.

Wolchko glanced up at her, saw her gaze drifting along the horizon, and followed it. He rose to his knees and saw a Great White—as big as any they'd seen—passing right by them, only a dozen or so feet away. It kept going northward without turning, without circling back. When it submerged, its fin vanishing into the water, it seemed to stay its course. Away.

Other fins were nearby, but they also seemed to be shifting direction. For so long they had been circling the sunken boat with such ominous intent that it was easy to see the break in the pattern.

Even the seals began to disperse. And Wolchko knew it wasn't the sharks' hunting pattern that had broken but the signal. *His* signal. Even with all of the blood that had been spilled in the water, the sharks were leaving.

They'd had their fill.

He stood and began staggering up the incline of the fallen tower, careful not to fall through, thinking of Kat and Tye and Captain N'Dour and Bergting and Naomi— *damn it, Naomi*—and then he heard a splash behind him. Rosalie shouted and pointed and Wolchko knew it had been too good to be true. Just a trick of his imagination, a tortured hope. He knew the sharks were turning around, coming back to finish them.

Then he heard Walter's voice.

"Hey, you assholes, I could use a little help here!"

Wolchko stared in astonishment as Walter swam toward the rusted tower, dragging Naomi with him. She looked unconscious or dead, and that snapped Wolchko out of his momentary paralysis. Sharks had tried to kill her once. If they could save her, if he could help to save her, maybe he could learn to live with the horror their experiment had caused.

Maybe.

"Here! Over here and we'll drag her out!" Rosalie called.

Then Wolchko and Rosalie were on their knees again, just like with Tye, only this time there was no more blood. No more screaming. They lifted Naomi from the water and then Wolchko helped Walter climb up onto the broken tower as Rosalie began CPR. It took only a few breaths and two pumps of her chest before Naomi coughed seawater, head lolling sideways as she choked and coughed and let it spill out of her.

"Look at her leg," Rosalie said.

They all did. Her prosthetic had been mangled beyond repair, the lower half of it torn off, but the leg had been secured so well that the upper half had remained in place.

The prosthetic—the fact that she'd had one in the first place—had saved her life.

CHAPTER 47

Naomi is surprised to discover that she's been sleeping. Her face scrunches when she feels the light drizzle on her skin and she opens her eyes, squinting against the daylight. Confusion swirls and for a moment she wonders if she's dreaming.

"You're okay," a voice says. "You're alive."

She blinks and looks up into Rosalie's face, realizes that she's been sleeping with her head in Rosalie's lap. The un-likeliness of this earns even more confusion, but she sees how exhausted Rosalie looks, the dark circles under her eyes, and the stray locks that have escaped her ponytail. Naomi feels the salt on her skin and reaches up to wipe grit from the corners of her eyes.

"How long have I been out?" she asked.

Rosalie shrugs a little. "Less than an hour, I'd guess. But not much."

A small groan escapes Naomi's lips. She's still exhausted and she feels so stiff. Then she notices the way

Rosalie is sitting, the awkwardness of her body, the way she's propped up on her hands, and the strangeness of their situation crystallizes. Naomi sits up as quickly as she can without making it seem like revulsion.

"Hey, be careful," Rosalie says, gesturing toward her legs.

Naomi starts to shift, to turn to face Rosalie. Her clothes are stiff and rimed with salt. Not completely dry, but crinkling like papier-mâché. The wind still blows strong, but less so, and only a light sprinkle falls from the still ominously gray sky. They sit atop the wreckage of the rusted watchtower, but it's the wreckage of her own leg that gives Naomi pause. The prosthetic doesn't even look like a leg anymore. It's a useless twisted appendage, a ruin all its own. But the leg can be replaced.

"Are you all right?" Naomi asks.

Rosalie has been wearing a brave face, stern and tough. The question causes the mask to slip. Her lower lip quivers a bit, but then she nods.

"I think so. I will be, anyway. It's just . . . Kat and Bergting and the captain, that was all bad enough, but Tye . . . I saw it happen. The blood was bad enough, but I saw the life just go out of his face, like someone flipped a switch and he was just . . ."

She can't finish the sentence. Naomi reaches over to cover Rosalie's hand with her own. The woman has been less than kind to her, but they are past all of that now. In the wake of such horror and terror, floating in this sea of grief, they can only be quiet and kind.

There's the sound of something scraping the rusty metal, and then Eddie Wolchko's face appears over the edge of the fallen tower. It occurs to Naomi that he looks older. The gray stubble on his chin and the pain in his eyes makes him look worn and a little crazy. But then she thinks how she herself must look and suspects they're all a bit older now. All a little crazy, from now on. Forever, from this day.

"You feel asleep," he says, watching her warily, like he's afraid she might start barking or horns might grow out of her head.

"I'm aware," Naomi replies.

"More like passed out," Rosalie says defensively, and it's never not going to be weird to have Rosalie on her side, in anything. But then Naomi has no intention of knowing Rosalie in the future. There are a lot of things Naomi has no intention of doing in the future.

"Are you all right?" Wolchko asks, still studying Naomi.

Who scowls. "Fuck no. Are you?"

Wolchko blinks, wincing at the question. He shakes his head. "Of course not."

"Where's Walter?" Naomi asks.

Wolchko hikes himself up and sits on the edge of the fallen tower. "Down with the seals."

Naomi shifts herself over, careful not to let the wreckage of her prosthetic catch on the metal lattice, and sits beside Wolchko. She glances down and sees the fisherman standing on the smooth rocky surface of Bald Cap. A swell rises—the ocean is still undulating with the powerful storm currents—but when it washes over the island it's only half a foot deep. Six inches of Atlantic foam rolls across Bald Cap and then subsides again, leaving the rocks glistening, wet and dark, but above water.

The seals are everywhere. Some of them are sleeping, while others lumber to the water and slide across the rocks, heads popping up a few feet out into the channel. Bald Cap is tiny, so only a very small fraction of the seals that followed them north can rest here, but Naomi glances across the channel at Deeley Island, and even at this distance she thinks the dark mass on the shore there must be more of the herd. How many of them will stay here, nest here, she has no idea. Did the WHOI team's experiment work? In her heart, she doesn't want to know. The answer will never matter.

What's odd is how quiet the seals are, as if they're also older now, exhausted and grieving. Walter stands down there among them, hands thrust into his pockets, still as a statue with its eyes westward, toward shore. He's so still that when he moves, just to take his hands out of his pockets, Naomi flinches.

Walter turns to look up at the three of them, there on the wreckage, and points to the south.

"Get your asses down here," Walter says. "They're coming."

Naomi hears Rosalie whisper a quiet prayer as they all look across the water to see the Coast Guard cutter rounding Deeley Island. She puts a hand on Wolchko's back and feels a dam break within her. Shuddering, breath hitching, she exhales loudly, expecting tears to fall. But Naomi doesn't cry then. The tears won't come, though they would have been relief. She wonders if she's dehydrated. After so much time in the water and after all the rain, the irony feels cruel.

Wolchko and Rosalie climb to their feet, stand on the edge of the rusted tower, and begin waving their arms to signal the cutter. The cutter replies with a blast of its horn to let them know they've been seen.

Naomi smiles, hates that she's smiling—after all that's happened, it feels grotesquely disrespectful—but she can't get the smile off her face. To make it worse, she blurts a single, shaky laugh.

And then the tears come.

Shock, she thinks. *I'm in shock.*

As the Coast Guard ship approaches, she watches the water, searching the swells and troughs for any sign of a fin. Her rational mind knows that the signal has been shut down, but the fear will lurk in her subconscious forever. She will always scan the water now. For as long as she lives, she will never trust the ocean again.

CHAPTER 48

The ship's horn startles Lorena. She glances over at Kyle, recognizing the flicker of hope and excitement in his eyes. They'd watched the unthinkable unfold across the channel. Sitting inside the tent, they had watched the tower on Bald Cap come down, and they'd known people must be dying. But then the sharks had gone away. As the storm began to subside, they had counted fins every five minutes or so, until twenty minutes passed during which they had seen only one. Since then, they've not seen a single shark. They're still out there somewhere, Lorena knows, but their frenzy is over.

The horn sounds again, and Kyle scrambles out through the tent flaps. Lorena follows, so happy that the rain has all but stopped. The wind gusts and droplets spatter down from the branches and leaves overhead, but she doesn't mind. Lorena isn't going to be bothered by anything now, not with help arriving at last. She's told herself that Jim and Dorian are safe. At first she feared the worst, but then she hated herself for surrendering to such dark thoughts, and ever since she has told Kyle she is certain his father and brother made it to Bald Cap, that they survived the tower's collapse, that the sharks have gone away and everything will be all right. She has told Kyle this over and over until at last she has come to believe it herself.

Only she hasn't. She doesn't. Not in her true heart, not in the dark rational core of her, the part she knows every person has, the piece of the mind that remains aware of its mortality. That piece of the human mind keeps quiet most of the time, and she's never been more grateful than now.

"Come on!" Kyle calls.

Lorena smiles in hopeful anticipation as she picks her way down from the tree line, over the rocks. The water has receded dramatically, but they can't get close to the water here. There must be two hundred seals spread across the northwestern shore of Deeley Island, and Lorena knows better than to get too close.

She and Kyle stand side by side, hearts pounding, as the Coast Guard cutter sends a little rescue boat over to Bald Cap, the rescuers just tiny figures in the distance. The survivors on Bald Cap are evacuated quickly.

"How many are there?" Kyle asks, eyes narrowed as he tries to get a count. "I wish your phone hadn't died. We could be sure."

Lorena takes his hand and gives it a squeeze. "They're okay, Kyle. I know they are."

She tries to let go of his hand, but he holds on and Lorena doesn't dare pull free. Together they watch in silence as the tide continues to go out and the tiny figures are brought aboard the Coast Guard cutter. Soon the ship is setting off again, looming toward them, approaching

Deeley Island with clear purpose. Lorena smiles. Even in the grim little rational core of her heart, she knows this is a good sign. The Coast Guard has left the small rescue boat in the water and it zips along, bouncing on top of the waves, outpacing the larger vessel. They *know* there are people on Deeley, or they would've hoisted that rescue boat back onboard.

A lightness fills her and she breathes deeply, watching the officers onboard the rescue boat.

Then she glances up at the approaching cutter and sees several figures on deck. She squeezes Kyle's hand and tugs him along with her as she walks nearer the shore. Seals bark at them but shuffle out of the way, none of the beasts bellowing a challenge. Maybe they're too tired for a fight today.

She watches the figures lined up at the cutter's bow railing, studies their silhouettes, their body language, her smile broad. Her first inkling is a knitting of her own brow, as if some part of her sees the truth before her conscious mind can recognize it.

If Jim were onboard that Coast Guard cutter, he'd be there at the railing, eager to be reunited with her and with his son. The nearer the cutter draws toward the island, the surer she becomes that none of those figures at the railing is familiar. Jim isn't among them. Neither is Dorian.

Kyle lets go of her hand, and Lorena barely notices.

The cynical little voice at the core of her heart feels no surprise at all.

But her feet go out from under her and she sits down hard on the rocks, numb and weak and bleeding hope. She ought to have known better, she thinks, than to believe in happy endings.

Then she hears Kyle's voice, parses the questions he's

asking. The rationalizations he's running through, speaking them aloud to try to make them real. Maybe his dad and Dorian are injured, being treated on board. That's got to be it, he tells her. And then he's calling her name and she can hear that he's becoming angry with her, frustrated that she's assuming the worst.

Lorena looks at him, hating herself for her selfishness. She's been thinking about her own life and what she has lost, but this boy had just lost his father and his brother, his two best friends in the world.

Realization strikes Kyle. Lorena watches it happen, sees the way his face crumples.

"No," he says, shaking his head. "No."

It's her own face that's done it to him. She knows that immediately. He's seen the pity in her eyes and that's what drives it home, that her heart is breaking even more for him than it is for herself. That's when he knows it's true.

"No," he says again.

The rescue boat reaches the rocks and one of the Coast Guard officers jumps into the water and starts wading toward them, finding an open path amidst the seals.

The cutter remains offshore, not daring to come any closer.

Lorena sits on the rocks, the surf washing over her legs, and stares at the distant strangers on the deck of the cutter, wondering why they get to live.

It's going to be all right, she wants to say. She should tell Kyle that. Really, she should.

But he's not a little kid. He's seventeen. He knows better.

The time for pretending is over.

CHAPTER 49

Walter keeps to himself as the Coast Guard cutter makes for Boothbay Harbor. It's disorienting as hell, sitting by himself on the deck with a blanket over his shoulders. A medic has checked him over, treated the cuts on his hands and a long scrape he didn't remember getting on his left arm. His thoughts keep turning toward his boat. He imagines it now, on the bottom, curious fish investigating its shattered hull, maybe a lingering shark prowling around it. Walter worked so hard for that boat, lived on a meager budget, just to ensure that he didn't have to rely on others for his living. Too many racists and homophobes out in the world. Too many assholes. Now that insurance policy is gone.

But it isn't the boat he mourns. The loss weighs on him, yes, but when he envisions the boat down on the seabed his thoughts slip over to Jamie. The way Jamie died. The way Jamie never gave a second thought to how different he and Walter were, always seemed surprised if someone brought it up. Now Walter's going to go home and the other guys he knew, the other fishermen, will talk about what a tragedy it is, but he knows that in no time they'll be making jokes behind his back about Walter and Jamie, just like they always have. Maybe they'll say Walter's a captain's widow now. They'll never understand that what he's lost is not only his best friend but the only person he's ever had in his life who has embraced him with blind acceptance, never wanting or needing him to be anything other than the person he is.

Micah will try to comfort him, of course. That's what a boyfriend is supposed to do. But he won't understand what Walter has lost any more than the fishermen will.

This is the loneliest pain Walter has ever felt.

The other people around him are hurting, too. The woman and the kid the Coast Guard picked up on Deeley Island sit together on a bench at the cutter's stern. They don't hug, but they're side by side and hand in hand, faces mostly blank. Here and there, the teenager starts to cry again and wipes tears from his eyes, straightening his back, trying to be strong. Tough. Maybe his dad was the sort who wanted him to "man up," or maybe he's just trying to wrap his head around what it's going to cost him to grow up right now. His father's dead. His older brother, Dorian, is dead. Walter thought he and Jamie had saved Dorian. He doesn't tell the kid and his mother—if that's his mother—that they'd pulled Dorian out of the water. It's not going to help them to know the older brother escaped the sharks once just to die twenty minutes later.

Gone is gone.

The cutter docks and the EMTs are onboard in an instant. Sheriff's deputies wait on the dock. Walter can see the cars, along with a news van from WGME 13, the CBS affiliate out of Portland. He's sure the others are on the way and doesn't want a thing to do with them. He won't be talking to any fucking reporters. He'll never understand the people who endure horrors and talk about it hours later with a camera stuck in their faces, as if telling the world about the pain of your baby falling out a window is going to make the hurting stop.

EMTs carry the one-legged girl off the cutter on a stretcher. *Naomi*, he reminds himself. Whose shark attack last summer set all this in motion. Walter knows it isn't her fault and he admires the hell out of her. Young woman has steel in her spine and ice in her veins as far as he's concerned. If not for her, he and the two Woods Hole scientists—Rosalie and Eddie—would all be dead. Walter doesn't doubt this at all. And he sympathizes with all she's been through.

But he hopes like hell that he never sees her again. If he could manage it, he'd like to never hear her name again, either, though once this fiasco hits the news he suspects he's gonna hear Naomi Cardiff's name over and over again for years. Every time he does, he's going to think about Jamie.

A light drizzle still falls, but the wind has all but died. The sea is calm.

Walter takes the arm of a Coast Guard officer. "Who called you? How'd you know to come and get us?"

The Coastie cocks his head. "Harbor master, sir. I guess you're Walter Briggs, which means it's you we were looking for. Harbor master didn't hear back from you and couldn't raise you on the radio. Raised an alarm, I guess."

Walter thanks him, lets go of his arm. He's been hanging back while the EMTs take Naomi off the cutter, in no hurry to go anywhere. Now he's watching EMTs talk to the woman and the kid, and Coast Guard officers escorting Eddie and Rosalie, and he realizes he wants off this tub. Right now.

He shrugs off the blanket. Doesn't thank the Coast Guard, doesn't stop to talk to any of the other people who almost died today, just walks to the gangway and gets off the damn boat. The dock shifts beneath him, but even that feels immediately better than being onboard a boat. The cops have kept the gawkers and the press back a reasonable distance, so while he walks off the dock nobody's bothering him. Walter feels a weight on the back of his neck, like the atmosphere itself is getting heavier.

He hears a voice call his name and thinks it must be Micah. His stomach gives a little twist as he realizes Micah is the last person in the world he wants to see right now. The sympathy, the sweetness, the false understanding, the awkward attempts at comfort, and the presumptions of an intimacy that isn't really there.

The voice calls to him again and Walter glances up. Past the cops and the gawkers.

It's Alice. Her face is streaked with mascara. She's still crying, but it looks as if she's been trying to get ahold of herself and now she wipes at her eyes. Walter heads toward her without even being conscious of altering his path. A cop tries to talk to him, but he keeps going. Most of the spectators stand aside, but one middle-aged guy with a handheld recorder tries to ask him questions, maybe a local journalist.

He reaches Alice. The rain has stopped. Walter puts his arms around her, sagging a bit and shaking, but not crying. All his life he's had extra motivation not to cry, not to let his feelings show.

"I'm so sorry, Alice," he says, knowing that she liked Jamie more than she'd ever let on.

Alice pulls back from him, puts her hands on his cheeks to make sure he's looking her in the eye. "No, honey. Don't do that. No. I'm sorry for you. I'm so, so damn sorry."

Then she pulls Walter into her arms again and he lets out a long, hitching breath. He still won't let the tears come— some lessons are too deeply ingrained—but he's never felt so grateful to anyone. The pain is still almost unbearable, but it's not quite so lonely now. He was wrong. There is at least one person who understands.

CHAPTER 50

—◆—

"I don't need an ambulance."

Naomi stares down the EMT who's inspecting her prosthetic. She's in the back of the ambulance already, still on
a stretcher because that's how they carried her off the
Coast Guard cutter. The Coast Guard medic has already
given her the once-over. Her hands are bandaged and she's
been drinking water to get rehydrated, but her biggest
problem at this point is an inability to walk on the wreckage of her prosthetic.

"What?" Naomi says, glaring at the EMT. "You think
you can fix that? The local hospital keep a bunch of spares
lying around? They're custom-made. I need crutches or a
rental wheelchair, and I need to borrow somebody's cell
phone. I don't need to go to the hospital and I don't need
a ride in an ambulance."

The EMT is maybe thirty, serious about his job from
the look of him. Former military, she guesses. But the

prosthetic is like a puzzle to him and he keeps glancing at it.

"You sure you don't—"

"Very," Naomi snaps. Then she softens. "Very sure."

Their eyes meet. He's just trying to do his job and she respects that. A silent acknowledgement passes between them. Naomi's made an assumption about his basic intelligence and it seems she was wrong.

"You're already on the bus," the EMT says. "Please give me a minute to call it in, so I don't get fired later for letting you walk away." He squeezes his eyes shut, opens them again. "Sorry. Not walk, obviously."

Another day, she would have smiled. But there are no smiles today. Not a one.

Naomi nods. "I get it. Call in. If you need me to get on with them and tell them to fuck off, let me know."

The EMT does smile, a little. He pulls out his phone and climbs out of the ambulance, taking a few steps away. Naomi exhales and lies back on the stretcher, but it's only a few seconds before she hears a soft rap on the inside of the open door and looks up to find Eddie Wolchko standing at the back of the ambulance.

"Knock knock," he says.

"That's not the opening of a joke, I hope."

The horror on his face is answer enough. It's Wolchko. He'd never have considered making a joke now and never have imagined someone would think he's joking.

"Jesus, no. Of course not," he says.

"I know. That's just me being sarcastic. It's my default defense mechanism."

Wolchko nods, but she can see he only half-understands her and it really comes home to her how different their minds are. She wonders how much it's going to haunt him, what they've gone through today.

"So I wanted to tell you—" he begins, but she cuts him off.

"Eddie, listen. Later, when it's all just bad dreams . . . when the shitstorm that's about to hit us has died down . . . I want you to know that you can call me. If you don't have anyone you feel comfortable talking to, if it's bothering you, but you have a hard time putting it into words or if you're just under pressure . . . you can call me."

He frowns, and it takes her a second to realize that he's not sure how to take this, that he might be wondering if— even after all of this and despite the age difference—she's flirting with him.

Miraculously, she finds herself smiling after all. Not for herself, but for him. So he knows.

"I'm saying I'd like to be your friend," Naomi explains. "If you'll have me."

Wolchko seems to relax. "Of course I will."

He doesn't have to tell her that he doesn't have a lot of friends.

"Thank you," Wolchko says.

The EMT interrupts them, halfway nudging Wolchko aside. "Just wanted to tell you that you're good to go. I'll just need you to sign something. Are you going to be okay with a ride to wherever?"

"I'll sign whatever you want," Naomi says. "And if I can borrow your cell, I'll call home and get a wheelchair and a ride sorted out."

She's thinking of what her mother must be going through right now, how she must be waiting for her cell phone to buzz. By now she'll have heard that Naomi's all right, but she'll be shaken by the story of what's happened.

They've had their differences, but Naomi misses her right now. All she wants is to go home.

She thinks of Kayla, wondering if the things that had been broken between them can really be repaired. Out on the island, she decided to find out, to give Kayla a chance. It worries her, opening herself up again like that, exposing an old wound that has never fully healed. But then she remembers the way Kayla used to look at her, the wonder in her eyes, and she knows she's only fooling herself. Of course she'll give Kayla that chance. Of course she'll take the risk. Love might break her heart, but it isn't going to kill her.

As the EMT goes around to the front of the ambulance to get whatever paperwork she's meant to sign, Wolchko studies her.

"You don't need a ride home, Naomi," he says. "I'll stay with you. Woods Hole is arranging for a boat to take us back."

Naomi stares at him, cold fear spreading through her. Her instinct is to fight this fear, to straighten her spine and show that she won't be beaten by it. But to hell with that—after the past thirty-six hours, she no longer has to prove anything to anyone.

"Sorry, Eddie, I'll pass."

Wolchko seems disappointed. "If you're sure."

"Oh, I'm sure," Naomi says. "I'm never getting on another boat in my life."

He looks like he wants to hug her, but she's still in the back of the ambulance and he'd have to climb in there, and even Wolchko knows how awkward that would be. Naomi sees the thoughts skim across his eyes and then he gives her a small shrug and promises to talk to her soon. Naomi tells him that he'd better, and then he's gone.

She sits up, maneuvers herself off the stretcher onto her one good leg, and then uses a handhold at the back of the ambulance to lower herself down so that she can sit inside the open doors. Her good leg dangles. The wreckage of the other leg juts at a strange angle.

She waits to use the EMT's phone, to hear her mother's voice, and as she waits she gazes out past the dock, past the Coast Guard cutter, toward the islands in the distance. Deeley is too far out to see from here. There are other islands in the way, so of course she can't see Bald Cap, either. She'll never see it again, and that suits her just fine.

Naomi watches the undulating surface of the ocean. The sight always used to soothe her, but today she studies the swells that roll into the harbor, scanning for the familiar curve of a fin. This is how she sees the ocean now.

And how she always will.